THE ROUGH RIDE

SANCTUARY, INC.

NONNA HENRY

May the flag unfurl to greet you
The stars fall soft across your heart
Bright stripes rest proud upon your shoulder
And until we hold you near again
May God gently guide you through the dark.

This book is dedicated to our military veterans.
Some of you gave more than expected.
All of you gave with honor.
Thank you for your service.

N ick Flannery tossed his towel aside and stepped into a serviceable pair of boxers, pausing to see if this latest scrubbing dulled the fire engine red ring on his johnson. His heart faltered. It was still bright as a vine-ripened, August tomato.

Damn that woman and her lipstick.

He'd stop at the pharmacy and buy a makeup remover because, sure as hell, his dick couldn't take another rough washcloth lashing.

He muttered a curse, raised the boxers, and pulled on his suit pants. Why in the hell did she mark him like that? It was one thing to find a love bite on his abs, but quite another to be sporting a crimson O on his pecker. *Shit.* He shook his head.

He shrugged into a blue-striped dress shirt and worked the buttons. This situation was his own damn fault. Nobody'd forced him to scratch his itch with a bar honey on the prowl. This was what he got for allowing his libido out of the box. His temples throbbed every time he thought about his stupidity. What had come over him? *What the hell had he been thinking?*

It didn't matter. He owned it. But he knew exactly *who* he'd been thinking about two nights ago when he acquired his scarlet letter.

Liz Nelson.

He'd worked with her a few weeks ago on a Sanctuary, Inc. rescue mission. The woman was a military analyst and a genius. But her refusal to acknowledge their close relationship during the mission confused the hell out of him.

She'd avoided him. Kept her distance. Shut down her computer and slipped away without saying goodbye at the end of the assignment. She'd left a business card with a P.O. address so they could mail a check. *Seriously?*

He and Liz had known each other for almost eleven years. She'd been his high school flame during his dark nights of family unrest and abuse. They'd been each other's first. Best friends. Confidantes. Lovers.

She'd encouraged him to leave home as soon as he turned eighteen. And leave he did. Two days after his eighteenth birthday and three days before their senior prom. He'd had his diploma mailed to him and boarded a bus bound for boot camp. Liz had never thrown it in his face that she'd gone to her prom with *the girls.*

He grabbed a subtle Swiss-dot tie and looped it around his neck. Ties were instruments of torture, but a day like today required one. First stop—a complete physical per the client's request. Second stop—a lunch meeting with said client to go over details of the assignment after he passed the physical. Ever since his honorable discharge from the military three months ago, his fledgling security company depended on his ability to sell discreet professionalism and a team in top physical condition. Starting with him. *Hoo-rah.*

He stepped back and eyed the dress shirt-and-tie combination. They complimented each other well.

Liz would approve.

Just how many more years was he going to harbor a hard-on for Liz Nelson and care whether she approved? Their lives had crisscrossed for a decade, and each time, the slow burn in their relationship erupted into a roaring fire until the call of duty rudely doused the flames and flew them to separate time zones on the globe.

No other woman was like his Liz.

Fierce. Honest. Smart.

Nick strapped on his watch and slipped his bulky shoulders into the suit jacket. In the past, he and Liz had been in tune with each other. But that was before she saw combat in Iraq and returned home with a prosthetic foot. The Liz he'd seen a few weeks ago was still the same brilliant woman he'd always admired, but she was more reserved, kept to the shadows, and spoke softer.

She had a right to her feelings and her pain. During the fifteen months since Iraq, she'd been distant. Told him not to visit and insisted that he date other women. She wrote thank you cards for his frequent flowers, instead of calling or texting. His gut churned thinking about how a passion like theirs had reduced itself to texts.

And the one thought that plagued and scared him the most? Maybe she wasn't interested in him anymore. That's exactly how she'd acted the past few months.

She lived in Alexandria, Virginia with her mother and had a cushy cyber job with Homeland Security. Good for her. Seriously—she deserved the best of everything.

So *that's* who he'd been thinking about when he'd accepted the proposition of the oh-so-willing bar honey. It was Liz's sweet skin he'd imagined as he nibbled and kissed. And when he'd thrusted, it was Liz's tight channel around his hard flesh. And when he came, it was Liz's name he groaned in his head. But now that he thought about it, he wasn't completely sure he hadn't said her name out loud.

He stilled from attaching an ankle holster. *Ugh. Damn.* Did he say Liz's name during a critical moment? *Aww hell...*he'd had a bunch of beers and couldn't remember. If he did, that would certainly explain the lipstick tattoo.

He adjusted his tie again, slid into a pair of wingtips, clipped his Glock onto his belt and slipped a Magnum into his shoulder harness. Not that he needed the hardware at the doctor's office, but the client would expect to see him armed to the hilt.

He wasn't looking forward to dropping his drawers for a prostate check, but if the doctor had a good sense of humor, he might enjoy a laugh when he noticed the emblem on Nick's member. Maybe the doc would even have a long-lasting lipstick remover for sensitive skin.

Nick could hope.

L iz opened the package of chocolate sandwich cookies, dunked one in her fresh mug of decaf espresso and savored the flavors as she chewed. Her body hummed with satisfaction. It was mid-afternoon, and she'd caught herself nodding off at the computer screen. The sweet treats would propel her to quitting time.

She reached for a third cookie, reconsidered her strategy, and fumbled around the top drawer of her desk for the bottle of all-natural energy she kept for emergencies. *Got it.* She poured half into her coffee and put the cookies away. In a little while, the B vitamins would kick in and this afternoon slump would be a memory.

She'd been up most of last night pacing and crying. And when the crying and pacing finished, the phantom pain in her AWOL foot started. There were dark rings under her eyes and lead in her ass today. All she wanted was six hours of solid sleep. Six hours to ensure she didn't drool on her keyboard at work and miss an important, life-saving detail.

Liz reached for her mug and took a couple hearty slugs.

She logged into a social media site and waited while it sprung to life with a list of notifications from her *friends*.

She didn't have *real* friends. Not anymore. Not since Iraq, and certainly not since Ella had been born. She had work and a fussy baby and a mother who'd taken an early retirement package from the postal service to babysit Ella. She had guilt. A shitload of it. Working mommy guilt, survivor's guilt, daughter guilt, and a case of baby-daddy guilt that she had no idea how to address.

Liz typed in the next name on her list. The social media page loaded, and she scanned for unusual posts, replies, threats, and possible hints at terrorism. Not exactly what she trained for but doable, and her mid-management position paid *very* well—like, six figures well. She had thirty names she was responsible to track via social media every day. Known abusers, traffickers, and religious and political extremists. Most of them had rap sheets and a half-dozen fake names. It was up to her to keep pace with them as they slithered between identities.

She rather liked the challenge, and her workplace persona at the moment was that of Dottie Ryan, a buxom, pouty blonde bombshell who liked *it* a little rough. Liz maintained eight to ten different online personalities for herself during any given week. When she wasn't this tired, she'd disappear into the cyber world for hours, hoping to thwart the next shopping mall bomber. Just last week, her efforts nailed a trafficker who lured young teens to his house under the pretense of being a math tutor. The week before that, she'd stumbled onto a bullied kid posting his suicide plans.

A co-worker stuck his face into her office. "There's birthday cake in the lunchroom if you need a pick-me-up, Liz. I figured you'd be interested because it's chocolate."

She didn't turn around but held up her coffee mug. "Already got some, thank you."

She glanced at the photo of svelte Dottie's persona on the screen and then at her own tummy that she hadn't firmed up since Ella was born. Dottie wouldn't stuff her face with chocolate to make up for lost sleep or lack of friends or a non-existent sex life or a missing foot that still felt like it was there sometimes. Of course not. Dottie would strut in her ho-red stilettos and drive the cyber-freaks insane.

This job was a bit like playing cyber-Barbies. Liz used a government program to invent fake people with pseudo lives. Not to be confused with the online sockpuppets who flooded the internet to sway public opinion. No, she used the faux identities to draw out extremists.

Her favorite persona was that of Marion Trent, a mousy, brown-haired librarian in search of a cause. Marion's homepage was a continual stream of invites from men wanting an American bride and religious and political zealots petitioning her to check out their videos. Marion was prime beef in the hungry world of cyber-hunting. She was unattached, advertised her virginity, and had more online boyfriends than any sane woman could handle.

A newish hire named Carmen jogged into Liz's office and plopped a laptop in front of her. "Read this. Does it impress you as boys preparing for a school shoot?" Carmen stood back and crossed her arms.

Liz glanced at the pictures first. Guns—lots of guns. Boxes of ammo. Two young men with hunting caps, pointing their trigger fingers at the selfie screen. The posts and replies were in another language. "I can't read it, Carmen. If it was Pashtu, I'd make sense of it, but my Spanish ends with *hola* and *gracias*."

"Oh yeah." Carmen leaned in and enabled the translation. "Here you go. Sorry."

The little office was quiet except for their steady breathing and the sound of the air conditioning system.

"I don't know," Liz murmured. "See, this kid is in a photo with a hanging deer. It could just be that they're hunters."

"I'd agree with you, but twenty-four hours ago, he posted on one of the cheerleader's timelines that he had something very special for her at lunch tomorrow. Three days before that, he and this cheerleader broke up. I checked. They're no longer *in a relationship* with each other." Carmen scrolled and highlighted the posts.

"He didn't happen to mention a birthday or making up or something?" Liz loosened her ponytail and massaged her head.

"No. He just said it was a *big* surprise and wanted to see her at lunch." Carmen fingered the silver dog-tag necklace she always wore.

"Well, these kids are either planning something, or stupid. Posting pictures of each other with guns online throws a red flag. They're underage, another flag. The reference to lunch is a red flag. I'd take it to the boss and let her decide if she wants to alert the locals and the feds. Erring on the side of caution makes sense."

She wheeled around and gave Carmen a big smile. "Great work. You may have found something. Report back and let me know what the upper crust decides. Otherwise, I'll worry about it right through lunch tomorrow."

3

Nick held the door for two people exiting the posh Georgetown restaurant, *The Town Crier,* where Senator Richardson had arranged for their lunch meeting. He was a bit early but hoped to use the time to test the security of the establishment. Its reputation was that of an eatery frequented by the Capitol Hill elite. He mentioned his name to the maître d' and was shown to a large table in the back.

Every place setting displayed a name card, and Nick walked around the table noting the names. The who's who of DC politics. Speaker of the House, the Majority Whip, and several members of the Senate Intel Committee. *Interesting.* Nick picked up his place card and swapped it with the Speaker of the House before sitting in what had been the speaker's chair. He eyed the room. *Much better.*

He declined the alcohol a waiter offered and ordered water with a twist of lemon and lime, then headed for the restroom. He used his scanner and probed it for bugs. There were two in the ceiling and several very discreet devices in the stalls. He retrieved a stepstool from the waiter's galley and removed the ceiling bugs. The others were easy enough to grab with a wad of paper towels he'd confiscated from the sink area. *Not bad for a first sweep.* He washed his hands and returned to the dining room after returning the stepstool to the waiter's galley.

Nick checked the senator's table for surveillance devices. Three of the chairs proved compromised and the underside of the table held an elaborate live feed. He removed everything he could detect with his scanner or eyes. He dropped all the pieces that he'd found into the senator's water glass.

The ceiling boasted several cameras. That was fine. An establishment had a right to protect itself with footage, but not in the bathroom, and certainly not at the tables.

Curious now, Nick scanned the chairs closest to the senator's table. He removed more listening paraphernalia, but couldn't very well continue sweeping the restaurant, as it was more than half occupied. He sat and enjoyed his fruit-infused water.

Five minutes later, the senator bolted through the front door with a staffer trailing behind.

"Nick," he waved. "Sorry, I'm late. The vote lasted so much longer than I'd expected." He shook Nick's hand. "Please, sit." Beau Richardson looked to be a youngish fifty, very fit, with a full head of thick, graying blond hair.

The male staffer set a stack of folders on the table next to the senator. "I'll be at the staff table if you need anything." He retreated across the room and joined a young woman at another table.

A waiter approached. "Would you like a drink, sir?"

"Uh—yes. Bring me a lemon-lime soda in a gin and tonic glass with lime, please."

Nick chimed in. "The senator needs a fresh glass of water, too."

Richardson picked up his water glass. "What's all this?" He looked at Nick.

"Twelve pieces of surveillance I picked up from the men's room, this table and chairs, and that table there," he pointed. "Most of them are simple audio, but the two I found in the men's room ceiling had both audio and video."

Richardson turned ashen. "What? That's unbelievable." He leaned back in his chair and crossed his arms. "Now I understand. My wife joined me here the other night for a late dinner, and she chatted with the speaker's wife about women things. The next day, one of the gossip columns announced the exact hair color specs my wife uses at the hairdresser. I know it bothered her, although she didn't say much about it. That's how they knew." He ran a hand through his hair and took a sip of his drink. "I could almost use a real drink after that tidbit, but I *never* imbibe until I'm done working. Just let them think I am."

Nick leaned back in his chair. "I'd be happy to check the ladies' room for devices. I only scanned the areas you'll use today."

"Thanks. Before you leave, I'll introduce you to the owner of this place. It sounds like he could use your services too." Richardson scrutinized the table. "You're supposed to be sitting over here," he indicated. "I gave my staffer the seating arrangement for a meeting to take place after you and I talk."

Nick smiled. "Sir, I can't see the front door, bathroom door, or kitchen doors from that seat. I switched the speaker's place card with mine. I wouldn't do you much good over there because I can't see a damn thing."

Richardson sighed. "That's why I need to hire your firm.

I'm new to all of this, Nick, as the freshman senator from Texas. I can't do my job and worry about my family's safety at the same time. Someone recognized my wife and a protest started the other day when she was buying groceries and household things. Angie's no wallflower, but she had the two younger kids with her, and it was terrifying to have people screaming and throwing stuff at her car. She had to call 911 to get an escort out of the parking lot."

"I see." Nick nodded slowly. No wonder the guy sounded so tense when he'd contacted him.

Richardson waved to the waiter. "You like cheesesteaks, Nick?"

"Works for me." Nick opened his iPad to take notes.

"Two cheesesteaks with the works—fried onions. Thanks." The waiter headed for the kitchen. "Dr. Thai cleared you to work for us. Your staff will need to pass the same physical you had this morning."

"Not a problem, sir. I'll get on it right away. How does your family feel about you hiring round the clock security?"

"Well," the senator removed the twizzle stick from his glass, "None of us are thrilled with the invasion of our privacy, but I'm counting on you to supply us with personable bodyguards who understand we're a normal family with our ups and downs. The last thing I want is for one of your employees to write a sensational piece for some media outlet detailing our personalities and routines."

Nick paused a second, and made a note to contact his lawyer about adding ironclad NDAs to his hiring package. He trusted all the people he'd hired, but the NDAs would reassure the senator.

The waiter arrived with their cheesesteaks. Nick set down

his iPad and contemplated. *As far as the personable staff?* He already had several employees who'd be a great fit for the Richardson's. That list did *not* include him. He could deal with *any* adult, but those kids? *Absolutely not.* They were way outside his comfort zone.

4

L iz pulled into the driveway at home and patted the dashboard. She hadn't owned a vehicle the entire time she'd globetrotted with the military, and the forty-five minute commute to and from work gave her a chance to decompress. She loved this car. It hadn't needed any retrofitting to accommodate her injury because the right foot did what the right foot had always done. Gas and brake. Her prosthetic left foot enjoyed the ride and tapped in time to the playlist on her iPhone. It was normal. She held a deep appreciation for normal these days.

She tiptoed into the kitchen and allowed the door to snick shut behind her. Ella wasn't crying, and the house smelled of meatloaf. Good meatloaf—her mother's meatloaf. Meatloaf with ketchup on top and onions in the middle. The kind of meatloaf that was so savory, she already planned on making a sandwich for lunch tomorrow.

Her mom stood by the stove humming to the music playing softly on the Bose speakers. She kissed her mom's cheek in greeting.

"I can't believe Ella's asleep. It feels like a miracle." Liz loaded a plate with mashed potatoes, broccoli, meatloaf and salad. "How'd it go today?" she whispered.

Arlene Nelson smiled. "Much better than the past few days. I figured out that Ella's cutting teeth. I'd forgotten that you cut your first teeth when you were her age. I paged through your *Little Milestones* baby book and remembered how fussy you were. Anyway, we took a field trip to the pharmacy, and I bought baby Tylenol and a cool teething ring. It's a good thing they worked. I was getting ready to rub some crème de menthe on her gums if it didn't," she chuckled. "And baby girl loves classical music. She's rocking in the swing in the dining room. I'm glad, for her sake, that she likes the softer music because I was ready to turn on some AC/DC and dance for her." Arlene winked at Liz. "The past couple hours have been peaceful, so I made dinner instead of calling for carry-out. I'd say that's progress, honey."

Hot tears pricked Liz's eyes as she reveled in her mother's words and the first bite of meatloaf. She owed her mother big-time. Arlene had dropped her own life and flown to the military hospital in Germany the day she found out Liz had been injured. She'd stayed for weeks, and when Liz had told her about the baby, Arlene flew home, had a new walk-in tub/shower combo installed in the main bath for her use, and started planning the baby's nursery. Her mother wasn't just her mom; she was her BFF.

Arlene pinned her daughter's hazel eyes with a look. "Nick stopped by today. He was on the porch when I got home from the pharmacy. I drove around the block a few times until he left. I wish you'd tell him about Ella, honey. He's going to find out sooner or later."

Liz's fork froze mid-air. She fought the panic rising in her throat. "I'm sorry. This situation puts you in an awful position. But how can I tell him? 'By the way, Nick, I know you don't want kids, but I have one, and it's not yours because you got that damn vasectomy?'"

Arlene took a deep breath. "Something like that, honey. It's not going to get easier with time. He's been home for three months." She slid the leftovers into the fridge.

Liz swallowed hard. "I know you're right. But I'm a decorated veteran who isn't brave enough to tell the man I love that I chose the baby over him. I'm afraid the look in his eyes will rip me apart inside." *Or he'll leave forever because I betrayed his trust and didn't tell him.*

"He loves you, Liz. You can't be sure of his reaction until you tell him. Maybe he's had a change of heart."

Right. Liz knew Nick better than anyone. *He'd freak.* "Let's talk about something else. You're off-duty now, Mom. I'll do the dishes. You've got twelve hours to yourself. Doing anything special?" Liz reached for the breast pump at the end of the kitchen table and unbuttoned her blouse. With Ella asleep, she just *had* to pump. Her boobs felt like torpedoes ready to explode.

Arlene handed Liz a soft towel and slid the container of sterilized bottles in her direction. "I was thinking of walking down the alley to Louise's to play cards, but I can stay here if you need help. I know you were up most of last night, honey."

"Absolutely not, Mom. Go play cards with Louise and enjoy yourself. Stay out late and do something wicked like watch a movie and drink margaritas after cards. Tonight will be better with Ella. I'm looking forward to snuggling with my daughter." She turned on the breast pump and sighed with relief. "And you need a break. I promise to start interviewing daycares in the next week or two." She smiled reassuringly at her mom.

Arlene put her elbows on the counter and leaned forward. "Don't rush it, Liz. I love my time with Ella. She brings back the sweetest memories of when you were little and your dad was still with us. I find it healing to remember those good times."

The back door flew open, and their wild-haired, nosy neighbor Vera whisked inside with a plate of cookies. "Yoo-hoo, I baked all afternoon and thought I'd share." She set the plate on the counter and whispered, "Is Ella awake? I'd love to hold her."

Liz covered her bare chest with the towel, cleared her throat, and raised an eyebrow at Arlene. How many times had she reminded her mother to lock the back door? This neighbor viewed an unlatched door as an open invitation to walk right in. "Hi, Vera. Thank you for the cookies, but Ella's asleep right now."

Vera's smile flattened into a grim line. "Darn, I was hoping to hold her, get my baby fix. Well, enjoy the cookies. Harold's waiting for me to watch a movie with him." She blew a kiss and disappeared as quickly as she'd arrived.

Arlene spoke the second Vera was out of hearing range. "Sorry, honey. I keep forgetting to lock that door, and Vera's more forgetful than ever. I've told her a dozen times to knock before she barges in."

Liz shook her head and offered a rueful smile. "This isn't Mayberry, Mom. I get concerned for you and Ella alone here during the day."

Arlene rolled her eyes and grabbed her purse. "I'll *lock* the door on my way out. I've got my keys and phone if you need anything." She kissed Liz's head. "Love you, sweetie."

"Love you too. Thanks for cooking." It didn't take her long to clean up the kitchen and check on Ella, whose little bow lips had an adorable spot of drool on the right side. Liz knew she was pushing it timewise, but she stepped into the walk-in tub and started a bath. The baby monitor on the sink counter was so loud she could hear Ella's breathing. She relaxed into the rising bubbles and sighed.

If the baby stirred, it would take her five minutes to drain the tub, dry off, dress, attach the prosthetic to her stump, and pick Ella up.

Arlene was right. This was progress.

5

M aybe it was a full moon. The crazies had cranked it up several notches overnight. There were so many cases in motion that upper management had moved into the huge work area affectionately called the bullpen on the seventh floor near Liz's office. They'd confiscated her phones, extra chairs, and all but one coffee mug.

The wall with the monitors was ablaze but muted with the closed captioning trolling and each major/minor network represented. The crew hated it when a reporter scooped a bust off a police scanner before the job was complete. When they lost suspects, it was usually due to a speculative broadcast before the perp was in cuffs. And when a suspect disappeared into the wind, months of good work was lost in minutes, and the bullpen had to start from scratch again. And in her bullpen? They were all hall-of-famers.

Carmen's kids with the guns were in custody, and it was only 8:00 a.m. Seems the principal of the school awoke to a 4:00 a.m. phone call and drove to the school in her running gear and curlers to unlock the place. The search warrants didn't wait for a shower.

The principal had been greeted by an army of locals and feds bearing paper cups of coffee. When she unlocked the boys' lockers, they found guns. Six, to be exact. Liz viewed the feds live take-down feed of the boys on the in-house monitor as she gave persona Dottie a new hairdo and makeup. One of the boys' mothers became so hysterical she required an ambulance. Not a warm and fuzzy pancake morning in that house.

Liz suspected the principal would never get a shower today since every locker would be searched, every staff member and friend of a friend on social media interviewed, and every parent notified as to why the school was closed for the next few days. But it was a far sight better than the alternative.

Liz knew many of the families from that school would sit down to a family dinner tonight, even if it was pizza—because they could. Some of them might even say grace for the first time since Thanksgiving because they were grateful to a higher power.

And that cheerleader? Liz had seen it half-a-dozen times already. She'd never return to that school. Her parents were going to raid her college fund or their IRA and send her to a private school so exclusive the sweet girl wouldn't get to kiss a boy again until her senior summer.

That was the way of families when the horror of what could have been hit home. They hunkered down. Hormone-infused kids would hug their fathers, and mothers would peek on their teenagers late at night in their beds. Something they hadn't done in years.

And by God, there'd be a metal detection system installed in the school before it reopened because the parents would insist on it. They'd protest, start a Go-Fund Me page, and retired law enforcement would offer to help the school resource officer staff it. And finally, after a ton of negative press, some councilperson would suddenly find money in the budget to protect the kids.

Liz caught Carmen's eye across the big room. She raised her coffee cup high in a toast with one hand and gave her a thumb's-up with the other. Carmen beamed with pride over her first catch. Liz had hired her specifically because of her age (she understood the online slang), bilingual abilities, and work ethic—just twenty-three and fresh from college.

Carmen swiped her cheek with the back of her hand. A tear? Maybe. Liz remembered crying herself to sleep the night of her first catch. There was something humbling about *being the one* who recognized evil before it detonated.

Well done, Carmen, well done.

Liz slipped into her office and uploaded Dottie's new look.

THE REST of the day proved to be as fruitful as the morning.

Her bullpen nailed a sex trafficker and intercepted a well-coded message concerning a large shipment of cocaine approaching the Florida Keys on a private yacht. The brass monopolized the bullpen until 3:00 p.m. and then, one by one, returned the mugs and chairs to her office.

Dottie's yummy new profile page garnered some interesting comments, among them an invitation from a recently divorced man wanting to escort her to the Washington Nationals playoff game in a few weeks. Liz tracked him through his profile and IP address. Nothing masked or hidden. Just a lonely guy endeavoring to get his mojo back after a divorce.

Liz checked him out on the over-50 dating sites where she maintained a couple of hot mama profiles, but he hadn't joined them yet. She declined his invitation via Dottie and steered him in the direction of the safer dating apps, throwing in a few compliments so he didn't feel squashed by his attempt to reach out. Every once in a while, an innocent wandered onto Liz's profiles. Most she didn't reply to, but the divorced guy was so squeaky clean—she threw him a bone and hoped he'd move on.

On the other hand, the virginal Marion Trent received a job offer to nanny a large group of children. The pay was enormous. Liz traced the IP and came up empty. She flagged it. A front for child trafficking? Perhaps. They often hired virgins (and yes, they checked) to watch the kids.

A uniformed woman in her mid-forties stuck her head in the office. "You got a minute?"

Liz spun around in her chair, recognizing the voice of her immediate supervisor, Natalie Chan. "Major, nice to see you." She stood and smoothed her skirt. "What can I do for you?"

The major gave her a head-to-toe glance. An old habit from years of making sure uniforms were up to snuff. "That was some great work out there today." She cocked her head toward the bullpen. "Congratulations to you and your team. I got to know some of them. Humorous and hard-working bunch."

"Thank you. They're all very talented. Dedicated, too."

"Just make sure you include yourself in the kudos. You're their leader, and you've given them the freedom to take risks, to stretch their cyber legs. It's good. They're worth the taxpayers' money."

"Thank you, Major. I'll pass your praise on to the team."

The major retrieved a glass vase containing a dozen red roses and baby's breath from beyond the doorway and handed it to Liz.

"Flowers?" This workplace didn't participate in fluff. The biggest treat they could bring in was a birthday cake or donuts, and even then, security sometimes mutilated the food beyond recognition during their inspection. *Hell.* Liz couldn't even have her phone during work hours. It was locked up in the security room.

"They were delivered for you earlier this afternoon. They're safe. Security already cleared them. You're aware of the policy of no deliveries allowed here, correct?"

Liz took the flowers from the major's hand. "Yes, of course. My mother is the only person with the emergency contact number and address for this place."

The major shrugged. "Just make sure your mom isn't chatting-it-up with the neighbors or prospective men for you, things like that. We'll let it slide this time."

This time? Liz swallowed hard. "I'm sorry. I can't imagine who sent them." She set the vase on her desk.

"Don't apologize. You obviously didn't expect them. After you read the card, just let the person know they should send all future deliveries to your home. And relax, Liz. Forward whatever you're working on to the next shift and go home. Beat the rush hour. You came in before dawn this morning."

"Okay, but that reminds me." Liz sat and tapped her computer. "I need to ask you about a post Marion Trent received today. Got a minute?"

"Of course." The major pulled up an extra chair and read Liz's detailed notes. She clicked into the online site. "Might be scammers looking for info for identity theft or could be an untrained recruiter."

"I thought the same thing. Want me to forward it upstairs?" Liz crossed her arms and waited.

"I want you to go home. *I'm* forwarding this to the dark web guys. Last time I checked, they were waiting for something juicy to work on." The major added her online signature, marked it highest priority, sent it off, and chuckled. "I'll bet if I go up there in a few minutes, they'll be all over it like a pack of beagles on a hunt." She slid her chair back into place. "See you tomorrow."

"Great—thanks so much." Liz rolled her chair toward the flowers and grabbed the card to see who sent them. The message read, *"Thinking of you."*

No signature.

LIZ DIDN'T LISTEN to music as she drove home.

The flowers had to be from Nick. He'd been the only man to send her flowers for years. He always sent them on the anniversary of the date they'd met in high school, her birthday, and *if* she was stateside, during the holidays. Except lately, he'd sent them every week or so because she'd been avoiding him.

But Nick always signed his name.

She could send him a thank you note, but then it would be days before she knew if he was the person who'd sent them. *Damn.* She'd need to text and thank him. But then, he'd start texting back, and she'd have to deal with him. And above all else—she could not *deal* with Nick.

He'd given her a wide berth since they'd retired their military uniforms. He, the enlisted one and she, the officer. None of it made a difference anymore. Those protocols were simply dress uniforms hung in the back of a closet for posterity. Now, he was just her delicious Nick. The one man who could rev her engine with a glance.

She put her blinker on and moved into the lane that merged onto the D.C. beltway. Bumper-to-bumper traffic. It didn't matter what time she left work, there was always a solid back-up. It would've been nice to accept the recruitment job closer to home, but the work wouldn't have been nearly as engaging.

And it felt good to be satisfied with her work. She wasn't fulfilled in other ways, so it may as well be work that occupied the void. Some nights, she missed Nick so much that it was a hollow ache in her gut. They'd promised each other they would give their relationship a real run once they left the military. But hell—if he found out about Ella, his world would implode.

He'd been serious about never having kids by getting that damn vasectomy when he was just a kid. His sick bastard of a father imprinted his weaknesses on Nick from a tender age. Told him he'd be a bum, never amount to a pile of crap, couldn't do anything right, and someday, he'd understand because he'd beat his own kids. But Nick made sure he never had any kids to hit. He'd never inflict that kind of pain on a child.

All she'd ever wanted was to marry Nick and have a couple kids with him.

Tears flowed like a sudden rain on her face. Her breasts were full in anticipation of Ella's suppertime, and the traffic wound like a lethargic snake as far as she could see. She fumbled for the bag of breast pads in her tote and shoved them into place in case her fountains erupted. Then she grabbed another breast pad, wiped the tears from her face, and blew her nose.

Freaking hormones. She could cry on a dime. Gone was the military edge, the self-composure, the stone-faced decision maker. Maybe she'd end the nursing soon and wean Ella. Just a few more weeks, she promised herself.

But what if she never had another kid? What if Ella was an only child? She loved nursing her daughter. Yeah. She'd think about it some more.

But right now, she had to figure out who'd sent those flowers.

The traffic came to an abrupt halt, and Liz threw the car into park, using the moment to send a text to Nick, thanking him. The car behind her honked, and she looked up. The traffic in front of her had started moving. She tapped *send* and put the car in drive.

It took Nick all of an hour to reply. She had just parked in the driveway at home.

The flowers are not from me. When you find out who sent them—tell them you've already got a man who sends flowers.

A smile crept across Liz's face. It was just like him to be territorial where she was concerned. She leaned her head back against the headrest and stared at the garage door.

So then, who sent the flowers?

6

Nick leaned back in his office chair.

His iPad was full of notes on the senator's needs. The guy wanted 24/7 protection at his home and one man to protect him when he wasn't in the Capitol office building. The Capitol police offered protection during work hours and events but no personal protection off-grounds or after hours. The senator wanted new security systems at his homes in DC, Texas, and the Outer Banks. He wanted SecureIT to accompany his oldest daughter to school in the morning and after school activities. Nick tapped his pencil and brooded over that one. He didn't do kids.

Ever.

Hmmm. Derek would blend right in with the children.

Nick needed nine security personnel to fully staff a week with the Richardson family. Extended out, he was looking at well over a million a year for bodyguard services, and that didn't include the new security systems in all three homes.

There was nothing like family money, and Richardson was swimming in it. Nick had arranged to meet the wife tomorrow morning and install the new system in the DC home. According to Richardson, there was no time to waste. He wanted his family safe. Yesterday.

Nick's phone pinged with messages, and he remembered Liz's text from earlier. Some doofus sent her flowers. *Not good.* It was time to get her talking. He'd given her plenty of space and time to heal.

And he'd tolerated her request to keep their relationship open.

He'd been stateside three months and had seen her only four times. She'd looked more beautiful than ever a few weeks ago. She'd put on a little weight. Not so military lean anymore. It looked damn good on her. Accentuated her curves.

He entered Liz's mother's address into his phone and scanned the directions. Well, he'd been at the right place yesterday when nobody was home. Maybe he'd try again today. He could buy a spectacular bunch of flowers and personally deliver them. *Don't bother calling first.* She'd only try to meet in a restaurant, or on a Saturday at some park.

He'd been patient long enough. There was no way he'd let some dude move in on the lieutenant he'd loved since high school. He glanced at the clock. The traffic would be easing soon. It was only seventeen miles from his place to hers, but in rush hour, it could take him the better part of an hour.

He'd take a shower first and wear something casual. On second thought, he'd wear a fresh suit. His girl never could resist him in his dress blues. A suit would really grab her attention.

The last time he'd seen her during that Sanctuary, Inc. rescue, she'd worn a wetsuit. It'd been like perusing the latest hot-off-the-press swimsuit issue. His johnson had spent the evening bouncing between half-chub and full salute. A rather pleasant experience until he realized she'd left without saying goodbye.

He chuckled to himself. He'd do his damnedest to get her attention tonight.

7

The doorbell rang and Liz called out, "I'll get it, Mom." A satisfied Ella slept in her arms as she glanced in the peephole before opening the door.

Her body froze. *Nick.*

Oh shit! What was he doing here? Her pulse sprinted. He always called first or tried to set up a weekend rendezvous. She looked left—right—bewilderment seized her and she hurried down the hallway to Arlene's bedroom.

"Liz, what's wrong?" Arlene dropped the book she was reading and stood. "Honey?"

"Nick's at the front door, Mom. You've got to take Ella to Louise's for a little while. Please, please, hurry," she panted. She placed the sleeping Ella into her mother's arms and swung the diaper bag across Arlene's shoulder.

"Oh, no you don't, Elizabeth. You've got to tell him about Ella, honey. If he wants you, she's part of the deal now." The doorbell rang again.

"Mom, please!" The harsh, whispered command sounded odd to Liz's ears. Her mom deserved so much better. "We'll discuss it later, but he hates kids. You've got to go—now." She gave Arlene a gentle push and checked to make sure she had shoes on her feet. Tennis shoes. They'd do.

Arlene reluctantly moved toward the kitchen. "I want you to tell him, Liz. He has a right to know. He doesn't hate kids. He was abused."

Liz opened the back door and waved an arm for her mother to get moving into the alley. "I'm so sorry. I'll make it up to you, somehow." She kissed Arlene's cheek, shut the kitchen door, raced into the living room, picked up a baby blanket, pacifier, booties and a book on the first year of life and threw them into the hall closet.

The bell rang for the third time followed by a series of short knocks. Her heart galloped like a Preakness winner. She pasted a smile on her face and heaved a deep breath before opening the door.

"Nick—hey, what a surprise."

She ran a hand through her hair as coherent words fled her mind. Nothing prepared her for all six-foot-three of her Nick in a suit and tie. It was even better than his military dress uniform. Those piercing blue eyes, broad shoulders, and powerful chest all framed in a subtle black pin-stripe suit. His only accessory was a sexy smile.

"Hey yourself, beautiful." He leaned down and kissed her forehead, pressing a huge bouquet of vibrant flowers into her arms. "For you."

Liz took a step back from the sheer size of the bouquet. "Wow, they're stunning—thank you. You want to come in while I put them in some water?" She still couldn't get over the shock of seeing him in a suit. Her heart beat faster than when she'd been running around. Just the sight of him made her dizzy.

"I was hoping you'd ask." He stepped into the foyer. "Sorry to drop in on you like this."

"No, you're not. You planned this, Nick Flannery." She laughed. "Does this surprise visit have anything to do with my text to you earlier today?"

"Damn straight, it does. I was looking for an excuse to come down and see you."

She bit her lip as he peeked into the dining room. *One of Ella's little pink bears grinned from under the table.*

"There's a baby swing in there. You got a friend staying here or something?"

Crap. She'd forgotten all about it. Her brain froze mid-thought as her heart pounded. "Umm, my mom's been doing some babysitting lately." She hurried toward the kitchen and filled a vase with water.

"I remember you telling me she'd downsized after your dad passed away. This is a nice place, babe. I haven't seen your mom in what, two years? How's she doing?" He leaned against the kitchen island and crossed his arms.

"She's good. She likes being retired and young enough to really enjoy it." Liz trimmed a long hydrangea stem and tucked it into the vase. She glanced over her shoulder and caught him staring at her. "What?"

He loosened his tie. "Have you been doing yoga or some new exercise program you learned in rehab?"

"No, why?" She threw a pile of stems and leaves in the garbage.

"You've got curves, girl. Lookin' good." He shoved the tie into his jacket pocket.

"What?" Her cheeks warmed. He'd noticed the sixteen pounds that were the curse of her existence.

"Seriously. You look terrific." He smiled as he removed his suit jacket and draped it over a kitchen chair.

She cleared her throat. "Thank you."

He rolled up a shirt sleeve.

Her mouth went dry. If he removed another piece of clothing or gave her a peek at the tats on his arm, she'd dissolve into a pool of molten lust on the kitchen floor. Her hands shook and ached for one touch. She spun around to keep her wits about her and cleaned the counter. A gargantuan task with him in the room.

He came from behind, slid his arms around her waist and set his cheek on top of her head. "I've missed you."

She sucked in her stomach as his hands locked over the softness where Ella had grown. She trembled with anticipation as he leaned down and placed a kiss on her right temple, then her cheek. She slid her hands up and down his forearms, heaved a deep sigh, and leaned back against his chest.

No matter how long they'd been apart, it was always this way. Their unique intimacy rose from the ashes like midnight embers in a fireplace. One touch, and they flared. Hot tears stung the backs of her eyes. If she turned around and faced him, he'd nibble her bottom lip until she was blind with need and opened to him.

She would not turn around.

She and Ella needed forever. They were a pair. They'd been together ever since she'd awoken in Germany with a doctor murmuring in monotone that he'd removed her foot to lower-calf. Then something about lost blood supply, shattered bone and, oh, she was pregnant—very early. Might not remain a viable pregnancy considering the trauma, the blood loss, the drugs. She had options.

"Get out," she'd snapped at his emotionless face. He'd had

the bedside manner of a salt shaker. She leaned over the side of the bed and got sick once he'd left.

Nick massaged her shoulders. "Let's talk, go get a bite to eat."

She stepped away from his comforting warmth, shaking off the memories.

"Yeah, that'd be nice." Sex wasn't on the menu, but a huge slab of chocolate cake would be a somewhat tolerable substitute. She placed the magnificent vase of flowers on the kitchen table, swung her purse over a shoulder, and followed Nick out the door.

She paused on the front porch and texted her mom that it was safe to come home.

8

"You always did tell a funny story better than I could." Liz wiped the tears from her eyes and grinned at Nick. How long had it been since she'd laughed hard enough to have her stomach muscles ache like this?

"We've spent the better part of this meal smiling, babe. I needed this." Nick forked a chunk of dark chocolate cake and offered it to her.

She shook her head. "I'm full, cake's yours. And you're right. Tonight's been really special." She leaned back so the waitress could refill her coffee cup.

He stared at the fork and put it down. "I've missed our easy talks, the humor—us."

"Yup. Like old times, Flannery." Liz smiled wistfully into her cup. Her insides throbbed from resisting the urge to touch him. If only tonight was her new normal.

"Remember those two weeks before you were injured in Iraq? We had ourselves a real good time." He winked at her and gently placed his hand over hers, caressing her wrist with his thumb.

Her cheeks warmed and her wrist tingled with his every stroke. "Yeah, I was so happy to be on the same base as you. The first time in eight years."

Nick chuckled. "A two-way street there, honey. I couldn't keep my hands off you and to hell with the consequences. Linen closets, empty bunks and offices, the tower stairwell, that cubby thing in the mess hall."

"We *were* pretty shameless," Liz whispered as the memories flooded back and reminded her of everything she'd been missing. She shook her head and sat up straight before a blanket of sadness for what *was* ruined the moment.

"You are the sexiest woman alive. Knowing what was underneath that prim uniformed exterior set me on fire." His tugged her hand closer and kissed a knuckle.

How could she love him so much and have drifted this far away? "I wanted to rip the fatigues off your body and kiss you senseless, starting with your tats," she murmured as she fanned herself with a menu. The diner was stifling hot or was it the conversation? *I'm just one inch away from vaulting across this table into your arms, Nick.*

He raised an eyebrow. "Remember that breakfast when you told me you weren't wearing a stitch of anything under your uniform?"

She groaned and her insides melted with desire. "You gave me those looks all day, but we couldn't get together until late evening. It was so hard to work. Felt like I'd implode." *Kind of like now.*

Nick barked a laugh and wagged a finger. "Any woman naughty enough to go commando in a war zone deserves to burn for a while. And if I remember correctly, you did implode several times."

Liz kicked him under the table. "Stop it. You're the one who collapsed on top of me that night and said if we were attacked right then, you'd die happy."

He leaned over the table and planted a kiss on her lips. "You're blushing. I've always loved that you do that when the conversation gets sexy."

The reminiscing left her with an uncomfortable ache between her legs and a wistful melancholy draped across her heart. "Always the best of friends, Nick. In every way."

"Remember how we promised that we'd give ourselves a real run at a life together once we were honorably discharged?"

She nodded mutely. *Where was he going with this?*

He cleared his throat. "Are you involved with anyone?"

Whoa. "What? As in romantically? No."

Nick nodded and cocked his head. "There's this distance between us these days. We live less than twenty miles apart, and yet, we've seen each other only four times since I got back."

Liz swallowed hard. "I've had a lot to deal with, Flannery. First rehab, and then the new job." *Not to mention a new baby.*

He held his hands up. "Hey, your health is first. I get that. I wouldn't want it any other way, Lizzie. But I can't help feeling like there's something you're not telling me. I can't put my finger on it."

"Well, you know, starting a new career and life as a civilian is a challenge." What the hell was she doing? As if he didn't know what the challenges were.

"No, this is different. For example, you left the Sanctuary mission a few weeks ago and never said goodbye. You just vanished."

A stab of regret hit her heart. "I'm sorry. I had to get home." Her boobs had sprayed all over the inside of her wetsuit. It's not like she could've whipped out the breast pump in front of a bunch of guys.

"I'm not trying to pry, babe, but is your mother alright?"

"Of course, Arlene's good." Liz squirmed a little in her seat.

"Okay, just making sure." He took a sip of water, keeping his eyes on her face. "Do you remember when I proposed a couple years ago?"

Her pulse quickened. "Yes, of course." She'd *never* forget. In front of the Eiffel Tower, on bended knee, with holiday lights twinkling in the background. A stolen weekend rendezvous when they'd both had a five-day-leave and scored cargo plane jump-seats from their opposite locations.

He stroked her ring finger gently as he spoke. "And you said *not right no*w because you wanted me to take some time, see if I found a woman who didn't want kids." He leaned back and set his palms on the table. "Well, I'm done looking around."

"Oh?" Her stomach soured. She stared at his hand when he slid it across the table and laced his fingers with hers again.

"Look at me, Liz, please," he said in a low voice.

Crap. Oh damn. He was going to let her down gently. Her cheeks burned hot again. He must've met someone. Why on earth had she ever suggested that he look around?

"Babe, I met a girl…"

She knew it. She glanced toward the entrance of the restaurant, judging how long it would take her to get out the door and bolt. She needed air. "Okay, I kind of figured you would. I don't need to know the details, Nick."

"You're interrupting, babe." His index finger guided her

face back in his direction. "As I was saying, I met a girl my junior year in high school, and she is the only woman I've ever wanted."

Liz shook her head. "What did you say?"

"It's always been you. I don't want anybody else. I don't think about anyone else. I've tried it your way. They're not you." His fingers caressed the palm of her hand.

Wow. She inhaled a huge breath and relaxed a fraction. "I wasn't expecting that."

"I know we're at an impasse about the kids thing. You want them. I don't. But I'd be willing to consider adoption, maybe down the road. As long as the kid doesn't have my blood. It's a concession I'm willing to make to build a life with you. Please work with me on this, babe."

Nick's eyes were so sincere and his touches unbearably tender. She opened her mouth but words escaped her. It was probably just as well. Until he knew about Ella, any response would be a lie. She nodded. This was a huge step for him.

His brows furrowed. "You know why I don't want to pass on my genes to anyone. It's not fair to the kid. You were there that night," he whispered hoarsely. He pulled his hand from hers and scrubbed his face.

She reached across the table, setting her hand on his forearm. "Yes, I was. No family should end that way." She'd stood with him as the EMTs wheeled his mother out on a gurney and the police arrested his father for homicide. Nick had been only seventeen. "But that doesn't mean you'll do the same thing."

"To you? Of course not. I'm not worried about hurting you. You'd shoot me first." A small smile crossed his lips. "I couldn't forgive myself if I hurt a kid. I mean, some of that has got to be genetic. I'd rather die than pass on that monster's DNA."

Her sexy, battered warrior. His emotional injuries weren't as obvious as her foot. But they were there, and like her, he'd learned to compensate and set boundaries.

"The kids in Iraq didn't even approach me. I can't say I blame them."

"Nick, we didn't want the kids in Iraq to approach us. We never knew which of them carried a grenade and would pull the pin."

He nodded. "It didn't stop some of my crew from giving them candy and treats. But not me."

She traced a vein on his forearm with the pad of her finger. "That doesn't make you a bad guy, just a prudent one."

He reached across the table and touched her cheek. "You know, after Paris, I was willing to do anything to be with you. I tried to have the vasectomy reversed."

Excuse. Me. What?

Her coffee lurched down the wrong pipe, and Liz choked. "No kidding," she said when she could speak again.

"Yeah, I went back for all the tests, and they said it didn't take. Their exact words were *medically unsuccessful.*" He fumbled for his wallet as the waitress placed the check on the table.

Liz dragged in a calming breath. The air was thick with the smell of grilled burgers and fresh coffee. Her ears were ringing. "You, um, didn't think that was worth mentioning when we were together in Iraq?"

He cocked his head and gave her a puzzled look. "It's kind of a moot point, don't you think? It didn't work."

Her brain swirled with unfinished thoughts. By all that

was holy, she needed to tell him about Ella. But how? She had no idea. *She had to think.*

Nick shoved some cash in with the bill and leaned toward her. "The days of me dropping you off at your mother's house are limited, I hope. Soon, we'll live under the same roof."

The very thought sent another zing of desire between her legs. "Dream on, soldier." She slid out of the booth and stood.

"I have my ways, Liz." An ornery smile crept across his face as he joined her.

Oh yes, he had his ways. *Slow, erotic, pleasuring ways that might be responsible for my current situation. Was that even possible?* Ways that would have her moaning in public any minute now if she gave him half a chance. Her traitorous breasts started leaking. She crossed her arms and chuckled. "Get over yourself, Flannery." She swatted his hand away from her butt.

"Gotcha thinking, didn't I?" He held the door for her as they walked outside.

"Maybe a little." She grinned.

"You let me know when I need to report for duty, babe." He unlocked his truck for her. "I'll wear my flag boxers and be there ready to serve." He laughed and shut the door.

LIZ LET herself in at home, leaned back against the door and closed her eyes. *Oh. My. Goodness.*

All this time she'd believed that Ella was another man's child. She yanked the hair tie from her brunette ponytail and let it billow loosely around her face as she massaged her temples.

In all their years apart, she'd only stepped out once on

Nick. Just one night. After a frustrated, testy phone call when he'd reminded her that women didn't wear signs proclaiming *they didn't want kids.*

She'd been so furious with herself for encouraging him to look around that she'd gone to the officer's mess hall and whooped ass on a group of younger officers at the dartboard. Spitting mad, she'd pictured the women Nick was dating as the bullseye on the board. She'd annihilated all of them, and it hadn't hurt that her fellow soldiers had celebrated every victory with a sip of tequila.

She wasn't drunk. She'd known exactly what she was doing, and it had felt damn good to join in on the fun and comradery rather than sit in her quarters reading nerdy military material and missing Nick. Again.

And she would've been fine if she'd just gone back to her bunk, but she'd agreed to have coffee with the hot officer who walked her home. The minute they'd hit the shadows, she kissed him. If Nick could do it, so could she.

But every kiss, every sigh, she'd compared and pretended he was Nick. Yeah, they'd taken precautions, but she'd always figured the condom must've broken.

She'd awakened at dawn with a tequila headache and orders to report to a plane leaving for Iraq at 0900 hours—same base as Nick. She never gave the officer another thought until she woke in Germany after the minefield. A noise from the kitchen roused her from her thoughts.

"Oh, there you are," Arlene mused. "I thought I heard you come in a few minutes ago. You missed Ella's feeding. I used the milk you brought home from work."

A fresh wave of guilt washed over her. "Mom, I owe you a cruise to the Greek Islands. I'm so sorry I dumped Ella on you like that. It'll never happen again. Please forgive me."

Arlene cocked a hip and raised one eyebrow. "Did you tell him about our girl, honey?"

"No, but I found out Nick tried to have the vasectomy reversed after Paris, Mom."

The silence said it all. You could've heard a pin drop.

9

N ick arrived at the senator's home in McLean, Virginia promptly at 10:00 a.m. Even the trees swayed with power and dignity as they guarded the front of the massive three-story residence of the Richardson family. He avoided the circle drive and parked his truck in the back near what he assumed was either the kitchen door or the old servants' quarters. Either way, it wasn't the kind of neighborhood where a vendor gained entry through the front door.

He stepped out of his truck and surveyed the height and breadth of the building. It would take him all day, maybe longer, to secure this place and get it online with his newly designed security system. Good thing Derek was coming to help him. This graceful behemoth would protect like a fortress once they completed the installation.

Nick spotted Derek's van and waved him into the driveway. Derek parked next to him and leaped out with a wry smile on his face.

"Dude, I'm going to need a bunch of new suits to work in this neighborhood."

"We'll ask Mrs. Richardson about the dress code. Since you'll be working days with the kids and the nanny, maybe you can get away with relaxed business or casual Friday. How's Maggie?" Nick hoisted several bags of equipment over his shoulder.

"She's good. Looks beautiful but says she feels like a beached manatee. I had to tie her shoes for her this morning. It's hard to believe there's four more weeks until the baby's due. Doc thinks she might blow early." Derek slung some duffel bags over his shoulder and grabbed a box of supplies. "You're in a chatty mood. You see Liz last night?"

Nick purposely elbowed Derek in the ribs as he turned around. "Chatty? You're an asswipe, D."

Derek laughed. "I'm serious, man. You usually just grunt before noon. You're forming whole sentences today. Did you get to see her?" He stepped out of the way so Nick could shut the door.

"As a matter of fact, we had dinner last night."

"Cool. Did she see the pink shit on your dick?" Derek's grin went from cheek to cheek.

Nick rolled his eyes. "Pink shit? More like red, and no, she didn't. I'm taking it slow."

Derek nodded. "Probably a good idea. I gotta tell you, man, I'm waiting for the right time to ask Maggie to put some of that red stuff on me. It's not only funny—it's *hot*."

Nick barked a laugh. "You're unique, D." He leaned closer. "I'm not sure if there's a security system in place already. Cool it, in case they can see and hear us." He rang the doorbell. They waited in quiet, professional silence until the door opened a fraction.

"Are you with SecureIT?" The female voice lilted a distinct Texas twang.

"Yes. Mrs. Richardson? I'm Nick Flannery, here with Derek Johnson to install your new security system."

"Okay, hang on." After a few seconds of chains dropping, the door flung open. "Hi, I'm Angie, Beau's wife. This here is Precious."

A black Doberman with white paws and a rhinestone collar stood as tall as Angie's waist. It growled, revealed a full set of teeth, and growled again.

Derek took a half step forward and growled back, showed his teeth, and growled again.

The Doberman whimpered and took off into the house.

Angie's eyes popped open as she stared at Derek. "You growled at my dog?"

"Yes, ma'am. Had to let it know who the alpha is."

"YOU'VE GOT the attic and bedrooms done?" Nick looked up from the iPad he used to tweak the security system.

"Oh yeah. I installed the nanny cam and trained it right on the little guy's crib like the missus requested. That nursery is loaded with toys. I can't wait to play with my kid." Derek grinned as he grabbed a bottle of water from their cooler.

Nick grunted. The time his father threw his Lego boats out the bathroom window because he'd left them in the tub crept uneasily through his thoughts. He'd copped a glance into the kid's tub while securing the bathroom window. "Whatever floats your boat, dude. Personally, I can live without a shower filled with rubber duckies and plastic ships. There's a freakin' armada waiting to set sail in the hall bath. An adult would kill themselves trying to shower in there."

"You're a killjoy about little people, Nick. I *get* that's how you roll, but try to contain your excitement for my impending fatherhood."

"I'm happy for you, man. You and Maggie wasted no time getting knocked up once you were stateside again, and you've both wanted this. You'll be terrific parents." He placed a few small components and boosters into a duffel bag. "Ready to do the main floor? Bring the cooler and the box."

Nick took a few steps and stopped. Precious blocked the doorway with a half-snarl on her face. "Hey, D, where'd you put the dog treats?"

Derek looked up and chuckled. "They're in the tool box, dude. You'd best make friends with that beast, in case you end up working here while I'm on family leave. Toss a tidbit across the room and she'll leave the doorway to retrieve it. Stash a bunch of them in your pocket. You want her to think of you as a human treat jar."

Nick lobbed a bone-shaped goodie toward the corner of the room as the two men headed down the stairs.

There was no way Nick would be filling in with the senator's kids. Just the thought of it brought on a cold sweat. He'd already considered Derek's family leave and had made arrangements. "Hey, D? Mason's covering for you while you're on leave, and he's never sure when and if his National Guard unit could be activated. Take whatever time you and Maggie need, but if you can make it back before the six weeks is up, I'll pay you time-and-a-half for the leave you don't use."

"Cool. We'll see. Good thing we've got a few more weeks to get a routine going here."

"Absolutely." Nick turned on the dining room chandelier. "Let's sync the main floor together. You install the readers, and I'll get them online."

"Roger that." Derek felt for the pull-cord and swept open the dining room drapes.

A little giggle trickled across the big room.

Nick looked up, saw nothing, and refocused on the iPad.

Derek gave a quick whistle and pointed toward the corner of the drapes. A pair of sparkly, little, pink heels stuck out at the bottom.

Nick nodded. Oh well. His hope to get through installation without meeting at least one of the kids was unrealistic anyway since three of them lived here. This encounter would make Derek's day more kid-centric than it already was.

Nick focused on the logistics of the job. He'd been protecting people since the day he'd lost his mother. A military shrink would have a good time with that one if he ever dared verbalize it. Which he didn't. Because he couldn't change the past.

Why the hell am I thinking about this right now? He cleared his throat to get Derek's attention.

Derek secured the sensor on the window molding. His boots knocked against the pink glitter shoes. Another giggle tumbled through the room. He put his tools down and pulled the drape back. "Hey now, what have we here?"

A little girl no taller than his mid-thigh stepped into the open space and spread her arms. "Ta-da. I'm a pink princess today." Golden curls bounced around her cherubic face with huge blue eyes lasered on Derek. "Daddy said you're here to stall new piscurity."

Derek knelt on one knee. "That's right. Your daddy wants his pink princess safe. What's your name?"

"Natalie." She took a deep breath. "I'm four. Ollie's only one. Linzee and I are his big sisters. He's asleep in Mommy's office. She's on the phone with Hilde. Hilde's sick and didn't come to work today, so Mommy won't go to her 'pointment 'cause Hilde's our nanny. What's your name?" She did an off-balance pirouette and landed in a fluffy heap at Derek's feet.

"I'm Derek, and that's Nick," he pointed.

She glanced at Nick. "You're big."

He shrugged. "I guess I am. And you're little."

Natalie lifted her chin. "I'm bigger than Ollie. He's a baby. I'm a big girl." She returned to Derek. "Can you come to my tea party?"

He chuckled. "I'd love to, little princess, but I've got work to do."

She turned toward Nick. "Can you come to my tea party? Mommy's going to make cookies for it."

"No, I'm working, too. Maybe another time. We're here to get some things done for your mom and dad." He'd better shut up before the nostalgic trip down nightmare lane started. How many times had his father told him he wouldn't play games even if he'd had the time? The tension in his shoulders cinched tighter. *Where the hell was her mother?*

As if summoned by wishing, Angie's Texas twang cascaded across the house. "Natalie, where did you go, you little monkey?" The brisk clip of heels tapped closer and stopped in the archway of the dining room. She waved a finger and Precious sat next to her. "Ah, there you are. I told you to stay near the office, honey. Just because I was on the phone didn't mean you could wander off and get in the gentlemen's way."

Natalie hid her face behind the skirt of tulle netting and sequins.

"She's no problem, Mrs. Richardson. She was just telling Nick and me about Hilde being sick and the tea party."

"Did she now?" Angie glanced at her daughter and back at Nick. "I need to introduce you both to Oliver and Natalie in front of Precious. Our dog's trained to protect the kids. Do you have a minute?"

"Sure, no problem," Nick affirmed. If a formal introduction helped them navigate the house without the animal blocking them at every doorway, he was all for it.

"Come to Momma, Natalie." She swooped the little girl into her arms with the practiced ease of a mother. "Here, Derek, I'm going to hand her off to you."

Derek accepted the little girl from her mother's arms. Precious barked and stood. Angie waved a finger at the dog, and the animal sat at attention. Angie put her hand on Derek's arm and Natalie's back. "See, he's okay, Precious." She left the child in Derek's arms, walked around the room and then summoned the dog to Derek's side for a good sniff. "Your turn, Nick." She lifted Natalie from Derek's arms.

"That's okay. I won't be working with the kids. I'll be with your husband most of the time." *I'll make sure of it.*

"You don't understand. Precious tore the pants off of a FedEx guy a few months ago when Natalie fell off her scooter in the circle drive. Beau works from home now and then. You'll spend time here. I need to know that Precious trusts you."

Well, okay then. He preferred his pants on his body rather than in the driveway. "Yes ma'am, no problem." His heart thumped several errant beats. It couldn't be that hard to hold a kid, although he'd never done it. He'd held rifles, injured animals, women, and ahh—the little girl was surprisingly light.

Natalie leaned back, scrutinized his face, and ran her small hand over his close, cropped beard.

"It's kinda scratchy." She scrunched up her face and giggled.

The air whooshed from his lungs. Up close, her blue eyes twinkled, and that sweet face bathed him in a rainbow of vivid expressions. This is what Liz wanted? As much as he was against the idea, he couldn't blame her for wanting it. Holding Natalie was sort of nice. He'd give Liz anything she wanted if he could. But a kid? *What if I hurt it?* Even by accident. He couldn't remember a time in his life when he was as wide-eyed and innocent as this child in his arms.

The cool, wet slobber from Precious licking his free hand pulled him back. How long had he been standing there? Angie was talking, but damn, he'd missed most of what she'd said. He set Natalie down and rubbed the dog's head.

He looked around. Derek studied him as Natalie scampered into the kitchen with Angie and Precious.

Nick grabbed his iPad. "Ready to get back to work?"

Derek nodded. "You alright, man? Looked like you drifted off there."

"Cute kid."

"Most of them are."

He nodded. A damn shame he couldn't give Liz one of the things she wanted. But even if he could—he wouldn't. The genes from his drunken, murderous father *had* to stop with him.

"You like the job, Erin?" Liz popped open the container of salad and chicken she'd brought for lunch and addressed the new hire Major Chan had introduced her to earlier that morning.

"Definitely. I like administrative work, and Major Chan seems like a good boss. Tough but fair. I'm looking forward to the challenge." The twenty-something with jet-black hair scrutinized her sandwich.

"Good for you. That's great." Something about the girl was familiar. "Have we met before? What's your last name?"

"Erin Carson." She looked away and stirred her coffee.

Liz slipped a cucumber slice into her mouth, eased out a chair, and sat across from the young woman wearing goth makeup and trendy clothes. Liz had silently admired her black lace-up heels every time she'd strutted down the hall that morning. Sexy heels and a prosthetic didn't really work. *Damn.* She missed sexy shoes something terrible today.

"What's your name again?" Erin inquired, and then stared intently at her cup.

"Liz Nelson."

"Right. You're in the third bullpen on the left. You're the team leader, aren't you?" She lifted her eyes and looked directly at Liz.

"Yes, great memory. Major Chan appreciates qualities like that."

"What do you do exactly?" Erin took a sip of her coffee.

Liz leaned back and chewed a bite of chicken. "Internet security." She answered any question about her job the same way. Rule #1 was never talk shop in the lunchroom. An employee manual guideline insisted they never reveal what or whom they were working on outside of their bullpen. If case-loads crossed paths within the building, which was rare, they'd find out later during the catch phase. It was a simple first day mistake. The girl was new.

Erin laughed and tossed her hands in the air. "Well, duh, the whole building works on internet security. But what do you *do*?"

Liz poked at a squirmy piece of red pepper and thought for a few seconds. "May I ask if you've read your employee manual yet?"

"Um, not completely. Why?" She crumpled the aluminum foil from her sandwich, tossed it at the recycle can, and made the shot.

"You'll want to read it this afternoon. Especially the section on lunchroom etiquette. Honest to goodness, that's what the heading's titled in the manual. Just tell the Major you haven't had a chance to read it yet, and she'll understand." She punctuated the advice with a warm smile. The last thing Liz wanted to do was offend the new girl on her first day.

Erin sat back and crossed her arms. "Lunch etiquette? Are you kidding me?"

Liz shrugged. "I know it sounds weird, and it doesn't have anything to do with napkins or cleaning up after ourselves. There are a few choice instructions on conversation that you'll want to read up on. Most bone-up on it before their first day, but you came on board fast, so I get why you haven't read it all yet."

"Oh, okay," Erin shrugged. "Human resources mentioned it last week after I did the paperwork, but when I saw the size of the booklet, I set it aside."

Liz nodded and repacked her lunch tote. Human resources did more than mention it. Those hounds repeated it six times during her entrance interview. "By the way, I like your heels. They're beautiful. They look great on you."

Erin pointed the toe of one elegant foot. "You think so? Thanks. I love them. Got 'em at a clearance sale on Bloomie's website. My boyfriend likes them, too, if you catch my drift." She made a point of glancing at Liz's shoes. "Guess you dress for function being a boss and all?"

Ouch. Maybe she'd buy the girl a real book on etiquette. "I'm more comfortable in these shoes. Sometimes, I spend hours on my feet." Liz stood and gathered her belongings. "Sorry to cut this short, but duty calls. I've got more to do before lunch is over. Have a good afternoon."

Liz headed straight for the nursing mother's room. After that conversation, she was grateful to be the only nursing mother on this floor and to have the secluded space to herself. She set up the breast pump and attached the plastic bag with a little more force than necessary. It tore.

Shit. She pounded the table with her hand and grabbed another sani-bag. It was a rare stranger who could cut her to the bone with one slice like Erin did. That girl had no idea how much Liz wanted to wear a pair of high heels again. A practical impossibility, unless Liz could find the fifty grand to purchase a custom prosthetic. And she'd already been gifted a made-for-her swim foot from Johns Hopkins for her favorite sport and work with Sanctuary, Inc. She really wasn't in the running for a second prosthetic gift.

She took a series of cleansing breaths. Logically speaking, Erin didn't know about her foot. Liz had worn pants today and had only the slightest limp. She turned on the breast pump, leaned into the plush, leather seat and tried to relax. Her shoulders were one massive knot. She always got uptight when her breasts strained at her shirt.

She closed her eyes and let the pump do its thing. There was nothing intentional about Erin's comment. *Move on.* Chalk it up to one of those moments when a stranger says something and has no idea that they offended. It happens to people all the time.

Why would anyone see the size of the employee manual and set it aside? The major hired only the most qualified applicants. Erin must have a resume of redeeming qualifications.

Eh, what the hell. She'd forgive and do her best to forget. First day faux-pas. No biggie. *Get over it, Nelson.* Let it go.

Liz tapped a finger on the armrest.

What was it that was vaguely familiar about Erin?

LIZ PULLED BACK from her computer screen and glanced at the clock. She'd been sifting through her online identities for hours, answering posts, tweaking her responses, all in an effort to sift for more information. Nobody was biting today.

Not much chatter. The unusual lack of conversation left her eyes watering and her brain searching for stimuli.

She kept drifting to Nick, last night's surprise visit, and their dinner. The fact that he tried to have the vasectomy reversed after Paris revealed what? He was heartbroken that she had said no? He'd had a change of heart? *Did it even matter?*

Hell yes, it mattered. What if his test results got confused with someone else's? What if he just took longer to heal and wasn't shooting blanks anymore? She scrubbed her face with both hands and paced the small office. Fresh coffee would be nice, but she nixed the idea. The moment she opened the office door, she'd lose her train of thought.

She'd been sure the young officer she'd hooked up with was Ella's biological father. So sure, in fact, that she'd mentioned her pregnancy to him in an email while recuperating in Germany. She'd been appalled at his response. "Well darlin', guess you better get that taken care of real soon."

She didn't email him again.

It had been a deep, personal decision that came down to one thing.

Ella had survived the minefield, too.

If her little bean of a fetus had survived that blast, the cold shadow of death hovering over them as they'd waited for evacuation, the transport to Germany, the surgeries, the blood loss, and the drugs—then her baby had earned the right to live. It was the quickest and clearest decision she'd ever made in her life.

No regrets. Then or now.

Even if it cost her Nick.

And there was the sucker punch to her gut. The past fifteen months had been the loneliest of her life. She'd never lied to him before, and each day that she hid Ella's existence was another blow that might drive his heart from her forever.

She'd survived combat, but *forever* without Nick?

I have to tell him. But it would be so much easier if she knew if he was Ella's daddy. Well now, that's easy enough— not. How would she do it? Hand him a pee cup and ask for a sperm sample? Or maybe request a mouth swab because she wanted to investigate his ancestry?

Liz chuckled.

She knew her Nick. With any one of those options, she'd end up pinned beneath him laughing in a compromised position. And he'd love every minute of it. To be honest, so would she.

She needed to soldier-up and tell him. She'd hid it too long. At first, the physical recovery from the blast had overwhelmed her. She'd spent weeks between rehab and an armchair by her hospital room window staring outside. She didn't look ahead but digested, tried to accept the life forced upon her. She'd grieved for the foot that no longer existed. A fog had enveloped her as she struggled for purchase and worked to achieve physical and emotional balance.

And then she flew home to Walter Reed. The endless cycle of more rehab, prenatal visits, and the daunting challenge to jump-start her life consumed her. She could've told Nick. They'd talked on the phone a hundred times. But all she'd wanted was space and distance. If she'd allowed him in her life at that point, she would've had to deal with his tragic emotions about the baby. Ella was her decision and hers alone.

She'd always been Nick's sanctuary. He'd placed his heart in her hands years ago, and it would have been too much to deal with as she recovered. Especially because he'd made sure that children were never a part of their future.

And she couldn't blame him for that. The abuse he'd suffered as a child was unimaginable to her. While they'd both had middle-class upbringings, her family life boasted of love and support while his nights and weekends belied fear and terror.

She rubbed her arms in an attempt to drive the cold shivers away. The only way to heal their relationship meant she had to risk harming it.

She'd tell him.

She'd invite him over for dinner. Keep Ella at the house, introduce her to him, and spell out the situation.

Her heart pounded just thinking about it.

She had a lot of explaining to do.

11

I llusia's phone vibrated and shimmied down the couch
pillow, landing on a purple seat cushion.

She set the bottle of cherry nail lacquer on an end table
and glanced at the name on the screen. *Pffft...he could kiss her
ass.* That dweeb military guy she'd been seeing the past two
weeks? Let him ring a hundred times. Done with him. *Idiot.*

Plus, his breath was plain foul.

In just under a year, she'd contacted every veteran on her
list. Most of them were losers as far as she was concerned.
She'd posed as a journalist looking to write a series on the
military stationed in Iraq. Almost all had given her necessary
pieces of information like dates, locations, and even a few
confidential conversations. She collected facts, steered the
small talk, asked questions, and laughed at their bad jokes and
one-liners. One thing she'd learned? Vets loved to talk about
their time in the service once they had a few beers under their
belt.

She'd followed up on vets as far as California, Nebraska,
Texas, New York, and Louisiana. It had cost her a chunk of

savings to trek that far, but she'd had to follow the names she'd found in her brother's online journal, and that's where they led.

And none of them had any idea they'd been selected for a mission greater than themselves. Every detail they'd revealed added to her cause, justified the means, and brought her another step closer to revenge.

Except for Sergeant Nick Flannery. A real tight-ass who hadn't relaxed one iota until she instructed the bartender to keep the beers coming at twenty-minute intervals. She'd slipped a fifty in the barkeep's tip jar as a thank you.

Even then, the first two beers hadn't softened the good-looking sergeant's tongue or demeanor. He'd hardly given her the time of day, focusing on the music and ordering a cheese-burger platter. Out of patience and running out of cash, Illusia picked up the third round of beers at the bar herself and laced *his* with a full dropper of *Super Spanish Fly*. Not the cheap stuff. The trademarked brand with a money-back guarantee.

Not to worry—she'd needed a good boning, anyway.

She wasn't a heathen. *Of course, she felt bad* when she read the directions on the bottle of aphrodisiac the next day. Five drops would've been plenty to command his attention. But she couldn't stand there at the bar counting drops without *somebody* noticing. And so, the sergeant with the broad shoulders, tasteful tats, who kept himself in shape, and was a gentleman? He'd been insatiable.

But he *was* a distant lover. He muttered *that woman's* name when it counted, but she didn't give a crap. He'd stayed tight-lipped with his military stories but sure knew his way around a woman's body. And when the Spanish fly wore off, he'd passed out cold for hours. She'd cloned his phone (just in case) and tiptoed out of the room with heels in hand minutes before dawn.

Illusia sighed. *So sorry to see that one go.* He was worth the effort and price of a DC hotel room.

She'd marked him hoping he'd think of her when he whipped that bad boy out the next time. Make him gun-shy with other ladies for a while. She smiled to herself. *There was nothing wrong with being memorable.*

She finished the second coat to her nails and waved her hands back and forth. *Shit.* She'd forgotten to turn on the TV before she applied the polish. Now, she'd have to miss half her show because the freaking remote always dinged at least one glossy finger. These nails were important. She had to look professional.

She stood and paced. Getting primped and pretty for the business world sucked big time, but the bank account needed replenishment. She couldn't touch the offshore savings for a few more months and had to be careful with the identity theft. The last thing she needed were detectives ringing her doorbell. She had to blend in like the illusion she was and be a respectable renter in her gated condo community.

Illusia sighed long and hard. Sometimes, when she looked in the mirror, she couldn't see the woman she'd been two years ago. But that was the grief talking. She hadn't spent nine months in the womb and a lifetime afterwards with a twin brother to lose him one day in supposed service to his country. Not when his journal stated otherwise. And she'd located the decision maker who caused his death.

They'd pay with their blood.

She'd make absolutely sure of it.

Nick stubbed a toe trying to get across the pitch-black bedroom to answer his phone. He cursed the contractor who had neglected to fix the electrical outlet by the bed. *Fix it myself.* Nah—he valued his life. Merciful God, his foot hurt. He grabbed the phone. "Yeah, Nick here."

"Dude, it's Derek. Maggie's in labor. We're on our way to the hospital. Get a hold of Mason to cover for me at the Richardson's today. I gotta go."

Nick was fully awake now. Maggie's voice in the background urged Derek to stop driving over every pothole, followed by a moan.

"No problem, D. You guys go have yourselves a healthy baby. Give Maggie my love." He disconnected the call and plopped into the red leather chair by the window, glancing at the clock radio. It was 4:15 a.m.

It had been a smooth first week with the senator's family. Derek melded right in, and the kids loved him. Aside from the crew manning the Richardson's 24/7, another technician picked up the work debugging Georgetown restaurants. Nick had gained nine restaurants in three days once word got out about the number of surveillance pieces he'd found at The Town Crier.

Nobody was irreplaceable but Derek came pretty close.

He'd have to shift Derek's workload to Mason. Mason was a good guy. Not as warm and fuzzy with kids, but he had a sense of humor and solid security instincts.

There'd be no going back to sleep now. He tossed the duvet over the bed and paused to imagine Liz curled in the middle, right where she liked to sleep.

It'd been a long time since they'd spent a night together. Paris, actually. Almost two years now. Hopefully, she'd give some thought to their recent conversation during dinner. Try to believe in them enough to give their relationship a chance. They'd always promised each other when they left the service, they'd see if forever belonged in their future. He rubbed the center of his chest. It always ached when he thought about Liz maybe wanting someone else.

He fisted the pillows into shape and lined them up against the headboard. His version of making the bed made Liz laugh. She liked it tucked in real neat, decorative pillows arranged up top, and a nap afghan arranged just so on the bottom corner. He stopped and took a picture of the bed. Maybe he'd text it to her. Remind her she could arrange the space however she liked.

Aww...hell. He'd settle to have her between his sheets so he could hear the little snore she'd developed after a zealous fist broke her nose in a volleyball game senior year. How he missed the light scent of her perfume and the way her round derriere snuggled into his core and made him hard in an instant.

He glanced at his tented boxers. *Sorry, buddy, you're stuck with me again.*

Maybe he could take some parenting classes. How the hell does anybody learn how to do that correctly? Never lose their temper or yell at a kid? Even his mom lost it once in a while, though it was rare. Mostly, he remembered her kindness and encouragement. The way she'd hide him in different closets behind the clothes when he was little and tell him not to come out no matter what he heard. She'd promise to make his favorite dinner the next day if he'd stay in the closet until she came to get him. He'd never forget the fear lurking in her eyes.

As he grew older and bigger, he'd become aware of the bruises and welts on her body. She'd covered them well, but once in a while as he walked by her room, he'd catch a glance of her back as she changed into fresh clothes. He started standing in the gap between his father's fists and her body. When he was twelve, he began training on the punching bag in their dank basement. He took his father's abuse most of the time, but every once in a while he'd fill with rage and just flat-out deck him. Cold-cock the sonofabitch, drag his drunken body into the spare bedroom and lock the door.

Some would call that protective behavior, but to Nick it only proved one thing.

He could be as cold as his father.

13

W *hat?* Family members. Right.

Liz realized she'd left the names on her desk, so she raced through the bullpen and across the hallway to her office. She sifted through the small stack of papers and found the information the commander demanded while listening to the hostage negotiations on her headset as they took a turn for the worse. She grabbed the paper and shot out her office door, plowing straight into Erin carrying a box of papers. The box upended onto the floor, and Erin fell backward into a glass door.

Liz stuffed the list into her pocket and grabbed her head. "Oh Erin, I'm so sorry, are you alright?" She bent to help the poor girl off the floor. "I'm so sorry, let me help you."

Erin put her hand up. "No, no, my fault. Red light's on in the hallway. I should've stayed out of the way. Do what you have to do. I'll get up in a minute on my own."

"Who the fuck are you talking to, Nelson? 'Cause it sure as shit isn't me. I need that intel now," the commander bellowed in her ear.

Liz nodded at Erin and dashed into the bullpen, pulling the door shut behind her. Every monitor was in motion. Different angles of the same scene. The takedown of a drug smuggler on a fishing vessel endeavoring to cruise into the Florida Keys unnoticed.

Good luck with that. The Keys had as many cyber-eyes as a major metropolitan area. They were just more discreet.

"I have the list, Commander."

"How nice of you to join us, Nelson. Anytime you're ready, read 'em off," he huffed.

Oh, how she hated working with this hostage negotiator. Blevins was a surly bastard. She bit back a retort because the perp on the monitor had a cabin full of undocumented immigrants and held three of them at gunpoint. Concern creased everyone's forehead in the bullpen.

"Wife's name is Maria. Children—Carlos, thirteen years, Bianca, ten years and Cecelia, six years. Copy that, Commander?"

"Got it. You'd better be right, Nelson."

Liz closed her eyes and counted to three. What an arrogant prick. Of course, she was right. Her bullpen had worked feverishly for days to confirm the intel. Six government agencies worked together on this bust. A huge conglomeration of locals and feds pulling in unison for a live catch. And Blevins picked right now to threaten *her* while three innocent people had guns aimed at their heads?

She braced her hands on a desk and leaned forward. Every monitor displayed a different angle of the gunman and hostages. None of the snipers had a clear shot. A bullet traveling at high velocity would not only pierce the intended target but the innocent in front or behind him as well. This was no time to play roulette with the law of unintended consequences.

She listened as Blevins recited the names of the perp's family members and focused especially on the youngest, Cecelia. Was it really worth it to this guy to leave behind a wife and three children? Blevins tended to be successful as long as he didn't deviate from the script.

Liz touched the mouthpiece on her headset. "Commander, we'd really like to capture this guy alive. He's the only one we've apprehended who knows the entire food chain personally for this particular cartel." Her headset crackled with his response.

"Yeah, well, I'd like the Easter bunny to start delivering candy at Christmas time, but we don't always get what we want, now do we?"

She drew in a breath through her teeth. "You're right, Blevins, but perhaps we could offer him a small concession to reel him in. Like cheeseburgers and cigarettes in prison? Twice yearly visas for his family to visit him? Think. Something that would make his life more bearable going forward. He's worth a lot to Uncle Sam alive."

Blevins snorted. "You damn people don't realize that scumbags like this need to be terminated."

"We're on the same team, Commander. Let's work together." *What was with this guy?* He was as insubordinate as she'd ever seen. She waited and listened.

After a brief pause, Blevins launched into a speech in Spanish. She eyed the cameras; watching the young woman in front of the perp break down sobbing.

Carmen hurried across the bullpen and translated. "You need to let those people go. We'll sweeten the deal and offer you cheeseburgers in prison. Anything's better than allowing the cartel to haul your sorry ass into the desert and kill you. Your family probably won't want anything to do with you if the cartel even lets them live. Put the gun down, asshole, and let those people go."

And with that, the perp raised the gun and fired at his own head. That fast. Negotiation over. Blood spattered the hostages and deck of the boat.

Carmen gasped, Liz dropped into a chair, and the major rose to her feet. The bullpen rumbled with a steady murmur. That translation was so *not* the heart and essence of what she'd suggested, and anger surged through her like a bolt of potent heat. She stood, touching her headset.

"Commander Blevins, you're relieved of your post. Please hand your headset to your second."

"Now, wait just a minute, little miss. You don't have the authority to dismiss me."

"Blevins, I am not your little miss but the lead analyst here. You are relieved of your post. Return to your company for reassignment to more compatible duty. I'll let your superiors decide what that might be, but I never want to hear your voice on a DHS headset again. Do I make myself clear, sir?"

"This will never stick, Nelson."

"I disagree, sir. The entire negotiation was recorded by six different government entities. The message you delivered did nothing to encourage the perp to surrender without further incident. You effectively stripped him of any hope. I have the translation in front of me. Please hand your headset to your second."

Major Chan's voice piped in, "She's right, Commander. Do you need the MPs help to leave?" She placed a hand on Liz's shoulder and whispered, "I've got it from here. Go take a break. You've earned it." Then, in a louder voice, she announced to the bullpen, "Twenty minute break, everyone. Go walk it off. Fresh coffee in the lunchroom."

Still stunned, Liz strode with her coworkers down the hallway, offering words of encouragement, thanks, and a few pats on the back. Fury fueled by adrenaline coursed her veins. There'd been hundreds of qualified people on site to handle the situation correctly, and it only took Blevins to muck it up. How could he have been so callous and narrow-minded? Why would the perp do that to himself and his family? There were people in this world who'd give anything for one more day on earth, shitty or not.

She headed for her office, stretched against the back of the door and tried to clear the image of the perp offing himself that reverberated in her brain by focusing on the picture of Ella on her desk. She'd taken this job to protect all the sweet Ella's in this world. How dare he use his commission in opposition to the unit's goals? She moved into a deep breathing routine that never failed to energize her and contemplated.

Nick had done hostage negotiation in Iraq. She'd never witnessed him in action, but the stories were famous around the barracks. He'd once talked a group of enemy deserters into surrendering themselves and their Russian tank without a single bullet fired. The fighters had gone six days without food and water. Nick promised them an all-you-can-eat buffet in exchange for surrender and the keys to the tank. They'd laid down their arms after a tense discussion. Unharmed, they ate their meal in shackles.

Maybe she'd talk to Nick about her situation today in generic terms. She couldn't discuss work outside of this

building, but she could ask him to shed light on hostage negotiations and learn a few things she'd employ next time. A
longing sigh escaped her chest. Hearing his steady voice right
now would be a healing balm.

But there were three hours left to the workday and her
profiles wouldn't follow up on themselves. She perused
Marion Trent's homepage. As usual, it was loaded with new
posts.

There was an invitation to a VFW dance in Sterling, VA
from an older gentleman, a few advertisements for strip clubs
and swinger sites, and an invite from a local crochet club
asking if she'd be interested in joining.

Liz moved on to the friend requests. Three of them came
from scammers she either knew of or had handled in the past.
Flag and forward to the appropriate agency. One was from an
interesting young man in Brussels, and she made a note to
check him out later.

The final request was from a man who'd served time for
child pornography. Liz highlighted and copied the information onto a report for her contact at the FBI. *They'll shut you
down again, sicko.* Maybe this time, they'll keep your perverted
self in jail before you can harm the youngest members of the
public again.

She leaned back in her chair and crossed her arms. Stopping that child porn guy made her crappy day worth it.

There were thirteen private messages. There was no time
like the present, and she opened the list. Two messages were
from the same overseas guy who'd offered Marion a job as a
nanny for that large group of children. Liz made a note to
follow up with Major Chan on what the dark web guys had
uncovered in their search.

She moved on, opening the next message while picking up her coffee for a sip.

Are you enjoying the flowers I sent?

It took Liz a few seconds to process the question.

She read it again. The coffee cup in her hand tipped and the warm liquid dribbled onto her lap. She startled, set the cup down, and grabbed some napkins. Dabbing at her clothes, she glanced at the corner shelf. The wilting roses stared at her like frozen mimes. She'd forgotten all about them and hadn't watered them in several days.

And then it hit her like a semi. Marion Trent's profile had been compromised.

No. Omigod. No.

Though the adrenaline from the earlier bust had subsided, a fresh release tore through her system like a sprinter on steroids. She clutched her chest. *What the hell?*

Marion was her connection to the darkest, underbelly worlds. Marion was responsible for over forty busts in the past couple months. Marion was invaluable. Liz checked the DHS procedures book and slammed it on the desk.

If Marion were compromised and someone asked about the roses via her messages, then whoever sent the roses also knew Liz worked at Homeland Security in the cyber-security section. They knew who she was. They'd possibly gained access to her files. What else did they know? It was an invasion of the highest magnitude.

Sure, phishing happened all the time at government agencies. But here in the sanctity of this building were some of the greatest cyber experts in the world, defending the perimeter twenty-four hours a day. What happened here was massive, life-altering.

Liz took a screenshot of the message and hurried towards the major's office. She knocked twice and then barged in on a meeting.

"Forgive me, Major. I need you." Liz couldn't believe she was doing this, but it was protocol.

Chan stood and excused the person sitting across from her. "We'll finish this discussion via phone in the morning, Harold." Once he'd left, she looked at Liz. "What's going on?"

"Probable security breach. Your input, please."

Chan didn't say a word but gathered a binder, burner phone, and her eyeglasses. "Let's go." She locked her door on the way out and shoved the keys in her pocket.

They walked quickly and in silence to Liz's office. The major locked the door from the inside after she shut it.

"Show me."

Liz pulled up the social media post and stood back, allowing Chan the chair.

The major steepled her hands and sat for a few seconds. "This is a prime example of why we don't allow personal deliveries at work, Liz."

A wave of unfounded guilt rolled over Liz. "I understand, ma'am. Believe me when I say that I still don't know who sent them." She reached for the vase.

Chan leaped up and grabbed her hand. "Don't touch them. Forensics will be here in a few minutes to bag and remove them. Here, just sit while I make a few calls."

Liz listened in horror as the major requested a forensic team on the 7th floor, initiated a complete download of every computer, and called in a Code Blue to freeze online access for the entire building.

When the voice on the other end of the phone questioned her, she raised her voice. "Kill it, Victoria."

FORENSICS ARRIVED MINUTES LATER. In Hazmat suits.

The major unlocked the door and let them in. "Come with me, Liz."

Liz reached for her purse.

"No purse right now. The team will scan and search it. It'll be returned when they're done."

Oh. My. Goodness. "Okay." She followed the major back to her office and steadied herself in a chair.

The major sat next to her. "I need to ask you some questions."

Liz swallowed hard. "Yes, of course."

"Think back. Have you made any new friends? Mentioned to anyone what you do for work? Flirted with someone? Got a new love interest? A new daycare provider? Is there anyone new in your life, Liz?"

Liz pursed her lips and gave a definitive shake of her head. "No. There's no one new in my life. I never tell people that I work here. I've told people that I work for Homeland Security but never go into detail. You need to understand, Major, my life is very limited in scope right now. I have an infant at home. Most nights when I'm done here, I head home to nurse Ella and relieve my mother from her babysitting duties. The most socializing I do involves buying diapers at the Big4Less on the way home from work."

"Has anyone flirted with you? Accidentally bumped into you?" Natalie sat back and waited.

"No. No one new."

"Someone from your past, then?"

Shit. Now she'd drag Nick into this. "I've had an on-again, off-again relationship with my high school sweetheart for the past ten years. And for the record, he doesn't know about Ella, and I want to be the one to tell him. We had dinner together a few nights ago. The same day the roses arrived at my office. I hadn't talked to him in a few weeks, but texted and asked if he'd sent the flowers. He said *no,* and that night he showed up at my home with his own flowers and a supper invitation."

"Do you trust him?"

Oh no, she was not going there. That was a trick subjective question, which would lead to twenty other questions. "You'll have to make your own decision on that matter. He's a decorated veteran with ten years of service." She recited Nick's legal name and military ID. She'd memorized his ID years ago, along with a few others because she often had access to casualty lists and searched them first for those she loved.

A knock on the door ended the conversation. It was the Hazmat guys with her purse and keys.

Liz stood up. "Am I free to leave, Major?"

"Yes. There's nothing else you can do here today. Go home. Please remember that the questions and cloak and dagger protocols are not personal. They're procedures."

"I understand, see you tomorrow."

Liz held her head high, even though sadness for the hostage situation and Marion's loss weighted every step as she headed for her car. After dropping into the front seat, she turned on the AC, and checked her messages in the parking lot. An impromptu invite to dinner at Nick's renovated loft greeted her. *Hell, yes.* Dinner with Nick would go a long way toward shaking off the day's events. She checked with her mother. It was book club night at the house. There'd be plenty of loving arms and kisses for Ella. And Liz was so glad she'd dropped the late afternoon pump for Ella.

For once in her life, she didn't overthink or analyze it. She tapped Nick's address into the GPS and turned onto the highway ramp toward his place.

14

Nick swung the door open. "Hey, beautiful. Glad you could make it." He pressed a kiss to her forehead and tugged her inside.

She gave him a shaky smile and handed him a bottle of wine.

"Whoa, what's wrong?" There were worry lines on her face where there'd been none a few days ago.

"Thanks for the invite. It's been a hellacious day at work. An evening with you is just what I need." She all but fell into his open arms and held him tight.

Okay, then. He hadn't expected to have her so close, this fast, but he wrapped his arms around her, kissing the top of her head. It'd been a long time since his girl needed him, and for some reason, she needed him *now.* He reached behind him, set the wine on the entry table and ran his hands up and down her back, massaging her curves under his palms. "Your shoulders are tighter than a piece of plywood, babe. You want to talk about it?"

"No. Well, maybe. Just give me a minute," she sighed. "You

shouldn't have visited me the other night. Now, I miss you all the time."

That's exactly why he *did* go see her. "Perfect timing, then. I saw where you lived earlier this week. I figured it'd be a nice idea to show you my digs. A step up from the barracks." He kissed the top of her head to the tip of her nose and planted a light one on her lips. "I could end every work day with you in my arms."

"Yeah, that'd be nice." She kissed his neck and leaned back, waggling her eyebrows. "You promised wine?"

"So, I did." He slipped his hand in hers and urged her toward the kitchen.

"Wow, Nick. These quartz countertops are gorgeous. Stainless steel, chef stove, white lacquer cabinets. This is beautiful." She wrinkled her nose and laughed. "Did you learn how to cook?"

He grabbed a remote and pressed a button. "Built-in monitor over there for displaying recipes. Contractors finished only a week ago. I haven't used it. So, no, my culinary expertise hasn't improved yet."

"Impressive. You've been here only a week?" She accepted the glass of wine he offered and strolled to the picture windows facing the park. "Pretty view."

"I actually moved in a month ago and lived in the mess until completion. I couldn't very well run a security agency that caters to the Washington elite from the eastern shore of Maryland. I put a long-term renter in the bayside Cape Cod. I'm not ready to sell it. It's been in my mother's family for fifty years."

"I love that cottage. I remember going there with you our senior year. Glad you're keeping it." She looked at him over the rim of her wineglass.

"I remember doing a lot of things there with you our senior year." He laughed. The memories kept coming. That was part of the reason he couldn't sell it. Someday, he wanted to enjoy the place with her when they were married. He slipped a hand around her waist. "Do you want to see the rest of the loft?"

"Sure. I love the floors. Is this the original wood? Wow. It's spacious." She walked alongside him through a wide hallway.

"Yeah. It's got three bedrooms, three bathrooms, and an office. I was lucky to find it before they began the renovations. I had the chance to customize a little, and yes, the floors are original for the most part. First stop, master bedroom." He swept his arms open as they entered the room.

She ran a finger across the footboard of the king-size sleigh bed and turned around. "Look at the size of that closet. As much as I like your new suit-and-tie style, I can't imagine you filling that walk-in, Nick." She let go of his hand and wandered into the master bathroom. A huge stained-glass palladium window framed a soaking tub. "This bathroom is the size of my mother's living room."

He smiled. "Cool, huh? I asked them to take two smaller rooms that used to be offices and make them into a bathroom. I wanted a lot of comfort built into this room." He leaned against one of the vanities and drank in the sight of her. She fit in like she belonged here with him, using this space. He ached to free her hair from the ponytail holder and run his hands through it. *She really had no idea how sexy she was.*

Liz stopped mid-step. "You installed one of those sitting tub and shower combinations. They're handicap accessible. My mom put one in for me." Her voice drifted off as she traced the edge with a finger. "It has a lovely pearl finish."

"Of course." He had to be careful. *Don't push. Don't push. Just let it sink in. Let her do the talking.*

She looked at him, eyes brimming. "You put this in for me?" She yanked a tissue from the box on the quartz countertop and wiped her nose.

"You can't blame a guy for hoping that maybe you'd want to use it sometime." He congratulated himself. It didn't sound presumptuous at all. *Totally her decision.* He really couldn't take it if she pulled away from him again. Slow and easy did it when dealing with his injured bird.

"It's beautiful and tasteful. It doesn't look like handicap equipment at all." She turned away and softly blew her nose.

The doorbell rang. "That's our food."

She nodded and followed him. "Let me help. What's on the menu?"

He tipped the delivery girl and set two large bags on the counter. "Chinese. Italian. Ice cream and cookies for dessert." He shrugged. "I couldn't make up my mind. You unload the bags, and I'll get us some plates and napkins." He grabbed a stack of serving spoons. "I hope you're hungry. I know I am." He gestured for her to go first.

"This is lovely, Nick. I'm famished. I haven't eaten since early this morning."

He made sure she was comfortable at the table and loaded his plate. "I know they give you breaks at DHS. Why didn't you eat?"

"We got caught up in a situation. I had an older commander call me a *little miss.*"

He gave a low whistle. "I hope you hurt him?"

"No, he hurt himself in the long run."

"Good." Nick took a bite of eggroll. "And?"

"And I can't talk about the rest of it." She placed a napkin in her lap and dug in to her food.

He raised an eyebrow. "Ever?"

"No. But it was tough." She slid a forkful of manicotti in her mouth and sighed. "Good choice. Italian is a total comfort food."

He could think of things a lot more comforting than Italian food, but maybe later. "You signed an NDA for that kind of discretion at work?"

"Yup. I didn't even question the policy until now. After a day like today, I'd like to be able to talk things out with someone other than a coworker. I won't bring it up again. There's nothing you can do about it." She took a sip of wine and flashed him a smile that didn't quite reach her eyes.

He wiped his mouth with a napkin and sat back. "We've always had different security clearances. Let's try talking around the details like we used to."

She spooned Italian vegetables onto her plate. "I guess we could. I'm very uncomfortable right now. A week ago, I loved my job, but as of today, I feel like I should be looking over my shoulder."

"Co-worker problem?"

"No. For the most part, they're wonderful people." She forked a huge hunk of zucchini, then reached across the table and fed it to him.

"An outside entity, then?"

She was quiet a few seconds. "Pretty sure. With a big *I'm gonna ruin your reputation* sign on it."

Unease crept across his chest. He nonchalantly twirled fettucine around a shrimp on his fork. "You work in an office, not off the grid, right?" *Please say no fieldwork.*

"That's right. Just me and my computer." She exaggerated a

sigh and then snickered. "It sounds so lame. But the work I do really helps people. That was one of my employment goals."

Of course, it was. Her big brain had always been motivated by her superhero heart. "By the sound of this conversation, I hope you don't mind me saying that I'm glad you're working in an office instead of the field. So, why do you feel uncomfortable?"

She paused, set her fork down, and pursed her lips. "Did you ever have a feeling like something or someone behind the scenes was pulling strings and meant to undermine your professional life?"

Dammit to hell. The half-chewed mouthful slid down his throat in one gulp as the unease in his chest spread like an alarm. "Overtly—yes. But then I confronted the person and set the record straight."

Liz tapped a finger on the table and pointed at him. "Because you could figure out who it was, right?"

"Correct. Sometimes, it took a little digging to determine the who and why." He grabbed the wine bottle and refilled both their glasses.

She leaned back in her chair and crossed her arms. "Well, that's just it. I don't know if I can nail down who's doing this. My job is cloaked. It's all smoke and mirrors. I'm not sure I can determine the source of the problem." She bit her bottom lip.

He wanted to nibble that lip in the worst way, so he looked directly into her light brown eyes instead. "Babe, the federal government is a behemoth of great minds. Surely, one of them will help?"

"I've got a great boss. An awesome support team. I just feel like I'm working a puzzle missing a bunch of pieces. It's *my job* to find the missing ones. I recognize patterns that no one else sees. But this is out of left field for seemingly no reason."

Hell, if she was uneasy, so was he. He tore a hunk off the loaf of rosemary bread more forcefully than he intended. She usually balked at his protective instincts and with good reason. The woman could take care of herself. But still, he *had* to broach the subject. "Do you feel safe at work, babe?"

She waved his question away with a flick of her hand. "Yeah. The building is very secure. It was just a bad day. I'll get over it. A good night's sleep and everything will be right in my world again." She leaned across the table and fed him a bite of manicotti.

He hesitated with his response but decided to go for it, anyway. "If you ever question your safety, Liz, please don't take any chances. Let me fix you up with some kind of security. Sanctuary, Inc. would be glad to help you out after all you've done for them."

She rolled her eyes. "I am no senator in need of a bodyguard. Don't go all Kung Fu and guns-blazing on me. Thank you, though." She reached over and squeezed his hand. "You know, I'd forgotten how good you are at discussing a situation without really knowing the details."

How could he make her understand? She was worth *fifty* senators to him. He hadn't seen her this uneasy about a job since the night before the minefield in Iraq. She'd paced the barracks half sick with worry that she wasn't the point person on the mission. She couldn't stand waiting for umpteen tiers of brass to decide what *she* was going to do in a situation where her own team wasn't in place. Liz had always functioned better in the alpha position, and 98% of the time, her decisions were spot-on. Riding shotgun had never been her long suit.

"More wine or a coffee maybe?" Me, perhaps? *No, he'd need to bide his time and be patient.*

"No wine, it'll make me sleepy. A decaf would be nice, though." Liz got up and took their dishes to the sink and started running the hot water. "I can't thank you enough for the delicious dinner, Sergeant. Your timing and food choices were impeccable."

Nick rose and followed her to the kitchen. "You're welcome, and I haven't forgotten how much you love Aunt Bertie's chocolate chip cookies. I had them deliver a bag fresh from the bakery. Want one?" He really wanted her for dessert, but would she'd let that happen? He grabbed a cookie, broke it in half, and stood behind her at the sink gently waving it in front of her. "Want a bite?" The warmth of her body invited him closer, and he pressed against her.

"Oh, they have nuts. It's a temptation I can't resist." She pulled the cookie in, took a bite. "Next bite is yours, mister. Watching the calories these days."

He had nuts, too. Tempting nuts. Waiting for her soft bite. He admired the gentle slope of her shoulder as it turned downward into a firm but feminine arm. "Far be it from me to comment on your calorie intake, but from my vantage point it looks like you've put each and every one in the right place."

She chuckled. "That's because you've always been a rearview guy."

He laughed. "Right." His fingers slowly traced her back to her waist, down to her hips and up again. "You're beautiful, babe. Inside and out. It's nice to be with you and enjoy some time together."

She turned the water off, braced her hands on the sink edge, and rotated her hips against his hard-on. "We're definitely in the same emotional space, Nick. I've missed you. Terribly."

Thank God. "And?"

"This is just what I need." She let out a long sigh.

"I've longed for this, every day since Iraq." He placed a hand on each hip and pinned her to the cabinet. Her bumping and his grinding threatened to set him off like an ill-timed firecracker in that position. He slacked off to regain control.

She whimpered, undid her skirt, and let it pool at her feet. "Please touch me. If you only knew how much—"

Her breathy plea became his only focus. "Shh, just feel, my love."

He freed her dark hair from its holder and swept it to one side, tracing the sweet spots on her neck with his tongue. She shivered and reached back, pulling his hips close again. He could tolerate her gyrations this time, elated to feel their hips moving in unison.

"How do you want me, Liz?" His fingers danced down her hips and traced the outline of her lace underwear. She was even more stunning than he remembered. Her curves filled his hand and he was desperate to feel more, claim what was his. She'd always been his greatest temptation and desire. One moonless night ten years ago, she'd captured him, body and soul.

"Desperate, Nick. Want. You. Please."

"Like this?" He slipped her panties down to mid-thigh and ran a finger through her crease.

She whimpered.

"There's a nice big bed in the other room."

"No, like this." She threw her head back and sighed.

Of course, she wouldn't choose the bed. A bed represented more than comfort to Liz—it depicted a kind of permanence.

This was a quick after dinner romp. For all he knew, she'd bolt from his life like she'd done after the Sanctuary rescue. He tried to memorize the feel of her touch just in case the memory was all he had after tonight.

He slid an arm around her waist and slipped his other fingers into her slickened folds. She was so wet that his fingers easily swirled in and out and around. She bucked against his hand while he tightened his hold around her waist.

"I can't hold back anymore," she gasped with a moan.

"Let it go, Liz. Come for me, baby." He set his cheek against hers and held on.

She shuddered and groaned aloud in his arms as her knees buckled. And then, what the hell? She started to cry, gasping for air at the same time. The seconds morphed into minutes until she confided in a quiet murmur, "I've never had an orgasm that made me cry."

"I've got you, honey. I won't let go." A promise he intended to keep if she'd only let him.

She turned and unbuttoned his shirt, pulling him in for a tear-infused kiss. "I need you inside me." She undid his belt and zipper, shoved the pants down—taking his boxers with them and setting his erection free. He toed-off his shoes and kicked them away.

He scooped her into his arms and set her on the chaise section of the couch. *Damn furniture needed to be broken in anyway.* Her hair fanned out underneath her like a mass of dark bronze silk in the fading amber light of dusk. She took his breath away.

"Please, Nick. Now. I want you."

He almost asked if she wanted the prosthetic off, but she sat up, took hold of his shaft and stroked, fondling his balls.

He couldn't think straight. "Whoa, girl. Go easy. I want to savor this."

He slid inside, inch by glorious inch. She was like home, warm and comfortable, and his. He inhaled her every breath with kisses, felt her quiver as she tumbled over the edge, and then shouted with his own release.

"I've been so lost without you." She nuzzled her face into the crook of his neck and ran her fingers through his hair. "I love you."

"You're my everything, sweetie. Stay with me tonight."

"I can't, but come for dinner on Friday night. There's so much I want to talk about."

The exhilaration of their lovemaking faded with her refusal to spend the night. *Love had never been their problem. Permanence was.*

He set his head on top of hers and let the hurt wash over him. *Why won't you stay, Liz? What is more important than us?* He swallowed the angst and focused on her invitation. "Did you learn how to cook?" He kissed her nose. It tasted of dried tears.

She chuckled. "Very funny, but I've become pretty good with a crockpot."

Hell, to do this again, just skip the food. "Yes, to dinner at your place on Friday. Whatever you make or order will be delicious." He slid his hardening cock into her tight channel and punctuated his point with a couple thrusts.

Her lips parted, and she wrapped her legs around him again. "Ooh, you feel good, so deep, and so damn good." She took his mouth in a wanton kiss. "You're everything I wanted tonight, Sergeant. Let's do it slow this time."

A half hour later, as he tucked her in her car to leave for

home, she took his face in her hands. "You're the love of my life. Don't ever forget that. Okay?"

He kissed her cheek and nibbled her bottom lip. "I love you, too. Drive safe. I'll see you Friday."

As she drove away, his brows furrowed. She'd said she loved him. Then why did her words leave him with a sense of dread?

Like they stood on the edge of something unknown that might rip them apart.

15

I llusia dropped her binoculars and ducked before Liz's car rolled past her.

Wow. Judging by the show she'd seen, Nick and Liz were joined at the hip. Literally. She needed a shower. Peeping made her skin crawl and itch. She wasn't a pervert.

He really should invest in some drapes.

Nick had done quite well for himself judging from the gaze she'd had into that loft. Maybe she should've held onto him a little longer than one night, kept his phone number in her private contacts?

Nah. He'd only distract her from her primary goal with those piercing blue eyes and solid biceps. She'd sacrifice another round with him to reach her objective.

She never thought following Liz after work would lead to *this.* She'd wanted to light up Liz's night another way, get it done once and for all, but information was valuable. It gave her strategy more options.

She wouldn't move too fast. Her brother always had big ideas and moved quickly. That's how the feds nailed him for hacking into the social security website. Jazz'd been so excited he succeeded that he forgot to remove a smidgeon of meta-data on his way out.

A big mistake. No plea deal.

The big house or the military? *Don't believe them when they say it isn't an option anymore.*

Hacking for the military was an option he couldn't refuse.

It had cost him everything.

Illusia wiped the tears from her cheek and tossed the wrapper from the burger she'd eaten for dinner on the floor of the sedan. She was a better hacker than Jazz and *visited* government sites all the time. Maybe when this was all over, she'd work for *Anonymous* or some other unseen organization. She had serious skills to offer.

And patience—lots of patience.

16

L iz's hand trembled as she tasted the crockpot stroganoff and turned the knob to warm. The wide noodles and roast vegetable medley sat on a countertop warming tray alongside the garlic bread wrapped in aluminum foil, with a note to remind her to bake for ten minutes. She'd pop them into the oven while she and Nick talked and enjoyed their wine. If only her nerves would settle down. She'd been popping antacids all afternoon.

Ella entertained herself with the pull toys on her sit-and-spin. More verbal every day, she cooed and babbled in her own baby language with an occasional tug at the bow on her one curl of blonde hair.

Liz grinned. If she were lucky, Ella would tolerate the bow until Nick arrived. Her little princess had already eaten supper and wore an adorable, pink onesie pajama with an attached lace ruffle. Liz only needed to nurse and change her before bedtime. Once Ella was down, she'd focus solely on Nick. She wiped her sweaty hands on a paper towel.

Stop stressing. She'd planned this night for a year and had rehearsed what she was going to say dozens of times over the past couple days. She'd explain everything. The other night at his apartment had convinced her. They were still good and understood each other. It gave the hope she'd clung to for so long a set of wings.

"Alright, sweetie, I'm outta here. Off to the beach with my friends." Arlene rolled a small suitcase into the kitchen and swung her purse over a shoulder. "I'll be home Monday evening. I love Labor Day weekend. It allows me a chance to stay at the beach an extra day."

Liz pulled her mom into a hug. "Thanks for giving me the house for the weekend and for your help with the recipes. Wish me luck."

Arlene kissed her daughter's cheek. "Are you kidding? I'm so excited to get away for the weekend. I can't wait to have a Long Island iced tea on the beach and sit in a hot tub. It's that much sweeter knowing you and Nick will be here making things right. Call if you need me, okay?"

"Yeah, sure." She wouldn't call Arlene under any circumstance.

Her mom beamed like sunshine with her beach hat askew from their hug. She carried her suitcase down the back steps and rolled it toward her friends waiting down the alley.

Liz hurried into the house in time to hear the doorbell ring. Her heart gave a thud. *He's here.* She glanced at Ella still playing contentedly. She'd have given anything to be as peaceful and happy as her daughter right then.

She stopped by the foyer mirror, tossed her hair, and wiped her once-again sweaty palms on her jeans. *It's all good.* She'd get through this somehow. She opened the door.

"Hey, gorgeous." Nick held flowers and wine in one hand

and snaked his other arm around her waist and pulled her in for a kiss. "How's my girl tonight?"

The trace of his lips against hers helped her forget for a quick second why she'd initiated this night. She placed a hand on his chest and leaned in, savoring each spark and sensation. He tasted like peppermint and the scent he wore—yummy layers of ocean and pine. When he broke the kiss, she let her nose wander down to his chest while she slid her hands to the waistband of his trousers. Forget dinner. She was hungry for *him*.

He whispered in her ear, "I hope you're going to invite me in because I've got an impressive boner right now. I'll scare the neighbors and the dogs."

She laughed. Something she'd seldom done this past year. "After a greeting like that, I wouldn't dream of leaving you outside to face the hounds of the neighborhood." She stepped back and accepted the wine, waving him in.

"The house smells incredible. You really *can* cook something besides me, huh?" He wiped his feet and winked.

She grinned. "Watch yourself, buddy. There's still time for me to burn it." She forged ahead with her plan. "I need to talk to you about something, Nick. Could we sit on the couch for a few?" There was a clatter in the kitchen, and she wheeled around to make sure Ella was okay when she heard the familiar voice.

"Hal-loo? You-hoo...just me. I know your mother is out of town this weekend, and I stopped by to say hi."

Oh, no. Liz rushed into the kitchen. "It's not a good time, Vera," she blurted.

"That's okay, dearie. If you need any help with your daughter this weekend, you let me know. My number's on the fridge. Where is the little munchkin? I just wanted to see how much she's grown while I've been in Florida. Then I'll get out of your hair."

The air whooshed from Liz's lungs. Heat flooded her face. She braced her hands on the counter as Nick's slow footsteps echoed on the tile floor.

"Well, hello there, young man," Vera drawled as she removed her sunglasses. "I'm Vera, and you are?"

"I'm Nick, ma'am. If you don't mind, we were just about to sit down to dinner. Stop back another time, perhaps?"

The ice in his voice made Liz's blood run cold.

"Well sure, I'll stop by later in the weekend." Vera cast a glare at Nick and opened the screen door. "You let me know if I can do anything to help out, Lizzie, okay?"

Liz nodded and forced a small smile for her mother's friend. "Thanks, Vera." She closed the door, locked it, and hung her head in dismay. All that planning shot to hell.

A dangerous silence hung in the room like thick fog.

"She's beautiful. I take it this is what or should I say *who* you wanted to talk about tonight?"

She turned to find Nick squatting in front of Ella's sit-and-spin with her little fist wrapped around one of his fingers. Her daughter stared at Nick with a fixed intensity. *Must be the deep voice.* Come to think of it, Ella had rarely interacted with men.

"I didn't mean for you to find out this way. I'm so sorry." Sorry was only the beginning of it.

Nick's hand shot out, stopping her. "Need a minute."

She went mute. She'd only gotten *the hand* two times in ten years. Once when she totaled his car in high school, and again, right after she'd refused his proposal in Paris. She fidgeted with a pot holder, twisting and folding it with her fingers. The silence roared for an uncomfortable few minutes.

"Did you do this because I couldn't," he inhaled sharply, "*wouldn't* give you a child?" He ran his hands down his face.

Her chin lifted. "Her name is Ella, and she wasn't planned. She just happened." Oh wow, that sounded *really* bad. Desperation flooded her mind. She couldn't even begin to remember the speech she'd rehearsed.

"Just happened." His voice drifted off. "Did you give birth or adopt her?"

"No adoption, the old-fashioned way." The loop on the corner of the pot holder broke, and Liz tossed it on the counter. It wasn't the only thing broken tonight, judging by the pain etched across his face. She straightened and took a deep breath. At some point, he'd have to look at her, and she braced herself.

"Ella is my greatest achievement in life, Nick. She's way beyond the Purple Heart I received. She gave me a reason to pull myself together after Iraq. I hope I'm half the mother to her that Arlene has been for me."

"So, this is who your mom has been babysitting?"

"Yes." Her cheeks warmed again at his mention of her lie of omission. *Shit.*

"And this is why you wouldn't stay at my place the other night?" He traced a finger down Ella's chubby cheek.

"Yes. Well, I'm still nursing her. Sleepovers have to be planned in advance." Did she just call staying at his place a sleepover? *Like they were eight?* Her boobs started to ache, and she crossed her arms.

He stood, shoved his hands in his trouser pockets and gazed at Ella. "She's pretty—looks just like you."

"You think so? I don't see the resemblance at all. I guess she looks like herself. It's amazing how fast she's growing." Oh God help her, she was babbling. Liz swallowed hard. Seeing

Nick and Ella in the same room brought tears to her eyes. She'd dreamed of it. But, good lord, not with this kind of introduction.

He gave a sardonic laugh. "Is this why you wanted an open relationship?" He turned around and pierced her with a stare.

It was worse than she expected. His eyes cut into hers like slashes of watery, dark flint. His lips were a grim line.

All of her good reasons crumbled into flimsy excuses. "Absolutely not. I didn't plan to get pregnant. I wanted the open relationship for you. I couldn't commit knowing that you didn't want children. Kids are a big deal, Nick. Maybe there was someone out there who felt just like you."

He nodded. "So, Ella is why you've been avoiding me since I came home? The reason behind us always meeting at parks and restaurants?"

"Yes. I wasn't ready to tell you." Fat, sorrow-laden tears rolled down her cheeks. She whisked them away. The betrayal on his face cut her to the core. "I couldn't figure out how or when to say something."

He shook his head. "You had to work really hard to keep me from knowing about her."

Understatement of the year. "I know. I'm so sorry. I had my reasons, but right now, I'm not proud of them." The tension in the room was stifling. Even Ella felt it, and her lip quivered.

"I kept the baby awake to meet you, but it's past her bedtime. It'll take me about fifteen minutes to um, get her settled. Will you wait?"

He fixed a dark gaze on her. "I'm a combat soldier, Liz. So are you. I'm not about to cut and run with a skirmish at hand."

A rush of dread—or was it hope?—bolted through her stomach. If he left, she could nurse her wounds in privacy. If he stayed, she'd need to face—what? An ultimatum?

She wiped her clammy hands on her pants. "I don't want to fight, Nick."

He nodded. "Me either. But an explanation would be damn helpful right about now." He strolled to the counter and started opening the bottle of wine.

"I'll be back. It'll take me ten or fifteen minutes." She scooped Ella from her play seat as the baby broke into a full wail. Liz grabbed a pacifier from the kitchen table.

"By the way, who's her father? Do I know him?" The cork popped, and Nick filled a glass halfway.

"Let's talk about that when I get back." Ella's crying increased, and Liz hurried toward the hallway. But she heard his clipped reply.

"Damn straight, we'll be talking about Ella's daddy when you get back."

NICK TOSSED BACK the glass of wine and poured more for him and one for Liz.

Ella's existence explained a lot. Like the ever-present dark shadows under Liz's eyes. She'd looked tired every time he'd seen her since returning from Iraq. And no wonder. She'd been working twelve hours a day and went home to another full-time job, day after day. As much as he wanted to beat the shit out of Ella's daddy, he hoped the guy was involved and gave Liz a break once in a while.

Damn. He shoved the garlic bread into the oven and leaned against the counter sipping his glass of wine. If Ella's father was in the picture, why did Liz have sex with *him* the other night? That wasn't like her.

His lungs seized. It better not've been her way of saying goodbye. That would be the ultimate insult.

The residual shock still pounded in his chest. Liz had a baby. While he was in Iraq.

What. The. Hell.

Guilt swamped him. She'd never hidden anything from him before. Did she lie because of his aversion to having kids? There had to be something very wrong in their relationship for her to hide a child. The baby had to mean the world to her in spite of his feelings.

But to hide it this long? There had to be more to the story, and dammit, he'd push until he knew everything. He took the last swig of wine and set his glass in the sink. No more drinks tonight. He rarely touched the stuff anyway. He needed food.

Remorse for the vasectomy he'd gotten at eighteen churned in his gut. His SOB of a father had reached out with his brutal fists and affected the one relationship Nick treasured. The bastard had no right to live beyond his unmarked prison grave.

The timer beeped, and he pulled the garlic bread out of the oven just as the sounds of a lullaby drifted from the baby monitor on a windowsill. For all of Liz's talents, and there were many, she couldn't carry a tune to save her life. Yet, the tenderness in her voice arrested his attention as he listened. His own mother had sung the very same lullaby to him, albeit with the voice of an angel.

But there was no mistaking the love in Liz's less than perfect rendition. Her voice dripped with emotion. And while his own mother's voice had trembled on the chorus if she heard his father's footsteps downstairs, Liz's cadence held none of the shaky fear or hurried ending that his mom's voice had. He'd rather die than have his Liz afraid of him.

Surely, Ella's father was contributing and not leaving it all to Liz and her mom. Nick scanned the dining room where the walls were neatly lined with baby equipment. He had no idea what half the stuff did, but the dad must be involved. That was good.

A bolt of searing regret rose in his chest. This was the one situation where he'd let Liz go if he had to. But if he ever heard fear in her voice, he'd kill the poacher with his bare hands.

He didn't hear her footsteps as she came back into the kitchen.

"You must be starving. I invited you over for dinner and haven't offered you a thing to eat. Let me fix you a plate."

He turned around. "I can get my own plate. How 'bout I fix one for you, too?"

She picked up the glass of wine Nick had poured and sipped. "Okay. A small one. It's doubtful I'll be able to get anything down, though."

He set two plates on the table. "Just try. I know nothing about kids, but I've read that nursing mothers need to eat." She didn't look him in the eye.

She placed a napkin on her lap. "Yeah? Well, I'm still carrying around sixteen pounds that I gained during pregnancy. I think I can skip a meal here and there." She stabbed a piece of beef and some noodles onto her fork and started to chew.

Ah—now he knew where those exquisite curves came from. He closed his eyes for several seconds. *Don't think about the curves.* He remembered where he wanted this conversation to go. "Who is Ella's father?"

She shrugged a shoulder and answered in a hoarse whisper. "I don't know."

He gave a brusque nod and sat back. "Elizabeth, that doesn't sound like the woman I know. You plan everything. I'd really appreciate the truth."

He had enough in his stomach now to quell the effects of the wine, pushed his plate away and leaned toward her. "Who is Ella's father?"

Liz fidgeted with the cloth napkin in her lap. "Nick, I honestly don't know for certain."

He winced, moved his chair so they could face each other, and pried her hands from the vice grip she had on the napkin and took hold of them. "Look at me, babe."

She heaved a breath as tears cascaded down her face. "Go easy on me, Nick. You have every right to feel like the injured party here, but this situation hasn't been a slam-dunk for me."

"Please, honey. We've always discussed everything eye-to-eye, no matter what. Until now, I can't think of anything you've hidden from me. I know you like dark chocolate but it keeps you up at night, your political views, your favorite authors, the way you color coordinate your drawers and closet. For fuck's sake, don't hide from me on this one."

She yanked her hands from his and stared him straight in the eyes. "I wish I wouldn't have told you to date other women. Remember that fight we had on the phone right before I deployed to Iraq? You told me about the women you'd been dating and yelled about how you couldn't tell if they wanted kids or not?"

He nodded. He didn't remember that *exact* discussion, but they'd had quite a few heated conversations after Paris about her insistence on an open relationship.

"After I got off the phone with you, I won $200 at the officer's club in a dart tournament, and later that evening, I jumped some guy's bones because I was furious with you. It was awful. I wanted it to be you the whole time."

Nick nodded. That story sounded familiar, like what he'd done a couple weeks ago with the bar honey. He forced the scowl off his face at the image of another man enjoying her body.

"The next morning at 0900 I was on a plane to Iraq. You and I couldn't keep our hands off each other and hooked up in every closet, bunk, and laundry room we could find for the next couple weeks." She drew in a huge, shuddering breath. "And then the minefield happened."

"Why didn't you tell your commanding officer you were pregnant? They would've never sent you off-site with that knowledge." *Why didn't she tell him?*

She lifted her chin, raised her voice. "I didn't *know*, Nick. I found out after they amputated my lower leg in Germany. I decided to keep her because I might never get the chance to have a child again, and I kept hoping she was yours because the other guy took precautions."

What?

"She *can't* be mine, Liz." He resisted the urge to slam his fist on the table and leaned back in his chair. "By process of elimination, we know I'm not Ella's father. I'm not capable. So, the other dude must be. Did you tell him?"

Her face hardened. "Yes. He told me to get rid of it."

Nick grunted, but it sounded more like a growl in his chest. If she ever spilled the guy's name, he'd kick the shit out of him. *To hell with the assault charge.*

"Then, I made a decision. My body—my commitment. I wanted her, no matter what it cost me. I hated hiding her from you, and I kept waiting for the right time to say something. For all I knew, you'd come home and marry someone else. I'd given you that freedom of choice in Paris." She nailed him with a stare.

The sadness in her eyes destroyed him. "I can't believe you did this by yourself, without Ella's father there to help out."

Liz stood and poured more wine. "My mom's incredible. She's been on active duty as a grandmother ever since Ella was born. She helps every day."

His eyes narrowed. "You could've told me. You're the most important person in my life. I would've been there for you, helped out."

"Really? How? You were deployed—would be for eight more months. And according to you, you had nothing to do with Ella's beginning." She unplugged the crockpot.

His neck was getting hot. "Are you trying to light a fire under my temper, Liz?"

"No. Ella was my decision. But I would appreciate you taking that test again, just to be sure you're still shooting blanks." She poured *way* too much dish soap and ran hot water in the sink.

"There's really no need, but I'll think about it." He rolled his shoulders and grabbed the extra silverware from the table.

Liz wheeled around and pointed a finger at him. "You do that. All the way to the doctor's office."

"Don't you use that first-lieutenant voice with me, Liz." He didn't have to listen to this condescending crap.

"I'll use whatever tone of voice I want—Nick." She scraped a plate into the garbage can.

Yup. She was spoiling for a fight. He hadn't seen this side of his little commandant since Paris. Any other night of his life, he'd rub his hands together, crack his knuckles, and act on it for what it was, a mating call. An occasional favorite that often skipped the fight and went straight to the *making up* part. He'd always enjoyed this particular dance of theirs because *he* got to be the alpha.

"All I was saying earlier before you started pointing at me was that I would've appreciated knowing about Ella sooner. I could've helped."

Liz smacked a dish towel on the counter. "Really? Would you have pushed all eight-and-a-half-pounds of her out of my body? Would you have nursed her? No, of course not, you would've bought some diapers. What does it matter now?"

Damn, she was wound-up good. He brushed the hurtful words aside to mull over later.

"I thought we were friends, first and foremost. Friends help each other, babe."

She barked a laugh. "I won't blame you if you walk away, Nick. You've had no say in this parenting endeavor."

Oh man, it was way too early for decisions like that.

Liz continued. "I don't have friends anymore, anyway. My mother's friends are all a generation older than me, and Ella, well—she's not much of a conversationalist yet. There are the fake friends I have at work on my computer. I talk to them all day long. But you're the only true friend I've had, and we see each other here and there. It's okay if you walk away, Nick. I get it. Kids aren't your thing."

That's it. Enough was enough.

Nick strode across the kitchen, spun her around, backed her into the cabinets, and pinned her hands to the counter. Not hard. She could pull free if she wanted. Her face was only inches away. Defiant eyes glared up at him.

"Don't you *dare* kiss me," she spat.

"I wouldn't *think* of it." He adjusted his hips so she knew he was on to her, and her lips parted on a gasp. It'd take every good angel this side of the clouds and a ton of self-control to keep from kissing that full lower lip, but he had a few points of his own to make.

She pulled a hand free and shoved against his chest. "You're so calm. I just gave you the shock of your life, and you won't fight with me."

"No, death is a shock. A new life is an adjustment. I'm trying to bring a little perspective into the situation. Nobody died. Ella seems like a healthy little girl. She fulfills your dream of becoming a mother and global warming hasn't washed my beach cottage away. There are a few things to be grateful for."

He continued. "Inside, I'm not calm. I'm pissed as hell that you didn't tell me, but I'm trying to understand. I said I'd *consider* adoption down the road. Right now, is not *down the road*."

His face hovered an inch from hers. "I'd have moved heaven and earth to help you as much as I could. You shut me out. You've been carrying around this two-hundred-pound gorilla for how long? How old is Ella?"

"Six months."

"Right—plus nine equals fifteen months. That's a long time to carry a burden this size alone, Liz. What's wrong in our relationship that you'd want to hide anything from me for fifteen months?" He held her teary gaze for a few seconds.

She looked away. "I'm sorry. I should've told you."

"Don't apologize anymore. You made a life choice. Not the choice I'd have made, but I'm glad for you because you've wanted to be a mom. But here's the kicker. That baby of yours in the nursery? She's got no control over the way she's treated. She's an innocent bystander at the start of her life." He swallowed hard.

Love for this gorgeous, headstrong, fierce woman ached in his chest. He'd feel like shit later for saying these words.

"You can't trust me with her, Liz. I could hurt her; say something she carries around the rest of her life. God forbid, raise a hand to her. I have no idea what I'm capable of with children, considering what I survived as a kid. I won't have that responsibility forced on me. She's *your* baby."

Liz turned her face away from him. "And where does that leave *us?*"

Whoa. His hands shook and the room was thick with heat. He needed space.

He lifted her chin with a finger. "I don't know. What I *do* know is that I'm leaving now. I've got a date with the boxing bag in my building. I'm going to pretend it's Ella's deadbeat dad until I get it out of my system."

He released her hands and stepped back.

"I've got the house to myself until Monday evening and lots of leftovers. You could stay here, and we'd have the privacy to talk."

Nick's gaze travelled the length of her body. "We wouldn't talk. You know us. We'd end up horizontal."

She nodded. "Would that be so bad?"

"You've had a year-and-a-half to digest this situation. I've had less than an hour. I need time. But, Liz?"

She looked up.

"You did real good. She's a beautiful baby."

He locked the door on his way out.

17

She eyed the Pilates chair in her room. *Nope. Not tonight.* Liz barely mustered the energy to peel off her jeans, pull down the sleeve, a liner, two pairs of thick socks, and a silicone liner. She set the mid-calf artificial limb aside.

The sensation rivaled taking off her bra at the end of a long day. An exquisite freedom, cool and heady, bathed her legs.

She stretched her right leg and wiggled the toes. The graceful muscles from foot-to-ankle and calf-to-thigh obeyed her every command. She lifted it high and pointed her foot. The stretch tugged at her glutes as she held the pose and breathed. Relaxation undulated up to her toes.

Now for the left. She took a deep breath and held it out straight, tightening her core muscles to get the best stretch. She grimaced as the muscles reluctantly slacked. They screamed in protest as she lifted it high. Divots from the shrapnel had gouged chunks of flesh repaired by surgeons, but the scarring was still prominent. She lowered her leg to cross her knee and massaged the stump. A residual limb is what they called it. She was grateful. She had a lot more residual than many.

The stump craved touch, and she indulged it every day with soft strokes and gentle massage. While watching TV or reading a book, she often caressed the stump like a lost stray resting on her lap. For the next five minutes, she grunted through a charley horse and whimpered every time she stretched the leg high. Without a pretty ankle and graceful toes to guide the process, her leg protested, balked, searching for muscle memory and nerve paths to rely on.

A foot was a powerful ally.

She needed another pedicure. Her mother's friend, Louise, gave her one every month, always painting the toes on her prosthetic the same color. And Louise massaged her good foot and the stump, treating them like equal parts. *God bless her.*

Liz detested pity.

Time and again, she'd informed the stream of doctors and physical therapists that she would not limp. Most said she needed to be realistic, swallow her pride, and accept her limitations. A select two helped her accomplish her goal. One was a prosthetist and the other a physical therapist. Together, they'd adjusted, tweaked, stretched, massaged, and pushed her to strengthen her left side with exercise. Sometimes without mercy and while barking orders to exert herself one more time.

Again. Again. Again.

That's when she escaped to her memories of basic training. She'd abhorred those long jogs in full uniform and the songs that accompanied them. Oddly enough, those recollections of running on two legs and the humorous chants had become unlikely friends during rehab.

She'd recovered enough to bear Ella the natural way when

the time came. She'd waddled, but didn't limp, into the hospital that night.

And Nick never saw any of it. The rehab, the growing belly, her learning to walk again with a prosthetic, Ella kicking a bowl of popcorn off her belly at thirty-nine weeks, her birth, first car ride, first bowl of oatmeal. Liz had kept it all a secret and robbed him of the worry and joy. The familiar stab of guilt panged in her chest.

But his emotions would've overloaded the delicate mental balance she'd worked so hard to achieve. Ella wasn't his responsibility anyway. She couldn't offer Nick the love he deserved back then. It was more than enough to learn to love herself again.

A sad melancholy draped her heart like a thick blanket. She'd hoped to spend the weekend with Nick and Ella making new memories. But she'd hoped too big on that one. Tears slipped down her cheeks.

She had no reason to be upset with Nick. She hadn't expected him to be thrilled with her decision to keep the baby. He had every right to take some time.

But the burden of secrecy that she'd carried for fifteen months had been harder than any hundred-pound backpack she'd hefted during ten-mile survival training hikes. And now that she didn't need to hide Ella anymore, she was free to live with the decision she'd made.

Her heart skipped a beat and adrenaline slammed her system. Tonight had jump-started her life. For the next three days, she'd be solo with Ella.

She hadn't been alone for this much time in years. There would be no physical therapist to massage her. No nurse with a pain shot, no doctor interrupting a nap, no orderly getting a wheelchair, or Arlene to make it all better. No help with Ella.

An emancipating wail of gratitude flowed from her chest, followed by another, and then dozens more—each sob a cleansing breath. Her stomach calmed, and the emotional weight she'd been carrying lifted from her shoulders.

Maybe she'd plan a trip to the beach with Ella and they'd play in the surf's edge. Perhaps she'd introduce her to an ice cream cone, take a long stroller walk through the zoo, or just take her daughter clothes shopping and show her off.

Maybe she'd call a few of her friends from college and catch-up, tell them about her beautiful daughter and share the joy.

One thing was for damn certain. She didn't need to hide anymore.

18

Nick landed one last ruthless upper-cut to the punching bag and stumbled forward, grabbing it for support as his chest heaved. He'd danced with this freaking bag non-stop for over an hour, landing blow upon blow, kick after kick. Another ten minutes at this pace and he'd fall flat on his face.

Yeah, he'd feel it tomorrow. But honestly, if he could find his wind again, he'd go another round with the sucker. He swung a towel across his shoulders and wiped his dripping face. Even his feet oozed inside the boxing shoes.

The phone buzzed. He answered as he turned out the lights in the gym. At least a shower was only an elevator ride up the two floors to his loft.

"This is Nick." He was still breathing hard from the workout.

"Dude."

"Derek. How you doing, man?" He smiled for the first time in hours.

"I'm pulling out of my driveway now. Got time for a break?"

"Need a shower first. Where you going?"

"Anywhere I can be with a brother. Mother-in-law kicked me out. She said I was hovering. Maggie said I needed to go take care of me for a while and have some fun. Three generations of women in the same house for a week. I need a pool table and a beer. Wanna join me?"

Aww, hell. Any other night of his life he'd be on board, but now? "Not sure I'd be the best company tonight, bro."

"Yeah? Why not?"

"I had a battle with Liz earlier. I just spent over an hour showing the boxing bag who's boss."

"Wow, sorry about that. I'm heading your way and turning onto the interstate. Let's meet at that tavern by your house. I'll show you pics of my baby girl, and you can tell me about you and Liz. We drink too much; I'll crash on your couch."

Nick hesitated. The last thing he felt like doing was socializing, even with Derek. On the other hand, it'd be nice to gnaw the bone with a friend. And D was a brother.

"Yeah, okay. But we might want to pick a different bar."

"Why? That one's got two pool tables and three sports TVs."

"The bar honey hangs out there."

Derek's snicker didn't go unnoticed.

"You're gonna run into her sometime. At least you've got a wingman with you tonight to chase her off if necessary."

"Very funny, D. Give me thirty. I'll meet you there."

THE TAVERN WAS a throwback to the previous century with its dark, glossy wood and brass rails. The slow beat of country music twanged from a DJ in the corner, while the waitresses all wore their emblematic pushup bras and cleavage. "Congratulations on the new baby. What'd you name her?" Nick shoved a slice of lime down the neck of a Corona.

"Catherine Annabelle, a family name on Maggie's side. That's the long version. We both agreed on Catherine. I'm hoping for *Catie*. Life's too short to have a long name. I'll admit, though, I'd have let Maggie name her whatever she wanted after watching what it took to bring our little girl into this world. I've never been so terrified and happy at the same time."

Nick's thoughts snapped to Liz and Ella. *She'd brought that baby into this world all by herself.* "I've heard it's intense."

"Intense? Dude, I'd have jumped in there and pushed *for* her after the half hour mark. I just kept doing whatever Mags asked me to do. Rub her back...wipe her face...get the ice chips...I'd be surprised if she ever has sex with me again." Derek laughed. "One minute, she collapsed onto the pillows and said she couldn't do it anymore, and two minutes later, Catie was born. It was dope, man."

Nick swigged his Corona. "Who's she look like?"

"Herself, I guess, but that hair comes from Maggie's gene pool. It's thick and black. Sticks out all over her head. Girl's got a set of lungs, too. Nobody sleeps when she's hungry. That's enough about me. What happened with Liz?"

Nick twirled a french fry in the ketchup on his plate.

Derek elbowed him in the ribs. "C'mon, dude, you guys fight over something stupid and break up again?"

Nick shifted in his seat. "We've only broken up once, and that was high school."

"True, but there was the Paris thing if I remember—"

"Liz had a baby." Nick dropped the french fry on the plate and grabbed his beer.

Derek pulled the burger out of his mouth without taking a bite and turned to face him. "You're shittin' me."

"I'm serious, bro." *I wish I wasn't.*

"How the hell did she have a baby without any of us knowing? I mean, the woman has some serious contacts and friends. I haven't heard a whisper about this. We just saw her a few weeks ago during the Reardon Sanctuary rescue. She didn't look any different."

Oh yes, she did. Those curves. "The baby's name is Ella. She's six months old. Liz's had a chance to bounce back. Arlene, her mom, has been helping her."

Derek's eyes softened, and he lowered his voice. "Did she say who the baby daddy is?"

"A single officer who told her to handle it." Nick clenched and unclenched his fist on the bar top. "A one-time thing." He caught the bartender's eye and held up two fingers. "This conversation is confidential, okay? The last thing she needs right now is a bunch of emails congratulating her and prying for details."

Derek crossed two fingers against his heart. "Not a soul, man."

The bartender set two more beers on the counter and added two shot glasses and a bottle of tequila.

Nick shook his head. "No shooters tonight."

"I don't know, bro, it seems like a good time to indulge. My wife gave me permission to have some fun, and you just got kicked in the nuts."

"I've got to keep my eye on that weather channel up there. That hurricane that hit the Gulf states? Mason's already packed up. He's on standby to deploy with the Guard. I need to know if and when it happens so I can get a replacement over to the Richardson's."

Derek nodded. "How's he been doing with them?"

"Just fine. He's a solid guy. Still settling in. You've only been gone nine days."

"Feels like a month to me, but I'm wading through new territory on the home front. I wish I could help if Mason goes south, but my mother-in-law is leaving later this week, and then the fun begins. I gotta be there to help Mags, even if I just vacuum and get the groceries or some carryout."

"Yup. I get it. Family leave was in the incentive package I offered you." Although right then, he'd pay *triple* to get Derek back on the job.

"What are your thoughts about Liz and the baby?"

Nick tightened his hand on the bottle. "She told me it was her body, her decision, her life. I'm not running away, but I can't imagine being much help to her. I'm scared to death of even picking up that little girl. And I'm burning mad that she cut me out of the process."

Derek took a swig of beer and turned toward him. "Well, bro, we've both seen injured vets turn inward and seal themselves off from the rest of the world while they're recovering. We returned home whole. She didn't. And it isn't like you were married."

Nick's stomach clenched. "We're not married on paper, but in here—" He knocked a fist on his chest. "We've belonged to each other forever."

"Yeah, I get it. Maggie and I were the same way. But we've all known for years that kids aren't your thing. Don't you think that weighed on her mind when she found out she was expecting? Hell, I wouldn't have wanted to tell you." He shook his head. "I'm thinking she did the best she could with a shitty situation."

Nick grimaced. "Yeah, but to hide a baby that long? It just cuts at the foundation of our trust."

Derek squirted vinegar on the leftover fries and popped one in his mouth. "And we've circled back to the injured vet needing time to put their life back together. Remember Smitty? He lost an arm. I visited him every week for eight months. He never smiled, gave me one-word answers, wouldn't go anywhere but rehab. Just about the year mark, he called me out of the blue wondering if I wanted to go bowl with him. Smitty laughed and said he still had his bowling arm. Something just clicked, and he got back to living."

"You're probably right. I guess I think of Liz as being so fierce, she would've plowed through all that shit."

Derek nodded. "You pissed it's somebody else's?"

Nick shook his head and turned to face his friend. "You're a plain-speaking man, D. What a loaded question. Yes. No. I don't know. I can't give her a baby. If you're asking if I'm mad she slept with somebody? I'm not happy about it, but I've got no right to point a finger. I need some time to think it through."

Derek tapped his empty plate. "Don't take too much time, bro. A lot of brass would crawl in their dress whites to hook up with retired Purple Heart recipient First Lieutenant Elizabeth Nelson. I was at her heart ceremony, and the room overflowed with officers who respect the crap out of her, and you know, she's gorgeous. There were lots of divorced majors looking to start over, stuffing their business cards in her hand, and a baby just makes the package more appealing to some. She's always been up front that you're in the picture—so hand's off—but word gets out that she's single?"

Nick stopped nursing his beer and barked a laugh. "Are you trying to make me feel better or worse?"

Derek laid a hand on his friend's back. "I'm just telling you like a real friend, dude. I stepped in three times and took her elbow, steered her toward the punch and cake table."

"Well, thank you for the heads up. I mean it. One of them already sent flowers to her workplace. He didn't sign his name and made her feel damn uncomfortable."

Derek glanced behind him. "I'm thinking it's time to blow this joint. The place is filling with ladies. I miss my girls. I'm going home. I've got five more weeks of penance until I get to visit Maggie's holy of holies again, and I don't need to be looking at women flaunting their goods."

Nick pulled out his wallet. He turned his head. "You can deal with a little celibacy. We lasted longer than five weeks overseas."

"In Iraq, I didn't sleep next to a rosewater-scented woman. Maggie's fragrance gives new meaning to playing with my rubber ducky in the shower," Derek added with a wry grin. "You going home?"

"Naw. I think I'll drive back to Liz's. I hate leaving it the way I did." And Derek's words *she did the best she could with a shitty situation* echoed in his head. D was probably right.

Derek looked at his watch. "Pretty late, man. What if she's already asleep?"

"Then I had a drive to clear my mind, I guess." Nick slapped a tip on the bar countertop and stood. But if he knew his Liz, she'd be up reading some book on military analytics or espionage during World War II.

L iz's phone rang. *Nick.* She answered before it had a chance to wake Ella.

"I'm sitting out front. I didn't want to ring the bell and startle you. May I come in?"

What? She set her book down and scooched across the bed, peeked around the curtain. His truck sat in the driveway behind her car.

"Give me five minutes. I need to pull myself together."

"You don't need to fuss, babe. I've seen it all before."

No, you haven't. He hadn't seen her leg without the prosthetic yet. "I need to put my leg on to get to the door. I'll be there in a few minutes."

She hung up and swung herself across the bed to the wheelchair with her leg and slipped on the silicon sleeve. *Damn.* She'd need to change into longer pants instead of the boxers she loved at night. *No—she didn't.* The tears from earlier in the evening had everything to do with full disclosure, freedom from pretense.

She glanced in a mirror. Her eyes were puffed-up like

tender plums. Oh, well. *Stop by without any notice and this is what you get, Nick Flannery.* She finger-combed her hair on the way to the door and waved him in.

Only steps from the porch, their gazes locked.

"Oh, babe—your eyes." His hand caressed the side of her face the second he crossed the threshold.

She placed her hand over his and leaned in a bit. "It was a good cry. Cathartic even. I feel much better."

"Do you want me to leave?"

"No, of course not. Although, I'll admit I'm a little surprised you're back so soon." A whoosh of relief flooded her system that he *had* come back at all.

Nick ran a hand through his hair. "I had a few hours to think and a beer with a friend. I'm still working my head with this baby thing, but I honestly believe you did the best you could with the hand you were dealt."

An instant lump gathered in her throat.

"I didn't finagle the open relationship to get Ella." She traced a finger down his cheek. "I wouldn't have done that to you—to us."

He kissed the palm of her hand and tugged her into his arms. "I know. I believe you."

Her arms slipped around him. "I'm so glad I'm not hiding her anymore, Nick."

"Yeah. Good decision, honey." He leaned back and gave her a once over. "Want something cool for your face?"

"No. Thanks. It'll look better in the morning." She chuckled. "Or worse. I don't care. I don't have to work. Are you staying?"

"If it's okay with you?" He looked at her with hopeful eyes.

"More than." She locked the door and flipped the living room light switch.

When she turned to him, he picked her up and ducked-walked her down the hallway.

"Which room?"

"First one on the left." The scent of his woodsy pine soap made her want to burrow into his shoulder.

"That's what I thought. Eh—same bed you had in high school."

She rolled her eyes. "New mattress, though."

Nick barked a laugh. "That's good. We put a real hurtin' on the old one as I remember." He set her down, toed-off his shoes, and pulled his shirt over his head. "Does the baby need to feed or something before you can sleep?"

Liz giggled. "She's not a vampire from one of those books you like. She doesn't feed, she eats. I nursed her a little while ago. She'll most likely sleep 'til morning."

"Very funny." He picked up the sexy romance she'd left in the middle of the bed and looked it over. "Speaking of reading habits, when did these become your thing?"

Her heart warmed. "Romance novels got me through rehab. I needed the happily-ever-after. I grew fond of them."

He placed the book on the bedside table. "Maybe some night you'll read me a hot scene? I could learn a thing or two." He smirked.

Liz stared at his massive chest, defined abs, the tats she loved on his arm and zoned out for a second picturing herself snuggled up, kissing his pecs.

"You don't sleep with the prosthetic on, do you?"

"No. I take it off. But I sleep on that side of the bed with the chair nearby and the leg propped against it. If I get up, all I have to do is swing myself over the side and put it on." She sat and removed the outer silicone piece. "You sure you're ready for this? You haven't seen it yet." Nerves danced in her stomach like the first time she'd undressed in front of him.

He sat next to her on the bed. "I've got buddies that came back with pieces. But yours is personal." He gave her knee a gentle squeeze.

She nodded. "Whatever you do, don't look at it and say they did a good job."

His eyebrows lifted. "What?"

"A lot of people say *they did a good job* when they see it for the first time. I guess they're uncomfortable or stuck for something to say." She slipped the final silicone layer off and removed the prosthetic, setting it aside.

Nick moved in front of her on one knee and caressed her upper and lower leg, running his calloused thumbs through the divots—favoring the stump. He gave her a tender kiss on the lips and gathered her hands in his, his sapphire eyes a darkened furious storm.

In a voice thick with emotion, he said, "Thank you for your service, Lieutenant."

Oh hell. Her throat slammed shut when her eyes brimmed with tears. "Thank you," she choked out. The tears she thought were over trickled down her cheeks as she leaned her forehead against his. "I'm so sorry. I should've told you about Ella. I should've dealt with it."

His fingers gently framed her face. "You had a lot to deal with, babe. I'm sorry, too. I should've pushed harder to find out what was going on. I wasn't there for you."

"It was my fault for pushing you away. You were discharged from a career you loved to be with me, and I didn't even greet you at the airport." Regret filled tears fell as she traced his jaw with her fingers. "I apologize from the bottom of my heart."

He kissed her forehead and her nose and nipped her ear lobe. "You were kind of busy. It was the day of your Purple Heart ceremony."

"Don't let me off that easy. I was scared to tell you about Ella." She placed a gentle kiss on his lips. "I've been such a coward, Nick." She grabbed a tissue from the bedside table.

He tilted her chin up with a finger. "You've a survivor, honey."

She swept the hair from her face. "Thank you for forgiving me."

He gave her a lingering kiss. "You're not the only one who needs forgiveness, babe."

She ran her hands through his hair. "C'mon, soldier. You're the perfect one here."

Nick shook his head. "No, I'm not. I hooked up with somebody a couple weeks ago. I gotta get past it. It's eating me alive inside."

Liz leaned back on her elbows and cocked her head. "Are you still seeing her?"

"No. Never was. It came at me out of the blue." He held up his hands. "I still don't know what came over me, but I own it. It'll never happen again. It was beyond humiliating. I'm pretty sure I shouted your name at some point."

Liz narrowed her eyes. "It served her right." She sat up and wrapped her arms around him. "You allowed yourself to be in a situation where you were an easy mark. I did the same thing. Stupid human stuff." If she ever met the woman, she'd have to hurt her.

He sighed against her neck. "We've both crossed lines that we wish we hadn't." He lingered at the little hollow beneath her earlobe.

His every touch ignited a slow burning flame of desire,

and Liz pulled him closer. "I want to feel again, Nick. Help me, please." She took his mouth in a deep kiss, her hands roving the breadth of his chest to the rose tat above his heart. She craved every sexy inch of this man. If only they could find their way back to the good that had defined *them* in the past.

He clicked off the lamp on the bedtable. "Ready to get some shut-eye? We both need it," he snickered.

She smacked his arm. "Always such a tease…"

His tone grew serious. "You're the only woman I want to love, Liz." He rested his nose against hers. "Gimme a heads-up here. Is sex any different when you're not wearing the prosthetic? Anything I need to know?" His index finger lightly traced the length of her arm.

Liz flopped back on the bed. "I've got no idea. Before the other night at your place, I hadn't had sex since *us* in Iraq." Someday, she'd figure out why that confession felt embarrassing.

"Well, then." He stood and lit the candles on her dresser, extinguishing the match between two fingers before tossing it in the garbage. "Knowing you the way I do, it's a wonder you haven't been consumed by fire." He gave her a predatory smile.

In the past, this had been her cue to take off running until he caught her. But now? She glanced at the prosthetic a few feet away.

As if he could read her mind, he strode over and lifted her chin with his finger until their eyes met. "Would you like to put the prosthetic back on? It won't bother me a bit."

Liz scrunched up her face and giggled. "No, I'll just stretch out here on the bed and do my best imitation of a pin-up girl." She shimmied backwards, gave him a wink, and reclined in a sexy centerfold pose. Her heart hammered erratically in her chest as she tossed her hair over one shoulder and crooked a beckoning finger.

He hovered above her and licked his lips. "Mmm, lucky me." He dropped his boxers and kicked them aside.

"I didn't know if you'd come back. I wish I'd worn something sexy." Not that it mattered. She'd be nude putty in his arms any minute now.

"Nice thought, but I'm much more interested in what you're not wearing." He nudged her hands over her head and slipped her roomy t-shirt off, tossing it on the wheelchair. He bent and nibbled her lips as his fingers danced across her breasts. "Elizabeth, I'm gonna take you apart inch by inch, and you're going to let go of all that angst you've been nursing for fifteen months. No pun intended. It'll take a while."

Her insides quickened with the husky promise in his voice. She could hardly wait. When Nick threatened a thorough loving, he fulfilled her every desire and then some.

He kissed her forehead and rested his nose against hers. She laughed out loud when he hauled her into the middle of the bed and removed her boxers in one swift move.

She reached down to tug off her lace undies, but he swatted her hand away.

"I'll get them when I'm ready." He stood proud as a bull for a moment before he straddled her.

Her pulse quickened at the intensity in his eyes. Finally, her Nick—hard-bodied and hot. All to herself in a soft bed.

She sighed with desire. He scooted behind and pulled them into a spoon position, his hands plucking softly at her nipples. *Oh, please.* She backed into him, longing for *closer,* and reached again to get rid of her underwear.

"Nuh-uh, sugar. I get to take them off." He slipped his

fingers through hers and guided them through the edge of her panties. "Show me the right spot, babe. I want to feel you."

Oh, she loved this man. They moved in unison, each touch forcing her higher, tighter. Her core quivered with anticipation. She threw her injured leg over his hip and arched her back in a consuming freefall of pleasure, his voice a whispered echo in her ear.

"That's my girl. Enjoy it as long as you can." He kissed her hair and shoulder. "In a few minutes, we're going do it again when I taste you."

She moaned. *He was always so thorough,*

He feasted on her body and soul until her legs gave out and she shrieked with pleasure.

And then, one teasing inch at a time, he nudged inside her, whispering promises while she murmured love. They moved together, not hurried or urgent, but with care and tenderness, reunited finally. In the soft glow of a nightlight, they melted in each other's arms, became one again, far from the combat area that had last separated them.

But how long could they keep the warzone at bay?

20

A soft, muffled sound pierced the night. Nick bolted upright and listened, his heart in a staccato sprint. He turned toward the baby monitor. It was Ella. He gently pulled himself free of Liz's warm body and sat up on the side of the bed.

More noises drifted from the baby monitor. *What the hell?* He didn't want to wake Liz for a false alarm. He glanced at the time. They'd had three hours of sleep. The baby whined, and his feet hit the floor. He crept to the doorway of her room and listened.

She babbled and whimpered off and on. Maybe he should get some eyes on her? He turned on his phone flashlight and tiptoed toward the crib, shining the light on the blanket. Her little head popped up with a squeal. *Judas priest! Shit.* He stumbled backward and killed the light in his sweaty palm. It was as nerve wracking as night ops.

He inched backward out of the room and leaned against the wall in the hallway. If she didn't quiet down, he'd turn the volume up on the baby monitor for Liz and leave. He *would not* pick that kid up under any circumstances. She was so small. One wrong move and he could break her. He stood there for the next five minutes while his heart jackhammered. Thankfully, it remained quiet in Ella's room. She must've fallen back to sleep.

His phone chimed, and he read the new text. *Damn.* It was from Mason. Nick found his clothes and dressed in the bathroom. The snick of the front door was a soft whisper behind him when he left.

Mason would cover his shift with the Richardson's today, but tomorrow, he'd ship out to the hurricane disaster area down south. Nick had less than twenty-four hours to find a replacement during one of the biggest holiday weekends of the year. *Crap.* How was he going to cover this work? His mind churned. He used a three-tier system in case of emergency with himself as last resort. Derek served as primary, Mason second.

The senator and Angie were flying to Dallas for a big fundraiser early the next morning. Beau had said they'd be socializing among friends and didn't need to have Nick along. He preferred that Nick stayed east and made sure the nanny and kids had coverage.

Nick shook his head. He'd hired quite a few personnel on a sub-contractor basis. He'd start making phone calls once the sun came up to see who was available.

He mentally browsed parts of the list he could remember as he drove home. He couldn't call the ex-mobster who'd cleaned up his act in the Army. The guy was a freaking mercenary these days and would scare the living crap out of the kids with the scars on his face and permanent sneer.

Nick turned onto the final road toward home. He'd start with the women on his auxiliary list. Yeah, he'd prefer a woman. They were tough as nails but with a softer face. That'd work. He'd get this taken care of by mid-morning. Talking to himself in the rear-view mirror, he grew positive. Who knew an entrepreneur required a lot of self-talk?

He parked in the garage under his building, and the elevator chugged him to his loft. He slid a mug under the coffee machine, punched the brew button and fired up his computer to open the document with possible temporary hires. A particular name and personality stuck out. She was a former CIA operative. She might work. He tapped the number and left the phone on speaker.

"Nick, you studmuffin. You've *got* to be on east coast time to be calling me at this hour of the night. What's up, darling?"

He shook his head. Her breathy Marilyn Monroe voice always cracked him up, and made her sound like a softie. Underneath the voice and sex-kitten looks, she was an expert covert operative. "Where are you, Lana?"

"At the moment, I'm extricating myself from under a beautiful sleeping Canadian Mountie on vacation in a super king-size bed in Maui. I had myself an exhilarating evening. And you?"

Aww hell. Maui was a longer flight than he wanted to pay for. But he'd do it if he had to.

"DC. You're on my back-up list. Any chance you'd want to fly back later today? I've got a senator's family that needs protection for a few weeks. Three kids, a nanny, and a wife." He mentally crossed his fingers and listened for something he could use to sweeten the pot.

"Ooh—kids. I love kids as long as they're not mine," she crooned.

That's exactly why he needed her now.

"Could you be here by tomorrow morning? What if I book

you a first-class flight to Dulles or National later today? I'll send a limo to pick you up." *Please, I can't deal with these kids.* She'd be an entertaining fit for the Richardsons.

"I'd love to, sugar, but I told you after I passed that grueling physical of yours that I'm not available until Tuesday. Bodyguard duty for two movie stars on vacation. I can't just drop them and ruin my rep."

Ah, crap. He'd forgotten about her date restrictions.

"I understand. I'll call you with work once you're home, or are you already committed going forward?"

"No commitments just yet. You know, cutie-pie, you sound so tense. I wish you'd take me up on my friends-with-benefits offer. I'd have you purring in no time."

Nick rolled his eyes. Lana was like an older sister but didn't look a day over thirty. She had the martial arts skills of a samurai and could pin him to the mat in three moves. Four, max. "I'm taken, Lana. Enjoy the sun. Don't exhaust too many Hawaiians and leave a little something for the other tourists. Catch you later."

"Kisses, handsome." She disconnected the call.

Replacing Derek and Mason would be difficult because they were irreplaceable. They excelled every day, manned the security office in the house, kept up with the hourly checks on the security, and somehow found the time to join Natalie's daily tea parties, escort Angie to appointments, and Derek even had the teenager, Lindsay, smirking at his jokes and calling him *boss*. Derek and Mason made the damn-near-impossible look easy.

Maybe the Sanctuary, Inc. guys could help. Nick had certainly volunteered plenty of times to help the private rescue organization. He placed a call to Mac Mackenzie, the guy in charge, who answered on the second ring.

"Mackenzie speaking."

"Mac, it's Nick Flannery."

"You got an assignment for us?"

"Not a legit rescue, but I could use some help. I'm short-staffed with Senator Richardson's family this weekend. Do you know of anyone who wants to work?"

Mac's reply was clipped and quick. "Describe short-staffed."

Nick cleared his throat. "Primary bodyguard is on family leave. Secondary just got called up by the National Guard. I'm no good with kids. I'd like someone who's dealt with children before to handle the day shift for a week or two."

"Is the senator's family in jeopardy?"

"No, everything's good. I'm just putting feelers out for someone who's kid-friendly."

An uncomfortable silence hung in the air for a few seconds. "Because you don't want to be around the kids?"

Nick turned the ceiling fan on. It was hot in his office. "I *can* be around the kids, but I'm thinking they'd be happier with someone less intimidating."

Mac heaved a deep breath. "Yeah. I know you've got this thing about kids. Remember the orphanage we guarded in Guatemala for four days?"

"Of course." How could he forget? *Didn't keep food down the entire time.*

"You were kind of amazing, bro. If I remember correctly, it was you who loaded each one of those kids into choppers while we were under fire. They all survived and landed in Miami. You underestimate yourself, Nick. I'd trust you with my life."

Nick took a slug of his coffee. "Thanks, man. The feeling's mutual."

"If it isn't a rescue team you need, I'm really hesitant to light up everyone's burner phone on a holiday weekend. Now, if things go south, call me back. Better safe than sorry."

Nick fidgeted with the paper clips on his desk. "Okay. I understand. No problem."

"Did you get the wedding invitation?"

"Oh, yeah. Thanks. I'll send my RSVP soon."

"Make sure to bring your *plus one*, bro. And remember, if you get in a sticky situation, call me back."

"Gotcha. Thanks." He disconnected the call. *Well, that was that.*

He looked at his watch. By now, Liz would be up and moving with Ella. How the hell would they make a relationship work with Ella in the mix? And he'd damn near had a panic attack peeking on the little girl this morning. He moved on, pushing the thoughts of Liz and Ella to a mental shelf and continued with the calls. An hour later, he came up empty. Two thirds of his list was on a beach somewhere, and the other third currently worked other assignments. The holiday weekend and bad timing didn't help either.

There were a few prospects he couldn't reach by phone, and he sent them a text. He'd wait to hear back. With any luck, one of them would be thrilled to have the work.

But just in case, because the whole *fail to plan and plan to fail* thing sat in his gut like a rock, he packed a briefcase and extra gear bag.

21

A ngie Richardson fluttered about the kitchen like an irritated bird, shoving little things in what she called a tote. It looked more like a duffle bag to him.

Nick eyed the five typed pages spread out on the counter. If she kept adding directives spit out by the kitchen printer, it would soon qualify as the size of the US constitution.

"I'll never understand why fundraising has to take place on holiday weekends. Holidays are for family, so *what* if Congress is out of session? Can't these fundraisers happen next weekend once Lindsay's back in school? I just don't get it." She tossed an exasperated look at Nick and shoved a pair of sandals in the tote as she continued.

"You don't need to bother yourself with those notes. They're for Hilde, who, for some reason, has chosen this morning to be late. She's got all sorts of fun planned for the kids. A barbeque, toasting marshmallows, crafts, movies in the big tent out back, watching fireworks on TV, and fun in the sprinkler and pool. Oh, but Lindsay is going to a friend's house this weekend. They're picking her up at noon."

Ah, yes. He'd run a background check on that family last week. They came up clean.

Angie looked at Nick again. "I hope you brought something besides the suit you're wearing. It'll be hotter than Disneyworld in July the next few days." She didn't wait for him to answer. "Just so you know, I put a whole bunch of leftover *Richardson family reunion* T-shirts in the security office closet, in case your crew ends up outside sweating like harvest pigs."

The senator rolled a suitcase through the kitchen and set his coffee mug in the sink.

Angie pursed her lips and shot her husband a glare. "I just hate being away from the kids on a holiday weekend, Beau."

"Me too. But duty calls." He tapped his watch. "We need to leave, like five minutes ago."

"We can't just yet. Hilde isn't here. She texted me at 6:30 that she's running late and will be here shortly." She crammed a bite of banana in her mouth and shoved an orange in her tote.

Nick offered her a tight smile.

"Ang, all three kids are still asleep. Nick's here to protect them. It isn't like we're running off and leaving them alone. Private jet or not, we still need to clear security and leave on time. The first fundraiser starts in six hours. Let's go, sugar." Senator Richardson zipped his wife's bag shut, tossed it on top of the suitcase, and headed for the garage.

"I'm not leaving until Hilde's here. If you have to leave this very minute, fine. I won't go. You can give the donors my regrets." She leaned against the sink and proceeded to finish her banana.

Beau walked back into the kitchen. "You *have* to go, sugar. You're the keynote speaker at three events, and you're introducing me at the other two. Remember all the work you've put into those speeches?"

"What kind of mother leaves her kids on the last weekend of summer? And Hilde's not here." She swiped at her cheek.

"The kids are sleeping, mama bear. When they wake up, Hilde will be here. They'll never know the difference," he implored. Beau drilled a serious gaze into Nick. "Do you mind if we leave? Hilde's on her way."

Nick shrugged out of his suit coat and laid it across the back of a kitchen chair. There were millions of dollars on the line here—not to mention the full-time employment of at least twelve people he'd hired. The panic clawing at his brain made him itchy. He was damn uncomfortable just being *around* kids. There was no way he could babysit them.

Nick plastered on his most chill smile and crossed his arms. "You should leave. Don't worry about a thing. Hilde'll be here any minute, and the kids are safe with me." *Yeah, right.* His stomach tossed his breakfast around, but he swallowed hard.

"See, sweetness? It's fine with Nick. Let's go." Beau placed his hand on the small of Angie's back and kissed her hair.

Angie looked around her husband to Nick. "Are you sure you're comfortable with this? I mean, Hilde's always been dependable. She was out sick two weeks ago, but she's better now."

Nick nodded. "Absolutely. It's only for a little while. The kids will have a great weekend. It's no problem at all."

"Oh God, alright. You can call me if anybody has any questions. Or text me. I answer texts pretty quick. Thank you, Nick. We won't forget this." She looped a purse across her shoulder. "Oh, and there should be three more pages in that printer for Hilde to read. Just line them up next to these." She tapped the counter. "You'll text me when she arrives?"

"Will do."

Nick followed them out, nodded at the previously cleared limo driver, and gave them a short wave as they pulled away from the house. His chest constricted like a rubber band pulled too tight.

He scrolled the contacts on his phone and located Hilde's number.

Surely, she'd be here before the kids woke.

Nick paced the long kitchen and sent an inquiring text to Hilde. She hadn't answered her phone, and the voicemail was full.

Hilde, are you on your way?

He'd already frantically read the eight full pages of notes Angie left behind, brewed coffee in the security office, performed the necessary security scans on the property, and let Precious out to relieve herself. He checked his messages. There was no reply from Hilde yet and he made sure the phone volume was up high. No sounds drifted from the baby monitor on the counter and neither of the girls had padded down the wide curved stairway.

Until now.

Out of the corner of his eye, a little hand trailed the bannister one step at a time. *It had to be Natalie.*

Nick stuffed his hands in his pockets. *God help me.* All he had to do was appear calm, like this was an everyday occurrence. The kid was sharp. She'd probably notice that he'd broken into a cold sweat, but he'd never let her know his heart pounded like a sprinter after a race.

He waited in the kitchen, his feet frozen in place. She'd turn into the long hallway any second now.

Blue fur slippers, cartoon nightgown, and every-which-way-curls. She clutched a pink bear, stopped dead in her tracks, and stared at him.

The scene eerily reminded him of *Shootout at the OK Corral*.

"Where's Mommy?"

"She left with your dad for Texas. They'll be back in a few days."

"Where's Hilde?"

"She's not here yet."

"Where's Mr. Mason?" She crossed her arms and cocked a hip.

"He had to report for duty with the National Guard. He'll be back in a week or two."

She let out a long sigh. "Can I hold your hand?"

"Uh, sure." He strode down the hallway. She slipped her hand in his, tugging him toward the bathroom.

"The light, pwease." She set the bear on the counter.

He flipped the light on. She reached under the cartoon nightie, dropped the panties to her ankles, and held up her arms.

"Lift me up?"

In the far corner of the powder room sat one of those little kid toilets. "Why don't you use that little chair over there?"

Her face contorted into a grimace of abject horror. "That's for babies. I'm a big girl. I don't use it anymore."

"Oh. Okay." He lifted and set her on the big seat. She was light as air.

"Don't look," she shrieked.

He closed his eyes and stood by the sink—waiting.

"Nooo. You have to go out there," she pointed. "I need p'ivacy, pwease."

"No problem." He stepped into the hallway, pulling the door behind him.

"Nooo. Leave the door open."

"Okay, I'll wait out here." He crossed his arms and whistled. He pulled out his phone, checked for a message from Hilde. Nothing. *Shit.* The sweat soaked his fresh-pressed dress shirt.

A few seconds later, Natalie started talking.

"Toiyets are too big for me. Daddy promised he'd put in a short one. I hope it's soon. This is 'barrassing, Mr. Nick."

"Sorry, kid. Your dad's a busy man. I'm sure he'll get to it."

"I asked Daddy to put a short one in the kid's bathroom, but Linzee fussed 'bout it. I like the house in Texas. All the poddies are short. Sometimes Mommy cries 'cause she misses home. And Precious puts her paws on Mommy's shoulders and licks her face when she cries."

And she was off and running in her usual tell-all-leave-nothing-unsaid manner. He'd heard the stories from Derek. Life in the big house from a child's perspective. Mommy and Daddy swimming in the dark at night, Daddy putting Precious in her crate so he could kiss Mommy. The pool company needing to sanitize the pool after Ollie's playmates pooped in it.

"Help me down, Mr. Nick."

He went in and helped her off the toilet, looking the other way as she adjusted her clothes.

"Ready to go?" He looked at his watch. This bathroom break had taken five minutes.

"No. I have to wash my hands. Mommy says not washing is 'izgusting.'"

"Use the stool there."

"Can't. I'm scared."

"Why?"

"I fell off and got a boo-boo." She held up an elbow with a large black and yellow bruise and pinned him with huge blue eyes.

One quick glance proved her point. The bathroom held nothing but granite, marble, tile, and porcelain. How many times had his father almost knocked him senseless in a bathroom? Fear washed over him, and his throat dried. There couldn't be any boo-boos on his watch. How would he explain that to Angie?

Natalie put her arms up again.

Okay, then. He straddled the stool and held her up while she turned on the water, adjusted it for warmth, soaped up, rinsed, soaped up and rinsed again. Somewhere in there, she bent low and rinsed her face. He moved her close to the hanging hand towel while she dried her hands and patted her face. Then he set her down and turned off the light.

Another look at his watch. Eight minutes.

Boys *had* to be easier than girls.

NATALIE RAN FOR THE KITCHEN. "I'm starving, Mr. Nick. Let's make bekfast."

He took a deep breath and hoped this wouldn't involve testing his culinary skills or lack thereof. He had to pull it together. Even *he* could scramble an egg on request. His phone rang, an unknown number, as Natalie pulled a box of

Pop Tarts from a lower cabinet. As a kid, he'd have chosen the same thing. They probably weren't on Angie's list of preferred eats, but desperate times and all that. He answered the phone as Natalie handed him the package to open.

"This is Nick."

"Mr. Flannery, you are the boss, yes?"

"Yes. Who's this?" He opened a bunch of different cabinets and finally found a plate for the Pop Tarts. The guy on the phone had some kind of Slavic accent. Russian, maybe?

"I am Edward, Hilde's husband. We are at emergency room."

Oh, shit. Nick slumped against the refrigerator. "What happened?"

Natalie yanked on his pants pocket while holding a little cup in her hand. *A drink?* He opened the fridge and pulled out the orange juice. She shook her head and pointed at the chocolate milk.

"Hilde's car had trouble this morning, so I say I drive her in my car. No work for me this weekend due to holiday. She no tell me how bad she's been feeling. We work opposite shifts and mostly see each other on weekends. Then she double over in car as I drive and cry out in pain. I say, 'Hilde, why you go to work when you so sick?' She say, 'the senator and his wife have to travel this weekend and she got to go for the children.' She loves those kids."

Nick set the cup of chocolate milk on the table as Natalie scrambled onto a chair, grabbed the remote, and turned on cartoons. He slipped into the laundry room to get away from the sudden noise.

"Okay. So, how'd you end up in emergency?" He ran a hand through his hair and paced.

"I drive couple more miles, and the pain no go away. She

cries out every time it comes to her. Then I know she's hurt real bad 'cause my Hilde is tough woman. How you say? She's no wimp. I say, 'Hilde, you my life. You no go to work. I take you to doctor. Hilde say no. I say yes, right now.' I see sign for hospital and bring her in. They take her back real quick and say her color no good. Her white count very bad. Then she gets sick on nurse and faint."

Nick could relate. The blender in his stomach had turned into a Magic Bullet at high speed. "Is she going to be alright?"

"They call it dicey fifty-fifty. They think her appendix real bad. All of a sudden, they cut her clothes, run with bed down hallway to surgery, bring me papers to sign. I worried for my little flower, she everything to me. We no have children. She love the senator's family so much. I try to reach Mrs. Angie, but no answer on her phone. You say a prayer for my Hilde, Mr. Flannery. She no be at work for a while."

"Of course. They'll take good care of her. Don't worry about calling Mrs. Richardson. I'll handle it. You just concentrate on Hilde and yourself. And call me Nick."

"Thank you, Mr. Nick. I call my sister now—she come sit with me."

"Can you send a text later and let me know how Hilde's doing, please?"

"I no text. How you say? Wrong generation. I am older than Hilde. My sister, she do everything on phone. I tell her to text you."

"Thank you. Take care. Give Hilde our best."

Back in the kitchen, Nick lowered the volume on the cartoons. SpongeBob and that annoying song. Who was Angie's back-up plan for babysitters? He didn't remember clearing anyone to take Hilde's place in the event of an emergency. Angie had a sister somewhere, but he couldn't put his finger on where she lived. He sent Angie a quick text asking her to call him ASAP.

He thought a minute and sent another. Just so she didn't get upset.

Kids are fine.

He was the one freaking out.

22

Natalie popped out of her SpongeBob trance and said, "Uh-oh," She leaped off the chair and grabbed his hand, Precious at her side.

"Ollie's awake, Mr. Nick."

He listened a second. She was right. The faint sound of baby chatter came from the monitor. The security scan was almost complete.

"Okay, let me finish this, and we'll go get him."

"Nooo, Mr. Nick. Now. Ollie climbs up his crib and falls down 'cause he wants to get out. Mommy says she needs to make his crib a big-boy bed soon. He gets a bloody lip when he falls."

What? Nick broke into a run, taking the stairs two at a time, passing Natalie on the way. *Which bedroom? Which bedroom? Closest to the master.*

He caught the kid with two hands as Ollie swung his second leg over the crib rail. It was too close for his comfort. *Hell.* The boy was solid as a brick and had some weight to him.

Natalie climbed on a little stool in front of a table. Nick couldn't help but notice she wasn't afraid of *that* stool. He tossed the little blanket and pillow from the floor into the crib and headed out the door, Ollie in his arms.

"Mr. Nick, come back. We gotta change his diaper."

Nick stuck his head back into the room. *Oh, the table.* He laid the little linebacker down and searched for buttons or whatever kept the kid's pajamas on, unsnapped the crotch, and wrangled the gurgling, happy, surprisingly fast-moving baby.

Natalie stood on the stool next to him, peeled back the little tabs, pulled out a new diaper from a shelf underneath, and set it to the side.

You can do this. How hard could it be? Like wrapping a hot dog.

Nick pulled the diaper back, slid it from under Ollie's butt and dropped it into a garbage can nearby, keeping a firm hand on the kid's wiggling torso. A steady stream of pee shot out. Natalie screamed and ducked out of the way as pee soaked his shirt and new tie. There was no way to stop it. It just kept coming.

Natalie ran out of the room yelling, "Linzee, Ollie's peeing on Mr. Nick, and there aren't any peepee-teepees, Linzee—." The rest was a blur. Nick dodged right and the left side of his shirt got soaked, he dodged left and the right side got soaked. How could one little kid pee that much?

Lindsay stumbled into the room and tossed a wad of tissues over the offending member during the last blasts and dribbles. She bent over with laughter, still half-asleep, her eyes alight with humor.

"You ever do this before, Mr. Nick?" Another giggle lit her face.

"Never in my life."

"No brothers or sisters?"

"Nope."

"No cousins or babysitting?"

Nick shook his head. He had cousins, but he'd refused to babysit them because, you know, he didn't want to hurt them, and he wouldn't leave his mother for too long in case his dad came home lit-up.

Lindsay moved closer. "Let me in there, I'll show you how to change a diaper. One time, and you'll never forget. Ollie's a real pee king. Half the time his diaper's dry until you take the thing off, and then he goes all over the place. Hand me the dipey-wipeys."

Nick moved aside and looked around. Natalie handed Lindsay the wipes she was looking for and took a long look at Nick.

"Your shirt's 'izgusting, Mr. Nick."

"Yep." *No kidding.* Reinforcements were in his gear bag.

"First, you put the baby belt on and snap it shut. Ollie's a mover. Before you peel the old diaper down, make sure you have a peepee-teepee in your hand to put on top of his thing. I guess Hilde didn't bring the bag back after washing. We have like a hundred of them. They're probably in the laundry room. I'll look when we go downstairs. But if you don't have a teepee, Mom says to place a couple tissues over him. Slide the old diaper out, use these wipes to clean him off, slide the new diaper underneath his butt and fasten just like this. Tight but not too tight. Too loose, it falls off. Too tight, he gets a rash."

Lindsay shot him a sideways smile. "Got it?"

"Yeah. Thanks. I appreciate the lesson."

"Might as well get him dressed now, too. Clothes are under here. He hates shoes, so he has thick socks with grips on the bottom. He's been trying to walk for a few days. If he starts walking while the 'rents are out of town, use your phone and get it on video for Mom." She pulled out a pair of shorts and a t-shirt, worked the pajamas over Ollie's head, slipped on the new clothes as she instructed Nick to *bend the fabric, not the baby* and finished with a pair of bright, red-striped socks.

She picked Ollie up. "I'll carry him downstairs. You're soaked." She giggled one last time. "Where's Hilde?"

"She's not feeling well today and isn't coming."

Lindsay's face fell. "I hope Mom doesn't ask me to babysit. I've been really counting on this weekend at the Benson's. We're going crabbing and waterskiing with an inner tube."

A pang of memories hit Nick's chest. How many times had he stayed home as a teenager working out on the bag in the basement, refusing to leave in case the old man wandered in and started on his mother? He'd missed sports, dances, and just hanging out with the guys. All to babysit his parents.

He took a deep breath. "Tell you what, Lindsay. You help me figure out how to make sure these two don't get hurt, and I'll talk to your mom."

N ick had Ollie and Natalie on the backyard swings when Angie finally called. Between pushes, he explained the Hilde situation in hushed tones.

When she got over her shock, Angie asked, "Is Lindsay still there?"

While everything in him had wanted to beg Lindsay to stay until the end of his shift, he just couldn't do it. Her infectious teenage excitement had been damn near contagious as she'd packed for her trip. He'd never forget the grateful look on Lindsay's face as he gave her a wink and closed the Benson's car door.

"No. I sent her off an hour ago with the Benson's. We're sticking with the schedule you laid out in your notes, and Lindsay was kind enough to explain any questions I had about the younger kids. She even installed their car seats in my truck, just in case."

"Let me find Beau."

Angie's heels a faint staccato in his earpiece, he threw another ball to Precious.

Angie didn't mute the phone.

"I need to go back, Beau. Hilde's in the hospital. I'll explain later. Nick's on the phone. He's by himself with Natalie and Ollie."

"Yeah?"

"I need to fly back to DC. Now."

"Is everybody all right, kids okay?"

"Yes. They're fine. But we didn't hire SecureIT to babysit our children. I don't want the kids to feel tossed aside, and it's not fair to him or his crew to leave them with two kids under five with everything they usually do."

"Mama bear, has any blood been shed?"

"That's not the point, Beau."

"Ask him. Any bloodshed yet?"

Nick heard the ding of an elevator in the background.

"Oh, for God's sakes—any bloodshed yet, Nick? I can't believe that's his standard for childcare."

"None at all. They've had breakfast and lunch. We're playing in the yard, on the swings at the moment." *He* was on his third fresh shirt of the day. Ollie's oatmeal having decorated the second. But the clothes were in the washer, and Lindsay found the peepee-teepees before she'd left. Although the painful, raw childhood memories of his father continued to sneak up on him, watching the kids wasn't as awful as he'd imagined. The house was a mess, but playing with the kids was kind of relaxing.

"No bloodshed, Beau. And that's not my point. I'm their mother. I should be with them, especially with Hilde out of the picture," Angie droned on through the phone.

"That's a good point, sugar. And my point is—you're needed here. I'm paying SecureIT a lot of money to take care of my family. I know it's unusual, but surely, they can watch over two small children until we get home. We're talking about combat-hardened vets protecting our kids. It doesn't get any more qualified than that. Have Nick call a nanny service and hire some help if he needs it. He's got access to discretionary funds. He knows what to do. I hired them because Commander Mackenzie gave them a five-star review. Nick is solid as a brick wall. Just trust him, sugar."

"I don't like not putting my family first, Beau."

"I don't either, but what choice do we have? Even if I wanted to fly you home right now, I can't. Ours was one of the last planes to land in Dallas because that damn hurricane has turned its snarling face toward Texas. The airport's closing soon, mama."

"Bless your heart, Beau Richardson."

"Now, don't you start cussing at me in southern, darlin'. It's not my fault. You give Nick my best. I have no doubt he'll handle the situation just fine."

Angie came back on the phone. "Did you hear all of that, Nick? Are you okay with it? I promise to get the first flight home once this weather clears."

"Everybody's fine, Angie. I simply wanted to keep you informed and let you know what was happening. Beau's right. We'll handle it. Try to relax. I'll text you with updates every few hours."

"I'm so sorry. I'd appreciate the update texts. Are the kids asking for me?"

"Not at the moment. They're having fun." He gave them both an extra high push on the swing and held the phone out so she'd hear the squeals of laughter.

"They sound happy. I won't ask to speak with them now. Hearing my voice might upset Ollie's apple cart. Call me if you need *anything*."

"I'm sure we won't, and I'll send those text updates." He ended the call.

He threw the ball across the yard to Precious again and texted Biggs, the next guy on duty for the three-to-eleven shift.

Don't even think about being late, bro. Bring a gear bag with shorts, tees, relaxed shoes. That means plural. You'll need them —heh heh.

24

L iz shared a dish of ice cream with Ella in her stroller under a shady, sugar maple tree with a bench. Her pretty munchkin shivered and made a different face with every little spoonful.

Liz couldn't remember the last time she'd been this relaxed and happy. It had been worth every moment spent in preparation to share this time with her daughter at the zoo. They'd already visited the ape exhibit, watched the elephants get a bath, and walked through the birdhouses. With each new animal, Ella pointed and cooed in delight.

Maybe they'd find the big cats and giraffes and call it a day.

Ella's little cheeks were pink with fresh air and sunshine as she yawned, ending with an adoring four-tooth smile for her mom.

Liz scanned her map for the closest restroom with a changing table. She followed the route with her finger and found one. It would be a short walk from their shady resting spot. She cleaned Ella's face and hands with a cloth, tossed the empty cup in the garbage and meandered her way to the restroom with a smile plastered on her face.

"This is the good life, baby girl." She pushed the handicap button and the door swung open to a large bathroom crammed with strollers and people. Oh geez, she doubted one more piece of baby gear would fit in there. She scooped up Ella, slid her into the baby carrier on her chest and grabbed the diaper bag. She didn't like leaving the stroller outside but there wasn't room for one more.

"Mommy first, then you, sweetheart."

She used the restroom, changed Ella on a just-vacated table, and followed a slow stream of women and children out the door.

Liz walked to where she thought she'd left the stroller, but it wasn't there. Maybe she came out a different exit on the other side of the building? She hoisted the diaper bag and walked all the way around the building.

Huh—no stroller.

She did another circuit of the building. Maybe someone had grabbed hers by mistake and had run back to correct their error, and left it in a different spot.

But nope. There was no sign of it anywhere.

Damn. Why would someone take off with her stroller? She loved that stroller. They didn't make that model anymore, and she adored the floral pattern and hidden pockets tucked here and there. Don't even get her started on how expensive a good stroller was.

Oh my goodness. She patted her chest area where she'd stored a credit card and cash. It was still there. She hadn't brought a purse, just the diaper bag, and upon inspection, her car keys were still in the zipper section.

"Well, baby girl—at least, we can get home," she muttered aloud.

But the situation burned her up. Who would have the selfish nerve to steal a stroller? Especially when the rentals were only two bucks in honor of Labor Day weekend. *That's just nuts.*

And then a wave of panic rippled through her. She'd slipped her phone into the back-zipper section after she'd texted Arlene and sent a selfie of her and Ella holding a bird on her finger in the birdhouse. The heat rose in her cheeks, and she clenched her fists. Not only was the stroller AWOL, but her phone with it and all the special pictures and videos she'd taken the past few hours of their afternoon together. Hopefully, the phone had updated and her precious memories were stored in the Cloud.

Liz whirled around in search of a policeman or rent-a-cop and spotted a security kiosk about a block away. She marched toward it at a brisk pace. With a little help, they'd find her stroller, and more importantly, her cell phone.

She waited behind a woman asking for directions to the birdhouse. Liz tapped her on the shoulder and pointed up the hill. "Straight up and on your right. It's painted yellow and green." The woman muttered her thanks and left.

The security guard glanced at Liz from behind the glass. "What can I help you with, ma'am?"

"Someone took my stroller when I used the restroom, but the worst of it is that my new cell phone was in the zipper pocket. I need help finding the stroller."

He scratched his head. "Let me get this straight. You parked your stroller outside the restroom and *left* it there?"

"Yes. The bathroom already had a dozen of them inside. It seemed the logical thing to do at the time."

The guy chuckled. "Lady, you should *never* leave your stuff unattended in a public environment."

A pissed-off heat rose in Liz's cheeks. She forced a smile because honey attracts bees and all that crap. "Thank you for the advice, but what I need right now is help finding the stroller."

The security guard shrugged and looked around. "I can't leave the booth, lady. You'll need to file a police report."

"Thank you. I'll do that. But in the meantime, could you call someone who'd help me look for my missing property?" She hoisted Ella onto her other hip.

"You got a picture of it?"

"Yes, sir, I do. It's on the new cell phone in my stolen stroller," she snapped.

"There's no need to get testy. I can't close down the park to look for your stroller, ma'am. We only close the exit gates for a missing child."

Liz heaved a breath. "Tell me what you *can* do to help me out here."

"I'll have someone bring you a replacement stroller—free of charge. The security pavilion is just outside the entrance/exit area. It's about a mile-and-a-half away. You can file your police report there."

Liz thought a few seconds. Ella was getting heavy in her arms. "How long will it take to get that loaner up here?"

"Maybe twenty or thirty minutes tops. We're a little short-handed today. Or I could request a golf cart and get you a ride down to the security office. But that would take the same amount of time." He peered over his glasses at her. "You want that golf cart?"

"No. Thanks, anyway. I think I'll walk and look for it along the way."

Liz fumed as she plodded down the hill, eyeing each stroller searching for hers.

A group of loud teens startled the bejeesus out of her sleeping Ella, who began to cry. Liz sank down for a moment on the edge of a flower planter and turned the baby around in the carrier so Ella could curl up on her chest. The walk took about forty-five minutes with a stop to buy a lemonade for the car ride home at the last concession stand. She had juice in the diaper bag for Ella.

"Mommy's going to need a time-out when we get home, sweetcakes." Liz rubbed Ella's little butt in her carrier when she stirred.

Liz chuckled a little, humored by the mental picture of herself sitting on a chair in the dining room alone enduring time-out. Her real time-out would involve a full glass of crisp Chablis and sharp, white cheddar with crackers while she fed her daughter some supper. But that respite was at least two hours away because she still needed to locate the Security building and file that police report.

She jerked through the exit turnstile and stopped, the family behind her almost knocking her over. Not fifty yards away was her stroller sitting by a bench occupied by an older gentleman.

Liz marched to the thing and walked around it. She tipped it over and inspected it. There was no damage. Surely, the phone was gone. Nope—the phone was in the same pocket she'd slipped it into at the bird house. She checked it out. All the pictures and videos were intact.

What the hell?

As she unloaded Ella into the stroller and hung the diaper bag over the handle, she questioned the older gentleman wearing a Vietnam vet hat, "Did you happen to see who left this stroller here, sir?"

He looked up from his book.

"Waiting for my grandchildren. Some lady in a black hoodie left it there about half hour ago. Kept thinking it was pretty strange she was wearing a hoodie in ninety-some degrees, and even stranger she pushed a stroller without a little one in it. Yours, huh?"

"Yes indeedy, it is. It disappeared when I was in a restroom a ways back."

"I'm glad you found it. That's a pretty baby girl you've got there."

"Thank you. She's a sweetheart." Liz pointed at his hat. "And thank you for your service."

"You're welcome, honey. I'm one of the lucky ones. Came home from the jungle at twenty-one and lived a full life."

"Good for you."

He smiled and tipped his hat.

Liz had every intention of living a long and full life, too. But first—she'd like to unleash some whoop-ass on whoever *borrowed* her stroller.

25

Thank goodness for packed restrooms.

Illusia sat in her car with the air conditioning on full blast, guzzling a coke. She'd tossed her brother's hoodie into the trunk where it awaited a good wash. Today was *way* too hot to be tromping around a zoo wearing the winter-weight sweatshirt, but security cameras lurked everywhere in this place. She couldn't risk her face on camera, just in case.

It had been the *longest* day ever. She'd followed Liz since that morning when her car pulled out of the driveway. The tang of victory was still fresh in her mind at the luck of it all. Liz Nelson rarely left the house, except to go to work. Yeah, it'd sucked to shell out the forty-five dollars for admission to the freaking zoo, but it had paid off big time.

She'd stayed twenty paces behind Liz and her kid all day, waiting for the chance to nab her phone. Ever since Liz's workplace went dark and the server shut down last week, she'd needed an access point to get back in. DHS had shored it up like Fort Knox.

Of course, she could hack in. She could breach anything, anywhere, but instead, she'd used her time wisely and invented a new worm that would remain undetected for several weeks. Once her little *Liz project* ended, she'd sell it on the black market, and then to hell with going to work every day.

All Illusia had needed to do was install the new program on Liz's phone. Once Liz stowed her purse and phone in the security area at work, it'd be a cinch to access a portal. It was *so* much smarter than chipping away at the dozens of security measures from the outside.

She'd been right behind Liz in the bird house, feeling Liz's pockets when Liz shot the video of the bird on her finger. Illusia ducked out of the way fast to avoid being in the picture and saw Liz slide the phone into the stroller pocket.

Seriously. Her luck was on the rise. She ought to buy a lottery ticket on the way home. Illusia grinned at the memory of Liz ditching that stroller outside the restroom. It was sitting right there for the taking. Illusia had waited for the door to close and nonchalantly rolled the stroller off the grass patch and pushed it into the flow of traffic. Then she'd found an unoccupied bench about a mile away and installed the program.

And just in case someone discovered the worm, she'd left the tiniest reference to SecureIT, so Nick's company would take the fall in the event of any backlash. As far as she was concerned, there weren't enough nasty paybacks in hell for a man who called out another woman's name during playtime.

The shame of it all? That little baby was all smiles and chubby fingers. It kind of hurt her heart that the kid would grow up without a mother like Illusia had, but that was the problem with Liz having been the command leader on a mission gone wrong.

At some point, heads had to roll.

Sorry, Liz.

26

A half-hour of television time was a glorious reprieve from Ollie's perpetual motion. The little urchin climbed onto Nick's lap and fell into a state of rapture every time the cartoon characters sang. And during commercials, Ollie entertained himself by pulling goldfish crackers in and out of Nick's golf shirt pocket, his fourth of the day. He hadn't been quick enough with the peepee-teepee before nap time and endured another spraying. The sliver of hope he'd felt with the possibility of hiring a nanny service had dive bombed after a few phone calls. They'd all required initial in-person interviews, background checks, plus their answering machines requested he leave a message and they'd get back to him after the holiday weekend.

Natalie enjoyed her tea party at the dining room table. She'd agreed to let Nick skip the event as long as chocolate milk and the little cupcakes confiscated from the pantry served as the treats du jour. The last time he'd looked, the three dolls she'd invited wore more chocolate icing than the cupcakes.

Biggs had settled into the security office, but not before remarking several times that Nick *looked real good with little kids hanging off him.* All in all, it had been an okay day. No blood, a few tears, and Nick never would've guessed it, but the knot in his stomach had eased.

Biggs' baritone voice invaded the room. "Hey Boss…"

"Yeah?" Nick's stomach growled as he chewed the goldfish cracker Ollie stuffed in his mouth with his chubby little hands. Biggs had ordered Chinese a half hour ago. It couldn't get there fast enough.

"You know that part-time staffer who works for the senator and attends Georgetown?"

Nick snapped to attention. "The student who stays on top of any news stories involving him and his family?"

"Yup. She just sent an interoffice email with a link to a broadcast. You'll want to look at it right away."

"Got it." Nick fished for his phone, watched the video, and then snapped the case shut. A reporter from one of the larger cable stations had posted a broadcast in front of the Richardson's street sign and had all but announced the senator's home address.

Biggs sat in a brocade chair across from Nick. "Remind me to never run for public office, man."

Nick hoisted Ollie to a different shoulder and shrugged. "It's just the opposition. There's a big vote next week. That's why Beau Richardson hired us. Let's amp up the sensors on the perimeter and be prepared for a few extra drive-bys tonight. I'll call the next shift in early, just in case."

His phone chimed with a text from the senator laced with fuming red-faced emoticons about the news broadcast. Nick replied and included a photo of Natalie's tea party.

I saw the broadcast. All is quiet. Kids happy. Will keep you updated.

The front gate buzzed, and Biggs left the room to answer it. He returned with two huge bags of food. "Kung Pao sustenance, bro. Are we eating in the kitchen with the kids?"

Nick barked a laugh. "That's the only safe space to eat with Ollie." He got up and moved to the kitchen where he slipped the little man into the high chair.

Biggs sidled up to him as they fixed bowls of food. "Delivery kid said the reason he was late is because of the protest against Richardson at the entrance to the neighborhood. The young man had to go all the way around and drive the farm roads behind the house. Resourceful guy, if you ask me."

They exchanged a look, concern creasing both their foreheads.

Nick opened a drawer and rummaged for one of Ollie's bibs. "I found that road when I walked the neighborhood. It runs along the farthest corral and is unpaved but usable in dry weather. It's impassable before harvest, but dumps right into the neighborhood. We're lucky it's not on Google Maps."

"Yeah. The kid says his aunt owns the farm. He grew up riding horses there. I gave the kid a big tip."

"Make sure you expense the meal and tip to me." Nick paused. "I wonder if the owner would allow us to position a few discreet sensors at the end of her dirt road?"

"It can't hurt to ask. Regardless, with the harvest over, it's golden to know there's more than one way out of this neighborhood besides growing fairy wings and crashing fences."

Nick nodded as goosebumps skittered across the back of his neck. "Hey Natalie, come in the kitchen and eat some supper. I got you and Ollie chicken fried rice."

"Nooo, Mr. Nick, I'm not done with the tea party yet. Can I eat in here with my dolls?"

He rolled his eyes. "No, kiddo. Ollie can't eat in the dining room. You come in here and finish the tea party later."

Precious sat at attention three feet away and stared. She'd been politely hovering since the food arrived. Nick filled her bowl with chow, got the kids started on their dinners, and the four of them sat and ate while laughing at Ollie's sticky duck-sauce fingers and Biggs' knock-knock jokes. It was the closest thing Nick had had to a family dinner in years.

He wanted to call Liz in the worst way and tell her about his day. But he'd save it for later. He planned on going back to her place tonight. Kids were actually…kind of fun. He'd been amused by the spills, not mad. Charmed by the tears—not pissed. The house was messy, but so what? The kids were safe and seemed happy, even if the whole boo boo thing still freaked him out.

Nick glanced out the window. The yard stood quiet in the dusky few minutes before dark settled in. One second, Biggs dangled two shrimp from his mouth imitating a walrus, the kids bubbling with laughter, and the next, Biggs' eyes flared as he dropped the shrimp and announced they had *tourists*. Nick's phone alarm pinged, the perimeter property lights switched on, and there were a half-dozen streaks of flame in the front yard. Nick hauled Ollie out of the high chair with one arm, scooped Natalie up with the other, tucked them close to his body and rolled under the big farmhouse table. Precious threw herself on top of all three and covered Nick's face with her head.

A crash shrieked above them, followed by a deafening roar. The shatterproof triple-pane windows nearest them held fast. There were several more thuds followed by tinkling glass and a whooshing hiss.

Biggs broke into a run toward the security office. "I called 911."

Ollie cried at the top of his lungs, and once Nick coaxed the dog off of them, he rolled into a sitting position. Little Natalie was white as a sheet and trembling. In the distance, tires squealed and sped off.

Nick peered over the tabletop and out the window. The azalea bushes outside the breakfast nook window roared with flames. A huge maple tree in the yard was split and ablaze. His best guess at the moment suggested a series of Molotov cocktails flung near and far, causing an inferno. And the recent three-week drought had left the landscaping dry as kindling, aching for a spark. He smelled smoke.

He gathered the two kids into his arms and hurried into a playroom to them and a safe room to the adults. He entered codes into the wall panel by the kids' bookshelf. In the next fifteen seconds, the steel doors swung shut and locked, steel panels covered the windows, and the separate ventilation system activated.

Nick tried to set the kids down on the rug, but Ollie hung onto his neck while Natalie latched onto his thigh. He sat in a rocker, pulled them onto his lap, and checked the security feed on his phone. Emergency vehicles whined in the distance, and a few minutes later, Biggs greeted the first police car with flashing lights in the driveway. The fires appeared to be limited to the front yard.

When Biggs sent him an *all clear* text, Nick disarmed the safe room panel and strode into the dining room with the kids in his arms.

Natalie took one look at the yard and started bawling her

eyes out, which only sent Ollie into a fresh chorus of hysteria. Their Chinese dinner was scattered as far as ten feet away. Ollie's high chair lay tipped near the hallway.

Nick paced and rubbed their little backs, murmuring *it will be okay, it's alright now.* His military training had included snippets on how to talk to adults after an emotional shock, but kids? He had no idea. If only Derek were here. Derek would have them calmed in a matter of minutes.

Hell. Derek *wasn't here now.* Nick needed to figure this out and fast. Forget that he'd go deaf from the crying—Nat and Ollie craved the calm. Ollie would never remember this night, but Natalie probably would, and somehow, he needed to put a positive spin on the situation like his mother used to do for him.

He dragged in a breath and set his shoulders. "Okay, guys, it's time to stop crying. That was scary, but you're not in any danger now. Hey, look at the fire truck," he cooed. "The firemen will put out the fires for us. Look at all the people who have come to help."

Hell, they'd seen the destruction. Now let them see the resolution. There was no use in pretending nothing had happened.

His mother's gravest mistake was thinking she could somehow fix the unfixable, instead of acknowledging that they needed help.

Biggs had total control of the scene out front. *Good thing.*

"Look, Natalie. The firemen are unwinding the hoses. They're going to put the fires out. You know, when you go to school, they'll teach you all about first responders. See that policeman? He's a first responder because he got here first to protect you."

Natalie sniffled and glanced out the window. Her face lit

with interest. "Look Ollie, there's a fire truck just like the one you play with in the bathtub."

Ollie screwed up his face and continued to cry.

Natalie threw an arm around his shoulder and kissed him on his cheek and forehead. "It's all better now, Ollie, I love you. Look at the big fire truck outside."

Ollie finally lifted his head. He gaped at the vehicles out front.

Nick shook his head. This was a hell of a lot more entertaining than another SpongeBob episode.

In between everything else, he called the Richardsons to alert them to the fiasco and continued keeping them in the loop with texts and pictures. Angie was now hell-bent on finding a way home early, despite the hurricane.

Nick heated fresh bowls of Chinese food and set Ollie's high chair in front of the dining room window next to a TV tray and chair for Natalie. They watched the goings-on in the yard with rapt fascination. Most of the firemen waved to them, and a female police officer made funny faces from the front walk. She came inside and interviewed Nick for her police report and left the kids with lollipops.

Precious sat at the door to the kitchen whining and staring, almost willing Nick to look her way. *Oh yeah, the Chinese food scattered around the breakfast nook.* He picked up Biggs' shrimp (because heaven forbid the dog went into anaphylactic shock with a shellfish allergy) and turned her loose on the chicken fried rice covering the kitchen floor.

Except for a few more shudders and Natalie melting down over her ruined tire swing in the charred maple tree, they watched the scene for the next forty-five minutes, along with Natalie's chocolate-covered dolls perched on the wide windowsill.

Bedtime came and went. Nick let the kids watch until the last police car quietly pulled out of the driveway. Ollie barely finished his milk and nodded off in the high chair when Kyle, the midnight security guy arrived early as requested and strolled through the kitchen.

"Hey man, busy night here. What can I do to help?"

Nick lifted Ollie from the high chair. "I'm putting this little guy to bed. Natalie's already upstairs changing into her pajamas. You can help Biggs secure the perimeter again. We're still running scans to see if we've lost any equipment in the fires. I'll be back down in a little bit. Biggs'll bring you up to speed."

"Okay. You look exhausted, man. Gonna go home and get some shut-eye? We can take over for a while."

He nodded. "Definitely thinking about it."

Nick headed for the stairs with Ollie asleep on his shoulder. Natalie stood in the hallway watching him with big fat tears running down her face.

"Please don't leave, Mr. Nick. I don't know that man. Please, Mr. Nick. You can sleep in Linzee's bed—she won't mind." She clutched her teddy bear and sobbed.

His heart tugged hard. *She's been through a lot today.*

"I'm not going anywhere, Natalie." Although, sleeping in Lindsay's ruffled canopy bed was off the table.

"You promise?" Several more tears cascaded down her cheeks.

"Sure. I promise." He reached for her hand as they started up the stairs.

"Do you really promise? Sometimes when I have a bad dream, Linzee waits for me to go back to sleep and then she sneaks to her own bed."

"I really promise," he said as they neared the upstairs hallway. "I'm going to sleep in the little bed in Ollie's room in case he wakes up. If you need me, I'll be in there."

"Okay." Natalie wiped her face with the sleeve of her Barbie nightgown.

"Let me put Ollie down, and I'll come turn out your light."

It only took him a few minutes to get Ollie in a fresh diaper and t-shirt. The bruiser was exhausted. It was hours past his usual bedtime.

On the way to Natalie's room, he texted Liz.

Won't make it back to your place tonight. Had an incident here. No matter what you see on the news, everyone is alright. Love you.

He found Natalie sitting among five teddy bears in her bed.

"You think you'll be able to sleep in the middle of all those stuffed animals, kiddo?"

She smiled. "Uh-huh. They're my night-night friends."

"Okay. I'm going to turn out the light now." He reached for the bedside lamp.

"Can I hug you, Mr. Nick?"

What? "Yeah, sure." He sat on the bed and leaned in, patting her back. "Now go to sleep, you little monkey."

But Natalie hung on to his neck and kissed his cheek. The kiss was soft as a rabbit's foot.

"I love you, Mr. Nick," she whispered.

The breath whooshed from Nick's body as he held her. No combat zone, counseling, not even Liz could've prepared him to hear that short phrase for the first time from an innocent small child. He closed his eyes when they filled and bit his bottom lip to keep it together.

He'd actually taken care of two kids for a full day without

hurting them. Could he possibly be a sort of stand-in dad to Liz's Ella? His heart skittered for several beats.

"Do you love me too, Mr. Nick?"

Was that what he felt? He'd thought it impossible, but it was somehow—*right.*

"You're easy to love, Natalie. Get some sleep, honey."

27

T he next day, Liz cleared security and met Major Chan at the elevator.

"Thanks for coming in on a holiday, Liz. Neither of us wants to be here today, but we don't have a choice. I need your input once we get upstairs."

"Not a problem, Major." But a colossal inconvenience, for damn sure. The last thing she'd wanted to do was leave Ella with Vera for what could end up being a long day, but she hadn't had an alternative with Arlene away.

They walked the quiet hallway in eerie silence to her office. The lights were already on, and the minute the major unlocked the door, the scent of brewing coffee hovered in the air.

"I brought the coffeepot in here. Figured we'd need some." The major locked the door from the inside and pulled an extra chair up to the computer.

Liz sat, put on her screen glasses, and logged in.

The major poured two mugs of coffee and joined her. "The first thing you should know is that we're being recorded.

Every word, every facial expression. It's protocol, and the only way I could avoid calling someone else in to act as witness. Got it?"

"Sure." Liz had nothing to hide. She didn't appreciate the cloak and dagger approach but years of government work had trained her to ignore the hidden microphones and cameras and be herself. Liz logged into her social media profiles. "What's our objective?"

The major scrolled to Dottie Ryan's page.

"As you are aware, the dark web crew works twenty-four-seven on holidays to monitor any new threats, posts, etc. Dottie Ryan's profile had a few concerning entries yesterday. They notified me as soon as the messages came in. We've already removed Marion Trent's profile because of the breach last week over the flowers comment. Whoever compromised Marion Trent didn't stop there. Take a look." She scrolled and leaned back.

Liz scanned the screen and found the post.

What kind of flowers are your favorite, Dottie?

Her heart sank. "What about the other profiles?"

"They all have posts about flowers. Even your nerdy Herman guy received a message about planting a flower garden next spring. The crew upstairs has been following the posts since last evening."

"Why haven't they removed the profiles yet?"

"Because upstairs moved your work to a separate server. We want to encourage this person or organization. Reply to a few messages. See if we can start a dialogue, figure out who's doing the hacking. And I know you've assigned different personalities, nuances, and mannerisms to each of your personas to make them appear realistic and genuine. Of everyone who works here, you've had the most online hunting success. It's due, in part, to the depth of the personalities you invent."

Liz nodded. "Do you want me to make a list for each persona?"

"No. On the rare occasions when we've lost an analyst to tragedy or illness, we can document that information ourselves, even though it takes time and resources to mimic perfectly. I brought you in today because you're up to speed with each account. We'll give you keystrokes to enter in a strict sequence. You're simply the front to lure them into a conversation. You'll have sixty words maximum to coordinate our sequence with your persona's nuances and reply."

Wow. Four years had passed since she'd worked on a project like this. It'd been like combat-crawling through her brain for the right word and puzzle piece.

"I need an assistant, Major."

The major raised her right hand. "That's me."

"It'd save me gobs of time if you manned the dictionary and thesaurus on the other laptop. It's not fun, kind of like playing *Wheel of Fortune* with a gun to your head."

"No pressure, huh?"

Liz smirked. "You're the one who signed up to be all that you can be when you put on the uniform."

The major chuckled. "Ain't that the freaking truth?"

"What's our time limit?"

"Each new sequence has its own time allotment, anywhere from thirty to ninety seconds. We'll find out when we open the sequence."

"And the purpose behind this exercise, Major? Give me a reason to be doing this, besides the fact I want to keep my job."

"Dark web covert division has hidden code and worms in

all the sequences. They can't trace the perp's entity because their signal bounces all over the globe and from satellite to satellite. So, they're trying to find out who and how proficient our hacker is. In other words, are we dealing with a gifted kid hiding out in their basement, or do we have a major organization or a foreign government on our hands? Our sequences are like slapping an ankle monitor on them. Every time they answer us is another opportunity to find them."

"You're hoping the hacker makes a mistake." Liz rolled her shoulders and cracked her knuckles.

"An inexperienced one will, for sure. Those people upstairs are smart and sneaky as hell. They know exactly how to corner and trap these bastards."

The air conditioning whirled on and gusted a cold draft over Liz's bare arms. She slid into the sweater she kept on the back of her chair. Espionage had never been her specialty. But, as daunting as this assignment looked, she was well acquainted with working on a team.

It was time to get to work.

28

Nick pulled up in front of Liz's house and parked. It sure was a friendly looking neighborhood. Flagstone ranchers lined the streets, each with a striking front garden, and different color front doors with matching shutters. Liz's yard distinguished itself with mounds of multi-colored impatiens and a pink crepe myrtle in full bloom. Judging by the combination of older folks and young children he'd seen on the neighborhood playground, it was a happy mix of every ethnicity and age. It looked like a comfortable place to live.

Liz should be home from work any minute now. Granted, her car wasn't in the driveway, but maybe she'd parked in the garage. There was a lot of commotion down the block. Two police cars and an ambulance. He narrowed his eyes at the scene before striding to the Nelson front door and ringing the bell.

No answer. He rang the bell again. Maybe she was changing out of her work clothes.

Still no answer. He banged the knocker a few times, walked to the garage and peered inside. The only car in there belonged to Liz's mom. He'd just hang in the truck until Liz got home.

As he unlocked his car, someone called his name. Arlene hurried toward him with Ella in the stroller.

"Hey Nick, I'm so glad Liz got a hold of you. Happy Labor Day." She gave him a quick hug and a peck on the cheek. "Follow me." She fumbled with the house key on her lanyard and unlocked the door. "Come on in."

"It's nice to see you, Arlene. Been what, a couple years? Your new digs are nice." He carried the stroller up the few stairs and set it down in the living room.

Arlene scooped Ella into her arms. "Thanks. I like it. Large enough for company but not overwhelming like the big place we had when Liz was growing up. Plus, with Hank gone, I needed to move near my friends."

"I didn't think you were due home from the beach until later tonight."

"We left early this morning and got home three hours ago. I could tell when I talked to Liz last night that she wasn't comfortable leaving Ella with Vera for a full day. We just left the beach a few hours earlier than expected, although, truth be told, I could've stayed at the ocean for the whole month of September. That sunshine and sand did my heart a lot of good."

He stuffed his hands in his pocket while the baby squirmed to get a look at him. "I'll bet. Liz said you've been a real help to her with Ella and everything."

Arlene smiled. "Aww, that's sweet. I love my daughter more than anything, Nick." She kissed Ella's head and straightened. "Okay. Let me show you a few things. I set her oatmeal and banana for supper on the counter. I already measured it. Just add a half cup of water and heat for thirty seconds in the microwave. I put her schedule on the counter. She gets a bottle after supper and one right before bed. Bedtime is seven or seven-thirty at the latest. She's been sleeping through the night, but if Liz isn't home yet, she may wake up and need another bottle and a diaper change around ten."

Whoa. Whoa. "I'm not following you, Arlene. I have a dinner date with Liz tonight."

"What? Didn't Liz call you to babysit Ella? I left a message for her at work."

"No. I haven't spoken to Liz since late Friday night. We've texted a few times, and yesterday, we decided to have dinner together when I was done work today."

Arlene rubbed two fingers up and down her forehead. "Oh, my. I thought Liz received my emergency message and sent you over to help with Ella." She slumped against the counter and shook her head. "I don't know what I'm going to do."

"What happened?"

She looked up at him with teary eyes. "My best friend, Louise, just did a Peter Pan down her cellar stairs while putting her suitcase away. I was going to take Ella with me to the hospital, but those places are full of germs. And I promised Louise I'd come with her to the hospital. Liz got called into work today. I thought the agency gave Liz my urgent message, and she sent you over to take care of Ella."

Nick gulped. *There had to be some weird conspiracy of the childcare universe going on.*

"Give me the baby, Arlene. Go take care of your friend." He stepped toward her and held out his arms.

She took a step back, clutching Ella. "Have you ever babysat before?"

"That wasn't important a minute ago." He forced a small smile onto his face. "And yes, I just spent fifty-two hours babysitting Senator Richardson's kids. A one-year-old and a four-year-old. It's a long story. You don't have the time to hear it right now."

Her eyebrows shot upward. "Wasn't it his house that got firebombed Saturday night?"

"That's the one."

"Goodness, I'm glad everyone is okay." Arlene kissed Ella's cheek and placed her in Nick's arms. "I gotta go. Louise is conscious but awful banged up. And you can't heat breast milk in the microwave. Just set it in a pan of warm water in the sink for a few minutes to take the chill off. My cell phone number is on the fridge if you have any questions."

Breast milk? Waaay different than Ollie's bottles.

THE HOUSE OOZED QUIET, except for the Cinderella clock in Ella's room. Its faint tick-tock reminded Nick he'd been rocking in this chair for over an hour with Ella. She'd dozed off a long time ago. Her little left hand clutched the neckline of his shirt while her right thumb nestled firmly in her mouth. Every once in a while, she'd stir and suck, then burrow deeper into his chest. He'd tucked a fleece baby blanket around her a while back.

He wasn't willing to put her in the crib just yet. Besides, she smelled like baby lotion, something he recognized but couldn't remember where or when the soothing scent had bathed his senses like this.

Truth be told, watching Ella was fun. She was such a happy

baby. Once he got over the trauma of changing a girl diaper, he enjoyed himself.

He scrolled the pictures on his phone with his free hand. He'd taken a slew of Ella. One of them caught the prettiest look on her face. It was the kind of picture you shared. Maybe he'd have it framed for Liz. He texted it to Arlene. It would make her smile, no matter what was going on at ER. Then, he sent it to his Aunt Eileen with a short text that it was Liz's baby.

He closed his picture app and checked the baseball scores. He'd just tuned into the Nats versus the Orioles when his aunt's reply pinged in his texts. Nick read it and inhaled a sharp breath as a potent mix of adrenaline and surprise sprinted through his body. She'd sent two pictures side by side. The one of Ella and one of him at roughly the same age.

They were almost identical. The breath whooshed from his chest as he read her text.

OMG. Liz makes beautiful babies, but it sure looks like you helped.

His hand trembled as he set the phone down, and his eyes filled with moisture. Emotions darted through his mind at warp speed. He looked at the picture on his phone again, just to make sure. *His aunt was right.*

In the distance, a car door slammed. It was eleven o'clock. The automatic porch lights switched on, and the sound of keys scratching against the front door drifted from the living room. It had to be Liz because Arlene texted hours ago and said she'd be spending the night at the hospital.

He couldn't get up just yet. His feet must've frozen in place while his heart did flip-flops. Liz would've seen his truck, and known he was there. She'd find him after she made her tea in the microwave. Sure enough, the beeps on the microwave sounded.

A couple minutes later, her fingers grazed his shoulder as she bent down, kissed his head, and whispered, "I'm so sorry you got roped into babysitting after your hellacious weekend at the Richardson's. I didn't receive my mom's message until later this evening, and by then, I knew Ella would be asleep. How'd you do with her? You okay?"

Nick swiped at the corner of his right eye. The words were hard to come by. It's a good thing they were whispering because his voice caught on the lump in his throat.

"More than okay. She really likes my beard. Kept trying to eat it."

Liz snickered. "Mom's been teaching her to give kisses. She was probably kissing you."

Oh? He chuckled. "Why don't you put that tea down and sit on the footstool here so we can see each other?" He forced his legs off the ottoman.

"Sure. What if I turn on the little lamp so we have some light? I could take Ella from you, if you want."

"No. I like it dark right now, and I'm not ready to let go of her just yet."

"I know that feeling." Liz set her tea on the changing table and sat on the footstool in front of Nick's chair. "What's up?"

"I took a few pictures of Ella tonight. She's a happy kid and easy to be with. I couldn't resist. I got some good shots, too."

"Really?" Liz cocked her head and gave him a tentative smile.

"And I sent one to my aunt and told her Ella was your daughter. You'd mentioned wanting more people to know that you had a little girl now, so I figured you wouldn't mind. I mean, Eileen's always loved you. She thinks the world of you."

The muted rays from the nightlights danced in Liz's hair and his fingers itched to slide through the dark silk.

"The feeling's mutual; I don't mind. May I see them?"

Nick pulled out his phone and scrolled down. "Take a look at this."

She gazed at the picture and paused. "Wow, that's a great picture of my girl. What app did you use to get the old-fashioned tint to the picture? It's lovely." She handed the device back to him.

"Yeah, well, here's the thing, babe." He cleared his throat and fought to control the waver in his voice. "That's a picture of me at seven months old. Eileen sent it."

"What?" She gasped and reached for the phone.

He located his aunt's text and handed it back to her.

She read the text and their eyes locked, the phone slipping from her hand to the ottoman.

Shock rolled across her beautiful face, and her expression froze. But seconds later, her eyes widened and her lips slowly softened into a trembling smile. Unabashed tears spilled down her cheeks.

"I'm not real sure what to say right now, Sergeant," she murmured.

He rocked the stirring Ella in his arms and slid his fingers over one of Liz's hands. He knew exactly where to begin. "I'm the one who never said a word about trying to have the vasectomy reversed. It never occurred to me that I wasn't shooting blanks. I'd read about some reversals healing over time but didn't even consider I was in that small percentage."

Liz stared at the baby picture. "You and Ella look almost

identical at the same age. Come to think of it, I've never seen a baby picture of you before now. The resemblance is uncanny."

"I know. You've never seen a baby picture because my mother hid everything she valued so my father couldn't destroy it. There were many nights I slept with photo albums and her jewelry under my mattress or in the toy box. When Eileen helped me clean out the house, I told her she could have whatever she wanted. During those bitter days, I wasn't interested in keeping anything. But I'm glad she saved that picture."

Nick leaned forward and placed a tender kiss on Liz's lips. "Ella's my daughter. I'll still get the blood test and make it official, but there's no doubt in my mind that she's mine." *Damn.* His voice was trembling. *Not* something he wanted to happen while conveying his acceptance of such a life-altering biological fact. "I'm not prepared to be a parent, babe. You'll help me figure it out?"

She grabbed a tissue and dabbed at her cheeks. "Of course I will. I can't imagine what changed your mind between Friday night and now. But, for the record, I don't blame you for this situation. This is *my* fairytale ending. It doesn't have to be yours. I'm the one who decided to have Ella."

His mouth quirked up on one side. "Yeah, well, it's pretty obvious I've been involved since her beginning."

"Let me put the baby in her crib now, so you and I can talk in the living room?" Liz gently removed Ella from his chest and tucked her in bed.

29

N ick stood, wavering a second. His knees were like rubber.

Never in his life had he imagined something like—like this happening. Yeah, sure, he'd watched movies where the guy ended up with a kid by accident, but he'd always shoved another handful of popcorn in his mouth and thought, *dude, you're in over your head.*

Liz took his hand and urged him down the hallway to the kitchen. She poured two fingers of Southern Comfort into a glass, took a sip, and offered it to him. "It'll take the edge off the shock, Sergeant. You've got that deer in the headlights look on your face."

He sipped slowly and paced the kitchen, guilt tugging on his heart. "I can't believe you've been through all this alone, babe. Honestly, I had no idea. I've spent a lot of time berating Ella's deadbeat dad in my mind, and as it turns out, *I'm* that dad." He ran a hand through his hair. "I wouldn't blame you for being really pissed."

Liz tossed her hands in the air and laughed. "Pissed is the

furthest emotion from my mind. I'm ecstatic." She took the glass from his hand and sipped. "I'm beyond thrilled that you're Ella's biological father. All along, I'd hoped against the odds that you were the one. I can't tell you how many nights I've yearned for a family, that you'd understand my decision to keep her and not hate me for it. You're all I've ever wanted, Nick. You're my best friend. I can never seem to get enough of your love."

He cupped her cheek and pulled her close. "You've been the love of my life since high school, honey. How can I possibly make any of this up to you? I'll try to be a good father to Ella." Emotion clogged his throat, and his eyes filled again. *Not just overwhelmed, but surprised and happy.*

Liz lifted her eyes and smiled. "It's the little things, Nick. Like how you held her until she fell asleep tonight." She gave him a firm but gentle kiss and whispered, "I believe in you. I believe you'll overcome the pain from your past and find joy in getting to know your daughter."

That was a very tall order. He kneaded the tight muscles in her shoulders. "Why did you name her Ella? Is it a family name?"

She wrapped her arms around him. "It's an acronym."

Of course, it was an acronym. Her brilliant mind would insist on something with significance. A chuckle rumbled through his chest as he ran his hands through her hair.

Liz sighed. "I didn't know if she'd ever have a strong male figure in her life, what with my dad gone and the baby daddy situation in the air, so I named her after strong, vital women. The E is for Eileen."

Hmmm. "After my aunt?"

"Yeah, she's amazing, don't you think? She was so good to you. Still is." She traced a soft finger along his jawline. "The first L is for Louise, my mom's friend. Her positive attitude and sense of humor encouraged me all through rehab and pregnancy."

"I don't know her very well. Guess I'll have to change that." He gave her an encouraging smile.

"Yes, definitely. The second L is for Liz because I'm her badass mom." She laughed out loud. "God help her."

"And the A?"

"For Arlene. Kindest woman I know. She's made of love."

His eyes filled again. *Wow.* Why did he want to weep? He swallowed hard. "Beautiful name, babe. It has a truly heartfelt meaning."

She stood on her tiptoes and planted a kiss on his cheek. "There's more, Sergeant." She ran her hands up his biceps. "Ella has a middle name, too."

He trailed kisses across her shoulder. "What's that?"

"Rose. Ella Rose."

His breath hitched, and he buried his face in her hair. His voice choked in barely a whisper. "After my mom?"

"Yes. She loved you so much, and she loved me. Bravest woman I've ever met."

"Honey," he sighed deeply. "She'd be so honored. I'm honored. Thank you."

"You're welcome. I always wanted Ella to be yours, if not by birth, then by love." Liz leaned back, dabbed the tears from her face with her dress sleeve, and swiped the moisture from his cheeks as well. "So, what happened at the Richardsons' this weekend to soften your attitude about children?"

Nick barked a laugh. "It's a long story. The short version is that I babysat the two younger kids for almost three days until Angie, their mother, arrived home early this afternoon. The first six hours were the most terrifying thing I've ever done."

She eyed him speculatively. "*Most* terrifying, huh? That's saying a lot since you've thrown a live grenade out of an airborne chopper."

"Yeah, well, I survived. More importantly, the kids did. Natalie, the four-year-old, broke through my shell. She got to me." *Slayed me.* He cupped Liz's derriere and whispered in her ear. "Why'd you work so many hours on a national holiday?"

"Somebody's sabotaging my work. That's all I can say about it. But they needed help straightening it out."

He raised his eyebrows. "And did you?"

"Sort of. I'll need to start from scratch, though. Once it's broke, it can't be fixed. Next time, I'll make it even better, more efficient." Liz shrugged. "I can't worry about it anymore. My brain is too tired."

"But you're okay? Can I help with anything?"

She rolled her eyes. "Always my watchful security specialist, aren't you? I'm fine. Work will be fine. Trust me."

"You, I trust. It's everyone else I worry about." But he wouldn't be concerned tonight. She was right here, where she belonged. He cleared his throat. "Thank you for giving me a daughter. She's a priceless gift."

Liz launched herself into his arms. "I love you. I will forever love you for saying that." She framed his face with her hands and kissed him. One kiss led to another and within seconds they swept each other into a swirling duel of teasing tongues and love bites.

Wait. Wait. He pulled back and heaved a breath. "I don't have any protection."

She peeked up at him with a sheepish grin. "Don't worry, I went on the pill before the Sanctuary rescue. I knew my resolve was cracking." She shrugged. "You know, just in case."

It was party time. In a nanosecond, he'd tugged her back

into his arms. Her hands grabbed at his hair, his hands searched for the zipper on her dress. She unbuttoned his shirt, tracing the outline of the muscles on his chest with her hands and nibbled her way across his six-pack.

He looked down. Nothing turned him on more than seeing his Liz kiss whatever she wanted when he could watch.

He wouldn't need his shoes, toed them off, and kicked them out of the way. He finished unzipping her dress with one hand while the other roamed her hair and guided her mouth to his favorite places. He slipped the dress off her shoulders, reveling in cleavage that begged for his touch.

Liz wriggled the dress down over her beautiful curves, and the slinky fabric pooled on the kitchen floor. She stepped out of it, snatched and tossed it on the counter. Her red satin bra and panties left him breathless. She took his lips in a searing kiss and made quick work of undoing his belt and pants zipper. *Thank goodness.* His erection bobbed free.

A sexy smile dawned across her face, and her eyes lit up with mischief. "Are we playing our strip version of *capture the flag?*"

Okay, okay. She'd seen his stars and stripes boxers. If either of them wore underwear with the colors in the US flag, it almost always led to this favored game. He'd play along. She was quite the competitor, but he always won. One way or the other.

LIZ SQUEALED with delight and made a bee line for the dining room. She stretched her arms against the farthest forest green wall and gave him a sexy shimmy.

He sauntered toward her and placed his hands on the

table. "I will win, you know. You often forget to count the pieces of clothing you've got left."

His confidence was adorable, but he was underestimating her. "Let's play, Sergeant. That's your side of the table and this is mine." She winked at him. "I go first. Pants, please."

"False start, babe. My belt's still on." He yanked it from the loops and cast it into Ella's baby swing. "Your turn. A shoe."

She removed the shoe from her prosthetic foot and tossed it into the living room. "Give me whatever piece you want, soldier."

He pulled off a sock and hung it on the draped crystal chandelier. "Your other shoe."

She bent over, giving him a wide-angle view of her ass, removed the shoe and lobbed it at him.

He knocked the shoe aside with his arm. "Hey, no roughing the passer. And, that sexy peek of your mons is an illegal formation. Do it again—I'll leap the table and sack you."

Her nipples tightened under his wolfish stare. "Then you'd be offsides."

Nick shook his head and snickered. "True. But thinking about your red zone distracts my defense. I'll break a rule or two if necessary. Your turn to pick."

"I want your shirt, Sergeant." She leaned against the wall and savored the erotic torture as he undid his cuffs, and shrugged it off. His body was a masterpiece of thick muscles. *Maybe turn in her panties and surrender?*

Nick held the shirt exactly halfway across the table. "Here you go, babe. It's yours."

She stepped closer and reached for the shirt. His big arms swooped around her and unhooked her bra.

"Hey, that's a flag. It's cheating and an automatic first down for me."

He nibbled her lower lip and smiled. "*That* was an honest interception. You read the play wrong. Gotta watch my eyes." He traced a finger up her throat and whispered, "Ready to declare me the winner yet?"

"Never. I play to win." She allowed the bra straps to slip down her arms. The tent in his pants stood at full salute. Her core throbbed and her underwear was soaked with lust, but all she needed to do was demand a forfeit or capture his boxers. She held her bra with two fingers and in one dramatic sweep of a hand, dropped it on the floor.

He whimpered and adjusted himself. "You're killing me, Lieutenant."

"How wonderful..." She gave him a short bump and grind show and smacked her ass. "Fork over the pants, Sergeant." His mouth fell open like a hungry pillager.

He snapped his mouth shut and set his hands on the back of a chair. "I can't. There's change in my pocket. You know the rules. I'll have to turn the coins in one turn at a time before you win my trousers." He raised an eyebrow and grinned.

Omigod. That could take forever. Nick was the only person she knew who still paid with cash. He could have dozens of coins. She'd spontaneously combust if she had to wait much longer. She tiptoed toward the table and peeked over his edge. "How many pieces do you have left?"

"Let's see, babe." He pulled the change out of his pocket. "Seven coins, one watch, the trousers and one pair of flag boxers. I believe that makes ten." He glanced at her side of the table. "You're an excellent strategist, Lieutenant, and I've learned not to underestimate you. But, from my point of view, you're down to those luscious panties. Ready to concede?"

His bare chest was *so* distracting. A sensual invitation. She bit her lower lip. *Hell, no.* "I've got two socks on each foot, eight pairs of earrings if you include all the tiny diamond studs, plus backings, the two sleeves on my prosthetic, my panties, and, if I get in a real bind, the prosthetic. I'm pretty sure that adds up to twenty-four." She mentally fist-pumped. Not bad at all, considering her mind was half-crazed and her body smoldered just looking at him.

He groaned and gave her a threatening smile. "Don't give up your leg, babe. What I have planned for you will require two feet." He tossed his loose change on the table, shoved his trousers down, and set them on a chair.

She waved a hand at him. "What are you doing?"

"Conceding, you little wench. Forfeiting. Call it whatever you want. I've got to touch your tits. My defense crumbled with the bra move." He sauntered around the table and pinned her body to an empty corner. "Claim your flag." His voice was low and husky and suggestive as hell.

Pressed against the wall with his face an inch from hers, she slid her fingers down his solid chest and snapped the elastic on his underwear. She suckled his bottom lip and dragged his boxers down with a painstaking slow discipline. Nick loved the tease, the erotic ascent, and tipping over the orgasmic edge almost more than she did. She'd give him as much as he could endure. She slithered down past the chair rail, fondling his engorged penis and swirling circles around it with her hands and tongue. When she stroked his balls, those pillars he called thighs trembled.

His boxers dropped to the floor. He panted loudly, and his chest heaved. "Enough."

He hauled her to her feet and kicked the boxers under the table. "That was an exceptional claiming ceremony, Lieutenant. Made me proud to wear the flag."

She giggled.

"You're wearing red. I get to have my way with you, too."
He fondled her nipples and kissed a trail of love nips down
her neck. Her breasts filled his big hands. "They're so
gorgeous, heavy and lush."

"I didn't get to pump or nurse Ella tonight. You're gonna
get sprayed, soldier." *Sprayed? More like hosed down.*

He licked and suckled his way from one nipple to the
other as he ran a finger inside her crease. "I love wet things.
Bring it on, Lieutenant."

The soft stroke of his finger ignited the burn she'd
hungered for, and she clutched at his shoulders. But when his
tongue traced a nipple, a quick climax barreled over her like a
train without a driver. She mewled a soft cry and collapsed
against him.

Nick straightened and kissed her mouth tenderly. "We got
a little cream off the top there, Lieutenant. Here comes the
one that'll help you sleep like a rock."

He set one big hand on her belly, held her against the wall,
and dropped to his knees, dragging the satin panties down
with his other hand. His tongue laved and circled her over
sensitized flesh until he found that one curve waiting for him.
She moaned and urged him on with her hands. She loved
being pinned like this—a flower opening to her warm sun.
Her heart hammered, faster and faster as the pleasure tightened. She threw her bad leg over his shoulder and writhed
against him until every taut nerve unfurled in cascading
pleasure.

Boneless, she began sliding down the wall. He caught her
and stood, her socked feet dangling at his shins, his breathing
heavy as he held her close.

"More, I want more. I want you inside me. Now."

He set her on her feet and smoothed her hair back. "You

sure? It's okay to be tuckered out."

"Definitely. Now." She'd swallow her pride and beg if necessary.

He tossed a chair pad on the table and bent her over it, massaging her shoulders, and ran his fingers down her back.

"I *need* to feel you this time." She reached behind and stroked his erection.

He spread her cheeks and nudged inside, his big hands around her breasts. "I won't last but a minute in this position after hearing you come twice, babe." He groaned and paused after each stroke.

"Slam me, Sergeant. That's an order. Don't hold back."

Nick's rugged flesh slapped against her smooth backside. His pace quickened, and her hips lifted with each thrust. The warmth, the slip and slide of his body against hers, and the scent of languorous sex covering them like an aphrodisiac were among the sensory treats she'd missed for so long. Her core tightened with his panting breaths and moans. He gripped her hips tight on a groan of ecstasy. Her core muscles squeezed and climaxed with his pulsing. The pleasure was delicious and raw and *them.*

Nick's body trembled as he rested his chest against her back. "That was the *best* game of capture the flag *ever*. Babe, we're made for each other."

Liz heaved a deep, satisfied breath and lifted her head. "Stay a minute, don't pull out yet." His chuckle rumbled against her back.

"I defy *that Vera woman* to walk in the back door right now, honey." He gently kneaded her shoulder muscles as they cooled down.

She burst into laughter. "Or my mother."

"Oh, please, no. That one time she busted us years ago will

haunt me a lifetime." He kissed her flushed cheek and withdrew. "Stay there. Don't move." He grabbed a fleece throw from the living room and wrapped it around her. "I'll be right back."

She couldn't remain splayed across the table like this for long, but the tufted chair pad underneath was comfortable and the fleece tamed her goosebumps temporarily. She relaxed into the cushion and folded her arms under her head. She could fall asleep right here. Every fiber of her soul yawned in afterglow relaxation. She was one thought away from the sleep abyss when he scooped her into his arms.

"I've got a bath all ready, my sweet." He carried her down the hallway and set her on the bathroom counter. "Tell me how to get this prosthetic off."

She guided him through the simple steps and glanced at the tub. "Honey, we're supposed to draw the water *after* we get in." She gazed into his deep blue eyes. By all that was holy, she'd love him forever. They were so *right* together. And tonight made everything she'd endured for the past sixteen months—worth it.

NICK SCOOPED his Liz into his arms and set her down gingerly in the frothy bubbles. He jogged back to the dining room and gathered their clothes. The memory of tonight went a long way toward rectifying the words he'd heard Vera speak into this room only days ago about Liz's daughter—his daughter. He'd better get used to saying it. His daughter.

He snatched his boxers and balled them in his fist—he'd save them forever. He tossed the armful of clothing and shoes into Liz's room and strode towards the bathroom.

"Here I come, Lieutenant. Make way for daddy long legs to join you."

Liz opened one sleepy eye. "What were you doing out there?"

He chuckled. "I hid the evidence, as in picked up our clothes. I have a feeling that once we soak and climb in bed, we're gonna sleep good, babe."

A grin spread across her face. "Thank you, so thoughtful. Here, you take the seat, and I'll sit between your legs." She leaned back against his chest and sighed. "We'll have to play games more often, Sergeant."

He lathered a bar of soap in his hands and washed her arms. "I'm already planning a version of the American League Playoff series for the pennant."

She burst into laughter and floated around to face him. "Your inner animal has been unleashed."

He ran a thumb across her lower lip. "You do that to me, babe. How many hours did you work today?"

She kissed his palm. "Eighteen."

"Time for bed, young lady. You look exhausted. Pull the plug, and I'll grab some towels."

Nick dried her off and carried her to bed. "I'll pull the covers down and tuck you in. Should I check on Ella?"

Liz kissed him one more time as he set her down inside the warm covers. "I really think she's out for the night. You can check on her, but if you wake her up—you're on duty." She yawned. "Welcome to fatherhood, Nick Flannery. I'm so glad you're here. We'll figure the rest out together."

He crept down the hall, minus the fear he'd worn like a wet coat the other night, and opened Ella's door. Judging by her breathing, she was fast asleep.

He slid in next to Liz and spooned with her heart-shaped

backside. It didn't matter if sleep eluded him. This was one of those precious days he didn't want to end.

He'd remember today for the rest of his life. Ella was almost seven months old.

But *this* was the day he became a father.

30

L iz plopped her purse on the conveyor belt at the security entrance of her Homeland Security building. Today was a day of celebration. If only a flash mob would pour out from the eight elevators to help her sing and dance a show tune in the austere marble lobby, and help her gift the ladies at the information desk with bunches of pink roses.

She'd spent yesterday with Nick and Ella. Her heart hadn't been this light in, well, let's see, maybe forever. *There was nothing to hide anymore.* Her precious little girl had a daddy, and someday Ella might even grow up in a family with two loving parents. What more could Liz possibly ask for?

She'd worn a red blouse today with a flamboyant floral scarf. It complimented her dark hair and livened up her plain black suit. Loud clothing was totally out of character for her, but this new lease on life demanded a colorful splash of fun. She was *over it.* No more contemplating what she could've, should've, would've done differently in the situation. And furthermore, she'd fought like a warrior to regain her life and personal balance. She was damn proud of her accomplishments.

Liz raised her chin, smiled at the security guy, and whisked the cross body purse over her head. She looked inside. Yup, they were on a no liquid kick today. Her hand lotion and antibacterial gel were gone. But somebody loved her: they'd left her favorite yogurt in the clear lunch bag.

The elevator opened as soon as she pushed the button, and she smiled at the mirrored door. Boom. She had this. Whatever the day threw at her, she'd overcome. The big stuff in her life? It was already handled.

She bounded from the elevator and strode toward her office, greeting a few folks along the way. She'd barely hung her jacket and purse on the hook in her office when Carmen rushed in, her brows furrowed.

"Hey. I can't see you on my system anymore. Is everything okay?"

"Oh yeah, don't worry. They moved me to a different server. New project. No big deal. I've got two laptops to stay on top of all the projects in the bullpen. You're here early."

"Four-day weekend. I got a lot of extra sleep and went to the gym at five this morning. I figured I may as well get started."

"Ready to catch some bad guys?" Liz fired up both computers and adjusted the window blind to reduce the glare, beaming a smile at her coworker.

"From your lips to God's ears," Carmen laughed. She leaned forward and whisked a finger through Liz's scarf. "You're mighty colorful today. It looks good on you. Happy."

"You're right."

"They had some suit from upstairs fill in for you yesterday."

Liz rolled her eyes. "Really? Who was it?"

"The guy mumbled an introduction at the morning meeting. None of us caught his name, so we referred to him as *the suit* for the rest of the day. We never saw him again until quitting time."

Liz leaned a hip against the desk and crossed her arms. "Huh. Did you guys get any work done?"

"Sure," Carmen hesitated. "Lots of research, but no catches. We're not used to having an absentee supervisor. We made the best of it."

"Okay. Let's change tactics today and see what we can find. I'm off to get coffee, check in with the major. I'll join you guys in a few." She let Carmen out first and locked her office door.

"Watch your step with the major. She's in full uniform and breathing fire. She already yelled at two people this morning," Carmen noted with a wink.

Liz poured coffee and hustled toward the major's office. Something was up. Usually, Major Chan projected a calm demeanor. Liz rounded the corner and almost ran into Erin, the major's administrator. Her arms were loaded with files. Her face held a worried expression.

"I'm so glad to see you here today. I need to talk to you, Liz. Really soon."

Liz helped her balance the heavy files. "Okay. What's up?"

Erin whispered, "Not now. Not here. Maybe we can take lunch together or something?"

"Um, okay. If not today, then tomorrow." Liz placed the last slipping file on top, close to Erin's chin.

"It can't wait until tomorrow. Let's *really* try for today, please?"

"Alright," Liz offered her a reassuring smile. "I'll do my best."

The major's voice boomed from her office. "Erin, are you chatting again? The colonel needs those files ASAP."

Liz held an index finger to her lips. "My bad. I'm the one who slowed Erin down. She's headed for the colonel's office right now."

Erin mouthed a thank you and hurried toward the elevator.

Liz approached the doorway. "Morning, Major. Just checking in before I visit the bullpen. Anything I need to know?"

The major looked up. "Intense morning around here. Come in and shut the door, lock it if you wouldn't mind. The last thing I need is another numb-nut barging in and slowing me down. Have a seat."

Liz sat on the green leather chair closest to the desk.

"We've got a ninety-two percent positive ID on the hacker messing with your online personas."

Liz raised her eyebrows and waited.

"He or she, although, we believe it's a *she* from the intelligence, is among the top twenty most wanted hackers in the world. Her screen name is Illusia. We're still digging for the birth name identity of this hacker. What we haven't figured out is why your files, why now?"

Liz swallowed hard at the information that just dropped a rock in her gut. *Breathe. Hackers don't physically reach out to harm people. Their currency is information. They attach and parasite themselves.*

The major pensively tapped a pencil on the desk. "For some reason, this Illusia found your DHS profiles a good fit for their needs. They're fishing for government info, I suppose."

Unease trickled across Liz's shoulders. "What about the flowers?"

"Yes. I'll admit the flowers are a deviation from the norm for this hacker. We've got a team of profilers and shrinks in for a consult on this, but I won't have their reports until tomorrow."

The major continued. "Unfortunately, you'll be starting from scratch again with your online work. The newer laptop on your desk contains state-of-the-art programs to build brand new personas. The software folks made sure there weren't blind entry points or back doors in this updated version. It's a slightly different platform, but you'll adapt quickly, I'm sure."

Liz rubbed her hands together in an effort to warm them. "Okay, I'll get to work."

The major leaned forward on the desk. "Look, Liz, I know this is a real bite in the ass. Your work is phenomenal in every sense of the word. Your world-building craft outshines people who've been here for ten years because you're smart and talented and you insist on doing things right. I wish I had a dozen of you. And your leadership in that bullpen is invaluable. The brass sent some stuffed shirt down yesterday to fill in for you." She shook her head and smiled. "And your bullpen looked like a team of prize dogs without a musher, all mopey and noses to the ground."

Liz chuckled. "You're comparing my infamous bullpen to a pack of dogs?"

The major laughed. "You know me, Liz. I love my dogs. Hell, the dark web guys have an *Eager Beagles* sign on the wall in their den that they made themselves. Any comparison is a well-deserved compliment. Just don't rat me out. Last thing I need today is some tight-ass giving me a lesson on political correctness. I know that each one of our people is invaluable and brilliant."

Liz stood and grabbed her coffee. "Your secret is safe with me."

The major nodded. "You look revitalized today. You had a good day off?"

"Best day on or off I've had in a long time." Liz smiled. "And you? Take any time?"

"No. I was here early again. I might take some extra days away in a week or two."

Liz unlocked the office door and opened it a few inches. "Major?"

She looked up. "Yes?"

"Are you sure I'm not in any danger from this person? Those flowers creeped me out, and I've got a family to think about."

The major stood, giving Liz a confident smile. "I suppose our imaginations could run a bit, but there's no evidence to suggest any danger. It's not part of the MO for these professional hackers. They leech onto an information highway and ride as long as they can. When Illusia discovers the intelligence has stopped, she'll go away. If DHS finds anything to suggest otherwise, you'll be the first to know."

Liz rolled her shoulders. "Okay. I'll relax once I get busy in the bullpen. See you later."

She wasn't halfway down the hallway when Erin fell in stride beside her.

"I *really* need to talk to you in private, Liz. It'll only take a minute or two. Are you going to your office?"

Inwardly, Liz sighed. It would have been nice to have a moment to breathe and relax. But if she avoided Erin now, lunch would be mandatory and judging by the time on the hallway clock, her lunch break would most likely take place at her desk.

"Sure, Erin. I'll meet you there in a minute. Let me nuke my coffee."

"I'll walk with you. Thanks for covering with the major. She's in a rare mood today."

"Perhaps Major Chan is dealing with a lot. She worked during the holiday weekend."

Erin rolled her eyes. "That's for sure. I came in yesterday morning and she'd stacked a week's worth of work on my desk while I was off. I don't know how she does it."

Liz slid her mug into the microwave. She focused on Erin. Something was unusual about her. "You look different today. Did you change something over the weekend?"

Erin smiled. "You noticed. No goth makeup. You like it?"

Ohh. "Well, the black eyeliner and lipstick worked for you, but this is definitely more professional looking."

"I'm so glad you noticed. My boyfriend asked me to get rid of the black for a week and see if I liked it. It's day five, and I'm kinda loving it."

Liz pulled her mug from the microwave and headed for the hallway. "I'm glad for you. It's important that you like the change, too." She unlocked her office door and waved Erin in. "We only have a few minutes."

"Right." Erin looked at the floor. "The major told me something last Friday, and I owe you an apology."

"For what?" Liz set her mug down.

"I was really nasty to you a couple weeks ago about your shoes. It's just that you're so pretty, and I couldn't figure out why you wore such plain shoes. I mentioned it to the major in passing, and she informed me that you're a decorated veteran and you'd lost a foot in Iraq. I had no idea. It isn't obvious."

Liz nodded. "I've worked hard to find my new normal, and when I wear a skirt, I wear tights so you can't tell."

A soft mewl escaped Erin's throat. "I'm so sorry. I really didn't know and have the utmost respect for veterans, especially those who give more than they should have to. Please forgive me. It was insensitive."

Well, what a surprise. "It's okay. Thank you for the apology. I appreciate it."

"I'd like to make it up to you somehow. Lunch is unpredictable around here, but maybe a happy hour drink after work sometime. Or a girl's night this Friday?" She grinned.

"There's no need for amends, Erin. It's fine. We're fine." So much penitence, it was hard not to believe her.

"Please don't say no. I'd really like to get to know you better, and we could invite some other work people. It'd be fun."

Carmen stuck her head in the open door and grinned. "Did I just hear you two talking about a girl's night this Friday? I'd *kill* for a happy hour after work. Say yes, Liz. For the sake of working women everywhere, say yes to the happy hour."

Erin chimed, "Just the three of us or invite the others from your bullpen. Whatever you want."

Liz crossed her arms. She *could* go if Nick or her mom didn't mind covering for several hours. Maybe she'd put herself out there. Although, she'd never considered Erin a friend, more like a coworker to avoid. "I'll think about it. It could be fun. Let me check with my babysitter."

Carmen reached over and high-fived Erin. "Best idea you've had yet, goth girl. Oh wait, no goth today?"

"Back to work, ladies. Chat in the hallway on your way to your desks." Liz shooed them out of her office. It had been years since she'd gone to a happy hour. *The possibilities.*

She sat and woke up the desktop and the laptops, checking the workload before heading into the bullpen. Something was different with the new laptop. The red camera light stayed engaged no matter what she did to turn it off.

She grabbed her landline, called IT, and ended up leaving a message for the department supervisor. "Morning, Pat. I've got a problem with my new laptop. The camera light stays on. There could be a short in it or it needs a tweak or something. You guys would know better than I. When you get a minute, send somebody over to fix it, please. Thanks a bunch."

Liz gathered the papers she'd printed and glanced at the new laptop as the camera light blinked off. *Odd.* She grabbed a piece of opaque tape to put over it but changed her mind. Maybe there were new security measures in her office she wasn't aware of.

She locked her door and walked toward the bullpen. An eerie unease tiptoed across her neck like a damp chill. *The same weirdness she'd felt in Major Chan's office.* She looked around, backtracked, and made sure her office door had latched.

Something was amiss, but damn if she could put her finger on it.

31

Liz pulled into the Big4Less lot and parked far from the entrance. She really needed to walk after sitting all day. And she *had* to get diapers, lots of them. Maybe she'd fill the backseat so she didn't have to buy them for a while. But what if Ella changed sizes? She'd be stuck with a ton of the wrong size. On second thought, she'd get enough for a month.

She gave the steering wheel an affectionate love tap. The accessories in this car were brag-worthy. Like a sound system solid enough for a block party, remote start, and frigid air conditioning for Indian summer days like today.

Liz grabbed her purse, locked the car, and headed for the entrance, pausing to claim a stray cart. She loaded up on diapers, wipes, two adorable blue outfits for Ella (because Nick had teased that Ella's drawers looked like a bottle of Pepto Bismol blew up in there) and a rotisserie chicken. Her stomach growled. The veggies and yogurt she'd eaten for lunch were long gone.

She stopped at the crosswalk, fished the key fob from her purse, and peered down the aisle for her car as she put on her sunglasses and looked again. It was *way* out there. She leaned into the heavy cart filled with purchases and got moving. *Hmm.* She'd only tried the remote start feature once at the dealership and then just never got into it. Today's weather offered a perfect day to give it a whirl and slide into a cool car.

But for the life of her, she couldn't remember how close she had to be for the thing to work. She tried the remote about halfway there. Nothing. Every two or three cars, she pushed the remote again. When she was ten cars out, the car finally blinked and engaged. She pressed the button to open the trunk, and *voila.* Why hadn't she used this awesome feature before now?

A hiss danced in the air, and she glanced left and right before a vicious force tore her fingers from the cart and launched her airborne. She landed in a heap with a thud.

Somewhere in the distance, her grocery cart crashed, followed by an explosion and a blast of heat. Voices screamed far away. Her head throbbed, and her ears roared. *What happened?* She tried to open her eyes, but the ache, oh, the ache. She couldn't do it. She'd just lie there, breathe a few minutes.

But the incendiary heat burned. Liz had to move. She forced her eyes open, insisting they blink. Once, twice. A two-story inferno raged in front of her. *Move. Move, soldier. Survive.* Another explosion and the heat rolled over her like a steamy, lead blanket. She couldn't lift a limb and curled in on herself.

Move. Now. Move.

Liz rolled, sliding down the front of the car where she'd landed. She covered her head with her hands and focused forward. She combat-crawled and slithered under a large vehicle, tearing her blazer half off. Blast it all, her brain was lost in a thick fog. But it was cooler here. She squeezed her eyes shut to think. Her only rational thought repeated several times. *Call Nick.*

People were running past her and screaming but she couldn't move. She remembered the phone in her pants pocket and fumbled for it. The space was tight. Good. Tight was safe. She turned her face to the side and tapped the screen, but zoned out as it rang.

"I was just thinking about you, gorgeous. Did you leave work yet?"

Liz lifted her head and hit it on something metal. Her mouth was so dry and her tongue was thick, like a wad of gauze. She spit out a pebble and tried to wet her lips. "Nick. Big fire. Help me." Her voice sounded like a distant echo in her head.

"What? Where are you? Liz? Dammit! Talk to me, honey."

———

THE LINE WENT DEAD.

Nick screeched onto the shoulder of the DC beltway and threw his truck into park. He grabbed his phone and checked Liz's location. He'd set their phones on *location sharing*. She could call him an asshole later.

"Come on, come on…hurry up." He shook the damn thing. Finally, the circle with her initial came into view. He enlarged the screen several times until it showed she was either in or somewhere near the Big4Less store. He was ten minutes away, but he could make it in five.

He slapped his left blinker on, churned up the stones getting off the shoulder, and re-entered traffic, calling Liz's cell every thirty seconds. Each time it went straight to voicemail.

He cautiously inched through a red light when two fire trucks and a police car whizzed past him and turned onto the road for the store. His adrenaline slammed into overdrive at the sight of several vehicles on fire. He parked rows away from the inferno and jumped out of his truck.

The phone locator didn't update fast enough to pinpoint exactly where Liz was, and he jogged the aisles calling her name until a fireman grabbed him by the shoulder.

"You're not allowed to be in here right now. We're roping off the scene. Get outside the tape for your own safety, buddy."

"My girlfriend owns one of those cars. She called me for help. I've got to find her," Nick yelled above the cacophony of noise.

"She called you *after* the explosion?"

"She needed help."

"I gotta tell you, buddy—no one inside those vehicles is alive. You sure she called you after?"

"I'm sure." His heartbeat stuttered. *Unless she couldn't get out.* His next thought knocked the wind out of him. He tapped a phone number and waited for someone to answer. "Arlene? Are you and Ella together?"

"Yes, I'm feeding her supper right now. What's all that noise? You alright?"

"I'm fine. Call you later." He hung up, slumping against a van. *Ella was safe.*

The fireman dropped his gear and got on his knees, looking under vehicles. "I can't stay. Gotta unload hoses, but if she's out here, she may have taken cover on the ground somewhere. Start looking under the vehicles, and shit; don't get any closer. There's gas everywhere. If you find her? There are ambulances on the way. Get her to one of them pronto."

Nick got on all fours and scanned the ground. He ran five or six car lengths and did it again, screaming Liz's name the entire time. She had to be here, somewhere. Five minutes later, Nick saw something under a pickup truck and sprinted in that direction.

He got on his knees and looked under the GMC truck. There she was—face down and still.

"Liz, babe. Can you hear me?" He lowered his body, stuck his head under, and slid his hand over hers. It was cold. "Liz. I'm here. Are you hurt?"

She turned her head toward him. Her eyes were glazed and wild; a row of scratches etched her cheek. She licked her lips.

"I told them not to send Jazz on the mission with us, but they did anyway."

Jazz? Oh yeah, the guy who'd died when she'd lost her foot. He only knew the bits and pieces he'd heard afterward. She'd never told him any details.

"I gotta get you out of here, babe. We can talk about it once you're safe."

"Not yet. Incoming enemy fire. Stand down, soldier."

He pulled his head out from under the truck and looked down the row of cars. The fact that there were no firemen in their aisle was a good sign. He could coax her out. It would take him a few minutes, but he didn't want to drag her out with brute force in case she was injured. He poked his head under again and laced his fingers through hers.

"Are you injured, honey?" He tried to slip a shoulder under the truck but didn't fit. At least the sirens had stopped, and he could hear her.

"Jazz was always twitching. Tapping that foot. Bucking the brass. No discipline. I ordered him to follow behind and he came up on my side." She heaved a huge breath. "He stepped on the mine."

Nick muttered a curse. She was reliving every detail of that evil day under this truck and there wasn't a fucking thing he could do about it. He stretched his arm and stroked her hair. "I'm here, babe. It'll be okay."

She lifted her head a little. "Wasn't okay. I heard the click, raised my arm. Everybody stopped, scared to breathe. Pete radioed from the Humvee for bomb detail. Bomb guys are bad asses. They could've figured a way out."

He stretched his neck to get a little closer to her. They locked eyes. "You're right. Those bomb guys rock."

Her lips smoothed into a grim line. "Jazz wouldn't stay still. A few minutes later, he cracked a joke, smiled goofy at me, and shrugged his shoulders. He lifted his foot on purpose." Tears cascaded off the end of her nose as she sobbed.

Nick's stomach clenched. *So, it was a suicide with intent to kill the others.* He'd heard rumors, but anybody connected with that day had accepted reassignments elsewhere.

"Liz, I'm so sorry, babe. You're the fiercest person I know. I love you." He stroked her hair.

She lifted her head. "It was dark and so cold. If it wasn't for Mac and that bomb dog, I wouldn't be here. I don't remember much after that dog licked my face and Mac gave me morphine. Sometimes, I dream about that dog. I don't think they're trained to lick a wounded soldier, but it whined and licked me that night as if I were its favorite human."

"Why were you even there, Liz? You were an analyst. Your brains were needed elsewhere."

"I had a gut feeling the intel was bad. I'm the only one who'd met the bad guy, so I'd recognize his face and mannerisms. I had to make sure before they put a missile in his basement. I insisted."

He tugged her hand and kissed a finger. "Do you know where you are?"

She gave a nod. "Big4Less store."

"Did you buy anything?"

"Yup. Diapers. Blue and chicken."

"Can you tell if you're injured, honey?"

"Head hurts, but I think I'm okay." She swiped the tears off her cheek with the back of her hand. "I really hate it when shit blows up."

"You crawled under a pickup truck. I'll come to your side and help you shimmy out."

"Still scared."

"I know." His heart twisted with compassion, and he shook his head. "But I promise to hold you close."

"Okay." She rested her face on her hand for a minute and started to move.

He moved to her side. "That's it, just a little at a time, brace your foot on the tire and push off. That's my girl." Once half of her body was out, he tugged, pulling her into his arms and kissing her. "You're out. I'll stand and then pull you up, okay?" She trembled in his arms.

"Yeah. I think I'm okay. Just my head hurts."

When they were both standing, he wrapped his arms around her. "There's an ambulance a ways down in the parking lot. I'm going to carry you there, make sure you're okay."

"No. I can walk; hold onto me. Where's my car?"

They took a couple steps together and walked slowly toward the ambulance.

"Your car is roasted, babe."

"Damn," she patted his chest with one hand, "I loved that car."

"I know you did. You'll get a new one."

She stopped and looked across the aisles at the burned cars. "It was the first time I used the remote start since the dealership. Whatever happened tossed me over on this side. I remember crawling until I found something I could fit under."

Nick took a whiff. No bomb material. He could identify that odor from ordnance training. Aside from the pungent burnt stench of auto parts in the air was the underlying scent of gasoline, lots of it. But four burned-up cars provided an awful lot of gasoline to ignite the next vehicle. He'd leave it to the professionals to determine the cause, but the situation rubbed him wrong.

They reached the ambulance, where the medics wasted no time checking Liz out. She had a nasty bump on her head and some bruising, but aside from that, they cleared her, leaving a trip to the hospital for full evaluation up to her.

The police and fire marshal both conducted short interviews while Liz sat in the ambulance nursing a bottle of water.

Once they had the information they needed, she looked at Nick and pleaded, "I want to go home and hold Ella and hug my mom. I want a hot bath and a bowl of soup. Take me home?"

"You betcha. Let me drive my truck over and pick you up."

As he jogged to his truck he thanked his lucky stars that the senator had decided to stay in Texas another week because he had no intention of letting Liz and Ella out of his sight until he knew exactly what had happened to her car.

32

J ustice was a dish best served flambé. The thrill of seeing those flames shoot high into the air would last the rest of her life. Liz should've considered the consequences before she'd allowed Jazz to die in the desert.

Illusia squinted through her binoculars through the first explosion. There was no way Liz survived it. Last she'd seen, the bitch was only a few cars away when Liz must've popped the trunk. It interfered with her view. She'd been hoping to see the last look on Liz's face, but it didn't matter. Even *she* could admit that was a tad macabre. No one could've survived that blast.

Damn, she was good. The inferno sent people screaming and running everywhere. Runaway grocery carts, fire engines, and police cars were an entertainment to behold. *You're welcome, good people of metropolitan Washington. One more public menace sent to hell.* It was such a shame she couldn't brag publicly, but she'd deal.

Who knew those two chemicals would ignite like that in the presence of a little gas and an electronic spark? All of her research had paid off big-time; thanks to the now-dead bomb specialist she'd played for days in Las Vegas. And unfortunately for the bomb specialist—what happened in Vegas ended in Vegas.

Illusia turned onto the DC beltway and headed for Georgetown. She had reservations for a much-deserved celebratory dinner. A nice bottle of wine, a thick steak, and a tavern full of people to blend with. There'd probably be something about the car fires on the news in an hour or, if she was lucky, rolling along the bottom of the screen already.

She parked out front, handed the valet a twenty, and sauntered into the establishment. She was a little early, so she flirted with a Fabio-type at the bar over a glass of champagne.

Halfway through her steak, a special alert trolled across the TV monitor about the car explosions. She almost knocked the waiter over trying to get close enough to read it. No one in the place was even aware they were eating with a famous person who'd just made history. This was excitement at its best.

And tonight, in the local news, several cars exploded at the Big4-Less store on President's Road. No injuries or casualties reported. More on your local news station at eleven.

What? She blinked once. Twice. Shook her head.

She stumbled backward and caught herself on a brass railing. *Impossible. She'd seen Liz a hair's breadth away from the blast.* No. No. They had it all wrong. The stupid police and fire just hadn't discovered Liz's cremated remains yet. They'd retract it on the eleven o'clock report, for sure.

Illusia waited at the bar for the special alert to repeat itself, just in case she read it wrong. The same wording crept across the monitor.

She clutched her chest and walked back to her table, grabbing the champagne and downing the rest in giant gulps. She cut another bite of steak, but it didn't taste the same and had gone cold. She guzzled her glass of dinner wine and flagged the waiter for a doggie box and the check.

She'd celebrate tomorrow once the truth came out. *Something* happened to Liz's body. Bodies didn't just incinerate and blow away like dust in the wind. They'd find her—yes, they would. And when they did, they'd have to explain to the public that they were a bunch of incompetent assholes who couldn't find a dead body in a parking lot.

She scratched a signature on the credit card receipt. It didn't matter if it was legible or not, it wasn't her card. It was one of the dozens she'd intercepted and had sent to her. The only places that checked for identification were the liquor stores, anyway. Furthermore, she stiffed the waiter because he'd gotten in her way when she'd tried to read the TV.

Illusia grabbed the doggie box, flung open the front door, and barked at the valet, "Bring my car around right fucking now."

Okay. Okay. She should've said please, but she was upset. She had every right to be livid.

Tapping her foot and waiting for the valet, the Fabio dude sauntered out and asked for her number. *Who the hell did he think he was?*

"Look, you conceited asshole, I gave you a few minutes of my time because you looked like you were worth it. Then you opened your mouth and convinced me I was wrong."

The Fabio guy held up his hands and took a few steps back. "Sorry, lady, my mistake."

Illusia yanked the car door from the hand of the valet and slid into the front seat. She fought with her jammed seatbelt and cursed, catching people out front staring at her and shaking their heads. Screw them. *It's the fucking law, you morons.*

The blink of a security camera winked at her from within the ornamental planters on either side of the massive wooden doors. *Shit. Damn.*

She peeled out of the circle driveway.

Well now, she'd screwed it up real good with that catastrophic dinner. She hadn't worn one of her wigs, and she'd removed the hologram from her license plate that made it blurry to cops and onlookers. *Great. Just fucking great.*

Now, because she hadn't said please, and she hadn't tipped the waiter, and she hadn't worn her Dolly wig, she was going to have to stay up all freaking night hacking the security footage from the restaurant and erasing it.

As if killing someone hadn't been enough shit to do in one day.

33

Nick clicked her seatbelt shut and slipped a blanket around Liz's shoulders. She was still shaking, her teeth chattering, and muttering random thoughts.

"I need to see Ella and make sure she's okay. Good God, my leg hurts. I have to see if there's any damage to the prosthetic."

Nick's body tensed. Right then, he'd have given anything to take her place and endure the terror she'd experienced in that parking lot. He gave her thigh a reassuring squeeze as he checked his mirrors pensively and turned onto the highway ramp. The questions that had gnawed at him while the medics and police questioned Liz sat like a rock in his gut.

"When did you buy that car, babe?"

"Nine months ago. Right after I received my second check from DHS. I didn't want to continue to use Arlene's car once I had a paycheck. Why?"

"Have you had any problems with it?"

"Course not. It's—*was* brand new."

An icy finger traced down his spine. He glanced in his

mirrors again as cars whizzed by. *No tail.* "New cars don't just spontaneously combust. I did some research while the medics looked you over. There's no fucking way that should've happened."

Liz hugged her middle and released a shaky breath. "Yeah. It *is* pretty weird."

"Not so long ago, you were nervous about something at work. Is that still an issue?"

She heaved a deep breath. "Nick, you *know* I can't talk about my work."

He glanced sideways. "Your car just *accidentally* blew up. You need to talk to somebody."

"Yes, well, I signed a contract, non-disclosure agreement. Ethics, moral code of conduct." A weak gesture of her hand indicated more reasons.

"Okay. So, answer me with a yes or no. Is your operating status covert?"

"I can't play twenty questions with this subject."

Stubborn woman. He gritted his teeth together. "A yes or no will suffice."

"No."

"Are you still nervous about something going on at work?"

"Maybe." She looked out the window for a long moment and sighed. "Yes."

"Do you think the work situation has anything to do with your car?"

Liz rested her head against the headrest and closed her eyes. "Maybe. But damn if I know how."

That was all the information Nick needed. Any inkling that the two crises intersected meant she needed protection. He caressed her knee. He'd be damned before government work put her life in jeopardy again.

He turned his blinker on and moved into the right lane.

She sat bolt upright and waved him toward the left. "Nick, this isn't my exit."

"I'm aware of that. This is *my* exit."

She grabbed hold of his arm. "But I need to go home. Please."

He nodded. "I understand. But we're going to my place. It's safe."

"I can't go to your place. I need to protect Ella." The panic in her voice inched toward high and shrill. "I need to hold her and whisper love in her ears."

His heart ached for her. "I get it, babe. Once you're safely inside my building, I'll go get Ella and Arlene. If your work and car situations are related, it's not safe for you to be with Ella right now. It'd be better to shelter in place. My building is the best location for that." He slammed on the brakes, glanced around the four-way intersection, and turned left, parking underground.

Liz startled when Nick unclipped her seat belt and slid his arms around her.

"No, no. I can walk. Let me do it myself. I need to move, everything hurts." She grimaced.

"Okay, but I'm right here if you need help." He grabbed her purse and torn jacket from the truck.

She limped toward the elevator he gestured to.

"My private elevator. This side opens into the dining room. That door opens to a small vestibule near the alley behind the building." They rode in silence to the loft.

The elevator doors opened and a pair of modern jacquard draperies swept apart in front of them. Nick used a remote sitting next to a pewter bowl on his dining room table to close the drapes and hide the elevator.

He dropped her things on the granite countertop, set a big mug with tea in the microwave, and pulled out a chair from the table where they'd eaten a few weeks ago, gesturing for her to sit. "Do you still have your phone?"

"In my purse."

"Text your mother a list of things you want me to bring from your house for you and Ella. Enough for a few days. I can get secure deliveries here, so keep the list compact. I haven't had time to order a real crib, but I did pick up one of those portable sleepover things and some bedding. Tell Arlene to pack the baby monitor. I don't have one."

He stirred a spoonful of honey into the tea and set it in front of Liz. "You want a shot of something stronger in that?"

She shook her head. "Maybe later when Ella and Mom get here." She put her elbows on the table and pulled her ponytail holder out, allowing her hair to cascade across her face. "I just want to protect our daughter, Nick."

He retrieved the phone from her purse and set it on the table next to her. "I promise to go get her in a few minutes. You've been through hell today, but I need you to send that list. I've got some things to show you before I leave." He squatted next to her, took the phone, and peered into her eyes. She'd stopped trembling, but her eyes were glazed and huge. "Why don't you dictate the list, and I'll send it for you?"

She shook her head and grabbed the phone from his hand. "No. I've got this."

He handed her a half-peeled banana after she'd sent the text. "Take a few bites. You're probably starving. Eat some while we take the security tour, honey." He held out a hand.

She stood and followed him, groaning every few steps.

"This building is a fortress. I bought it in case I ever needed to protect a client for a while. You already saw the private elevator. Every window and entrance on this level has triple deadbolts. With one swipe of my phone, I can lock and unlock everything. When I leave to get the girls, I'll lock the place down tight. You'll be safe." Nick gave her an encouraging smile and continued.

"I'm shutting all the drapes on this level. You can see out, but no one can see in. They can't even tell if a light is on. Let me show you the safe room."

Liz coughed on a bite of banana. "Safe room?"

"Yeah, state of the art. I learned all about them when I led the security detail for assorted dignitaries and brass overseas." He gave her a cursory lesson on the safe room buttons and protocols and headed towards the bathroom. He hung a fresh towel on the hook and set sweatpants and a t-shirt on the counter for her. He peered down the hallway. She was still standing in front of the safe room door.

"Let's go, babe. I know the medics gave you a once-over, but let's make sure the prosthetic and the rest of you are okay."

She hobbled through the doorway of the huge bathroom. "You don't need to stay. I'm really worried about Ella and Arlene. We've already been here for ten minutes."

He looked up from the drawer he was searching for a new toothbrush. "Yup, got my eye on the clock. But I'm not leaving until we check out your leg."

She bent down and struggled to untie her right shoe. "Dammit." She clawed at the too-tight lace job.

"Let me help." Nick leaned down and hauled her up to sit on the bathroom counter. He set the offending shoe on his thigh and poked at the wad of knots in the middle, found a loose one and pulled the jumbled mess free. He repeated the process on the other shoe.

"Thanks. My fingers aren't working very well right now. Could you pull them off?"

He gave a gentle tug, set them on the floor, and raised an eyebrow. "Pants?"

"Oh yeah." She slipped the tank over her head and unbuttoned the pants.

He gave a low whistle. "Those are some serious bruises on your left side, babe."

"I know. The EMTs saw them. But I didn't tell them I wear a prosthetic. The prosthetic area hurts more than my side. I didn't want them to look at my leg and keep me from getting home to Ella."

She was amazing. Always putting Ella ahead of herself. Nick helped remove her trousers and the layers of socks she wore under the prosthetic. The sock closest to her leg was soaked in blood.

"Oh, that's not good." She peeled the sock down, removed the prosthetic, and examined the stump. There were several large vertical gashes in her leg. Her eyes locked onto his. "I may need a doctor after all. I can't risk infection in this leg, especially that close to the stump."

Nick placed the socks in the sink and the prosthetic on the counter. "I've got a doctor on call. As soon as I get back with Ella and Arlene, she'll come over and take a look at you."

"Okay." Liz's hands shook as she brushed the hair away from her face. "I need to get in the tub and clean this leg."

Her face was drawn and tight. "Are you going to be alright with me gone a little while?"

She gave him a tight nod. "Yeah, fine. The sooner you get the baby and my mother here, the better off we'll be."

"Remember the rules. The building's impenetrable. Don't open any doors. Only answer your phone if it's me."

"Got it. Go get Ella." She gave him a wan smile, stepped inside the bath and started the water.

Nick strode to the kitchen and made a phone call. SecureIT was short-staffed tonight with everyone working. He had to find a back-up operative to watch the building while he drove to pick up Ella and Arlene.

She answered on the second ring. "Nicholas, twice in one week, you handsome stud. Want some company?"

"Cut it out, Lana. This is business. Are you in DC?"

"Got in yesterday and shook off the jet lag. What's up?"

"How soon could you get to my place in Georgetown? I need you to guard my building. I've got a very important client here."

"I'm thirty minutes away. Who's the client?"

"Her name is Liz Nelson. She's resting inside. I need you to watch the entrances and exits while I run an errand."

"Got it. I'll load up now."

"I'll be gone when you get here. Stay outside. Call me if you have any questions.

"Will she know I'm there?"

"I'll make her aware of your presence. You're the final layer of security. Thank you." He hung up, reheated Liz's lukewarm tea, grabbed a packet of peanut butter crackers and her phone, and headed for the bathroom.

Liz looked up as he set the snack on a built-in shelf by the tub. "Thanks. You're still here?"

"I'm leaving in a minute. In a little while, someone named Lana will be guarding the outside of the building. She's worked on Sanctuary missions before, but I'm not sure if you know her. Anyway, you won't be alone."

Her face softened as she picked gravel from the skin on her arms. "Thanks, Sergeant."

He gave her a kiss. "Stay inside. No one can get in. You're totally safe here. I'll be back in a little while." He pulled a Glock from one of the bathroom drawers, and set it on the counter. "You keep up with your target practice?"

"Always. Put it back in the drawer, please. With any luck at all, I won't need it or the safe room."

He slipped the gun back into the drawer. "It's locked and loaded."

34

I llusia hurled the vase of daisies at the marble fireplace. Shards of broken glass scattered across the gleaming wood floors of the open living area. *You fooled me, Liz Nelson. Shame on you.*

She touched the locator on her phone to be certain and looked around for her black running shoes. That vase was only the beginning of the destruction if Liz's phone pinged a location again. And ping it did. She enlarged the screen, and traced the map. The phone was in Nick's building. She slumped onto the bench in her small foyer and closed her eyes.

Logically, if the phone had been in the purse she'd seen on Liz's shoulder in the parking lot, and Liz died in the blaze, then the phone should've melted right alongside her. From the vantage point she'd had through the binoculars, Liz didn't have even a second to heave the purse aside and scream *save my new iPhone.*

Illusia frowned. Gallows humor was not her forté.

Liz lived, and that was an unacceptable outcome. Period.

Illusia hadn't come this far to accept defeat. She'd need to work smarter to complete the assignment Jazz had left behind. The diary on his computer specifically stated that if he died overseas and Liz lived, then she, as his sister and only living relative, would need to avenge his death.

She would *not* deny her brother his last request. Not when Jazz had sprung them from the endless system of foster homes they'd grown up in when they were only sixteen. He'd supported them both by hacking. He'd always had at least three new identities in his pocket and even paid for her beauty school tuition with some dead guy's credit card.

And yeah, Jazz'd been a little extreme in his attitudes about women, the government, and the military, but still, he'd been *the greatest freaking brother on earth.* Guilt swarmed her body, and she groaned. *She hadn't even been there to help him when he'd needed her at the end.*

Illusia stood, rolled her shoulders, and stretched against the wall, taking a deep breath. She'd figure this out. Nick's place wouldn't be a piece of cake to infiltrate. He'd invented a new layered alarm system with sequences that randomly shifted and rearranged. She'd captured the sequence a few times, but two seconds later, it had updated and locked her out.

And forget about obtaining blueprints of the building. She'd tried. The building inspectors acted like they didn't exist anymore, considering it'd been built in 1910. Even the guy she'd promised a little something-something couldn't uncover anything on the recent rehab. Like the place was some kind of urban Camp David.

She *would* get in eventually. But that required the luxury of time she didn't have. She yanked Jazz's military duffle from the front closet and planned while she packed. Balaclava, rope, handcuffs, loaded gun, black tape, blanket to cover the body, sensors she'd need to read the security system, extra cell phones, voice distortion equipment, climbing rope, rooftop anchor.

Shit. She hated climbing and heights.

She slipped into a black ensemble, including her custom-made jacket with the protective pockets for her electronic notebooks, and thought a minute. *This might take a while.* She crammed extra chargers into the big pockets and found her black lipstick. She'd need it in the dark.

While the coffee brewed, she stuffed her curly hair into a black cap. With thermos in hand, rope slung over one shoulder, and Jazz's duffle weighing down the other, Illusia avoided the elevator and trotted down the service stairwell to her parking garage. This time, she'd succeed in eliminating Liz Nelson.

Because—fool her twice—shame on her.

ILLUSIA DROVE past Nick as he pulled out of the lot and turned left in a hurry. Within seconds, he was gone.

She drove the block a few times before parking in the darkest corner of the lot behind his building. She put her sun shield across the front window to keep the motion sensor lights and cameras from detecting her before she got to work.

Liz's phone pinged from inside the building. *Hmm.* Nick had left her alone. She checked his location. He'd entered the highway. Good. He wasn't on a short run for Chinese food or something. Even so, she'd work fast. No telling where he was going or when he'd be home.

She didn't want Liz calling Nick for help tonight. She'd

make sure of it. She contacted the chip she'd left in Liz's phone at the zoo and tapped *disable phone*. On second thought, Liz wouldn't need the phone from now on anyway. She may as well erase the damn thing. Illusia cocked her head and thought a few seconds. *Sure, it was spiteful, but what the hell?* She tapped *erase memory*. If only she could've erased Jazz's mistakes this easily, he would've come home, and they'd be working together again.

Illusia set up her tablets and got to work. She'd investigated Nick's security one other time and navigated quickly, casually leaning toward the side window to peer up at the fourth floor. Not a light on in the place. That had to be a smoke and mirrors effect, because Liz was definitely in there.

Just like the previous time, the security grids were spaced every few inches or so and rotated constantly. Illusia checked her watch. They were shifting every four seconds. She scanned the four entrances on her monitor. There was the main lobby, a side entrance that led to the service elevator, and two entrances in the underground parking garage.

Last time, she'd tried to crack the code for the parking garage and couldn't get in. Tonight, she wouldn't give up until she strolled inside one of the first-floor doors or Liz came out.

Illusia slammed the notebooks shut and scooted down in her seat as the high beams from a sports car on the road illuminated her parked car. It was probably some neighbor, because Nick didn't have tenants.

During the next half hour, she isolated the security grid and endeavored to freeze it. The second she caught the sequence, the grid shifted from vertical to horizontal or vice versa and shut her out. Nick's system had the unique quality of unpredictability. It never repeated an algorithm. She slammed the notebook against the steering wheel and took a deep breath.

The feds could learn a thing or two from Nick's program. Their programs lumbered along like cyber manatees, changing only when challenged by an intruder. Nick's setup never stopped moving. It was like trying to catch grasshoppers.

She grabbed her coffee and sipped. A joint would really help her narrow her focus, but she didn't dare open the windows. And the last thing she needed was a clambake rendering her useless instead of a few mellow tokes.

She shook her head. There'd be no climb up the building tonight either. *If* she could even get the fire escape down, the stairs contained an electric current similar to the precision of a large dog's collar. Same thing with the windows and rooftop. And she'd bet her life that he'd replaced the old windows with bulletproof glass, because hey—Nick was just enough of a detailed freak to do that.

But Illusia hadn't earned her reputation by giving up. There had to be vulnerability somewhere. She poked and prodded for *anything* she might have missed previously. There was a possible back door she'd ignored during her searches thinking it a dead end. She backtracked through a dozen saved pages and found the spot.

One line in the system sat inactive. She worked on it for a few minutes and turned it on. The pulses resembled an old phone or intercom system. A quick search for public info on the property stated it had been a sewing machine factory in its heyday and converted to office space in the 1970s.

For the next ten minutes, Illusia traced the old cables to the fourth floor and activated them. They fired right up. But the only way she'd know if the wall boxes were intact was to listen and see if she heard anything. She clicked the first circuit and nothing. She tried the second and heard the faint sound of a hairdryer in the distance. When she checked out the third circuit, footsteps echoed on a wood floor. Illusia snatched a pad and made notes on which circuits worked and those that didn't. *She was a freaking genius.* Yes, sir, the truly intelligent in this world adapted to their circumstances and overcame.

If she couldn't get in the building—she'd motivate Liz to come out.

3 5

M ajor Chan scrambled from under the weight of her husband's arm and leg. She climbed over him to answer her work phone.

"Chan." She glanced at the clock. It was way after midnight.

"Sorry to wake you, Major. This can't wait." The young analyst's voice quavered.

"It's alright, Phil. Go ahead." She slipped into the bathroom and put the speaker on.

"That hacker we've been researching? She's been busy. Las Vegas police issued a warrant for her arrest tonight and issued a nationwide APB. They found the body of some Canadian demo specialist in the desert three days ago. He'd been there a couple weeks. Shot point blank through the head. He'd gone to Vegas for a work convention and never returned home. Family filed a missing person's report ten days ago. Vegas PD combed through his phone and computer. Illusia's digital fingerprint is all over his emails."

Poor guy. *Not good.* "Did Vegas PD get an ID? Did she check into a hotel?"

"Oh yeah. Penthouse suite. She spent the big bucks."

"What name did she use at check-in?"

"Genevieve Ralston. But that's just the name on the credit card. FBI's been chasing this perp for several years. Credit card fraud is one of her specialties. She's on a dozen security feeds up and down the Vegas strip. She left the hotel with the demo guy in a rented Buick and returned several hours later alone driving a rented Mercedes. And her fingerprints are all over the dead guy's belongings. She did nothing to disguise herself. Her real name is Paula Mumford, born in Wisconsin, age thirty-one. No rap sheet as an adult but there's a long juvie record, according to my source. I didn't actually get to see it."

"The condensed version, please, Phil." She fumbled for a Dixie cup and drew some water.

"Yeah, yeah. I'm getting to it. Paula Mumford's twin brother, Gerald, was a hacker, too. He made big money hacking for premier outfits but got busted a few years ago. Long prison sentence. The feds didn't waste the IOU and allowed him to do his time using his hacking skills in Iraq. He served with Lieutenant Nelson. She came home to a Purple Heart. He came home in a body bag."

The major swallowed hard and dropped the cup in the sink. "Do we know where Paula Mumford is now?"

"No known address under that name, but she flew Vegas to Dulles eleven days ago. Until this evening, we haven't had any fingerprints to connect Illusia and Paula Mumford. She got really sloppy in Vegas. Almost like she wanted to get caught. It figures she's a hacker like her brother, but according to her tax returns, she's been a nail tech in private salons all over the DC area."

"Good work, Phil. Thanks."

"Wait, wait. Here's an interesting tidbit. Liz Nelson's car caught fire tonight in a Big4Less store parking lot on President's Road. Preliminary findings state *possible malfunction or tampering.*"

The breath froze in her lungs. "Is Liz alright?"

"Yeah. Medics released her at the scene for follow-up with her primary care."

Relief rolled over her in a huge whoosh. "Thanks for the update, gotta go." She disconnected the call and immediately placed another one.

"Security—Hans speaking."

"This is Major Natalie Chan. I need to initiate protective custody for one of my analysts."

"Enter the file number, please."

Using her keypad, she entered a series of numbers.

"Special instructions?"

"Contact Alexandria Police immediately for a patrol car to guard her house until security detail arrives. I'll be at the location within an hour to brief the agents."

"Got it. Security activated and Alexandria Police notified. Good luck, Major."

She hung up and called Liz's cell phone. It picked up after several rings and repeated a message twice.

This number is no longer in service. Please check the number you are dialing and try again.

Unease raced through the major's mind. Of course, that was Liz's number. She'd reached her via cell just yesterday. She tore off her nightgown and threw on some khakis and a sweatshirt, stopping only to open the bedroom safe to grab her sidearm.

Dammit—why hadn't she seen this coming? Liz Nelson was like a daughter to her.

36

Liz wiped a few drops of water off her phone and tapped the screen. It blinked once and went dark. She powered it on again, but it shut down a few seconds later.

She shook her head. The car *and* her phone? *Unbelievable.* That's what she got for letting the phone get wet. She shoved it in her pocket. Maybe it would fire up in a little while.

She blew her hair dry and headed for the kitchen. Knowing Nick, he'd bring food back with him, but she'd give anything right now for something other than peanut butter crackers. His fridge was almost barren, but she found a brick of cheese and an apple. She leaned over the kitchen counter and nibbled while staring at the twinkling Georgetown lights outside his living room window.

If only she could explain her work situation to Nick. The Major was usually right. Top-tier hackers searched for information, but they didn't physically harm their victims. On the other hand, too many weird things had happened lately. What were the flowers about? Why had that hacker breached only her files? There were dozens of people working higher security projects in the same building, and their files went untouched. It didn't make sense.

A floorboard creaked. Her nape crawled. She glanced around the living and dining room, saw nothing, and told herself to calm down. *Old buildings had their quirks.*

Of course, she also understood Nick's point of view. She'd been edgy for weeks now, contemplating the ramifications of her ruined files. It would take her at least two months to rebuild her entire cast of online personas. And it had to be unsettling for Nick to know *something* was going on and not have details.

Liz wrapped up the remainder of the cheese, stowing it in the fridge. Now was a good time to set up the port-a-crib. She found it in the corner of the master bedroom. *Aww...he bought bedding with pink hearts.* She held them to her chest and smiled. *He's already planning for Ella to be part of his life.*

She wrestled the plastic cover off the linens when a door clicked shut. She set the bedding down, walked to the door, and peered down the long hallway. *Weird.* He hadn't mentioned tenants. She yanked the phone from her pocket, but it didn't even blink. So much for calling Nick to ask him about the eerie nuances of the property.

Maybe the security person he'd stationed out front had arrived? She sidled to the drapes and glanced down the road. *That must be Lana in the silver sports car parked across the street.* Liz huffed a laugh. Her nerves had sizzled during the car fiasco and ensuing flashback. Help was right out front—not that she needed it. Nick had assured her the woman was a Sanctuary, Inc. operative and a professional badass.

A distinct unease settled in her chest. Even if she wanted

to, she couldn't call Lana because her damn phone didn't work. When would she learn that phones and water weren't a good combination? She'd dunked one in a toilet when she was hugely pregnant with Ella and another in a gutter on a rainy day. She shook her head. It didn't matter. Nick would be back soon enough.

She threw herself into unpacking and setting up the port-a-crib for Ella. He'd purchased a really nice model, and it expanded and clicked into place with ease. It even had a comfortable six-inch-thick mattress. She made the little bed, pausing to appreciate each layer because Nick had picked them out. He'd outdone himself, right down to the two little heart-shaped pillows on top.

Liz flinched when a cat screeched outside followed by a barking dog. Perhaps it was time to make more tea, and she'd lace it with that shot Nick mentioned to calm her nerves. She usually enjoyed quiet moments, but with these creepy sounds tonight? She couldn't wait until he returned with the noisy fussing of Ella and Arlene. Not to mention, they'd all be safe under one roof.

Liz placed the mug in the microwave and set out in search of fresh towels for her mother. *Anything to keep busy.* But the guest suite was already meticulously equipped for visitors. Nick must've hired a designer because the curtains matched the bedspread, which matched the nautical themed towels in the guest bath. She giggled a second. The Nick she knew couldn't care less if anything was fresh or coordinated because more than once she'd removed thread-bare towels and replaced them in his duffle with fluffy new ones.

Liz headed for the master bath, quickly wiped the counter, hung her towel on the porcelain hook, and rinsed out the tub.

Something winked at her from the floor, and she got down on all fours in case it was glass. Little pieces of blacktop quartz must've fallen off her clothes, and she wiped them up. As she backed out of the bathroom, there was a noise. *Breaking glass?* The hair on her neck stood on end. She sat back on her heels and listened again. But all she heard was complete silence.

Just admit it, girl. She hadn't shaken off the willies since reliving that awful night in Iraq earlier. The same unease she'd experienced a year-and-a-half ago on that desert ops crawled through her gut tonight. She reached over to straighten the fluffy rug in front of the counter and cocked her head, resting it against the doorjamb, and listened again. *Omigod.* Now *that* was definitely the sound of breaking glass.

Liz scrambled faster than a jumping spider and flipped the light off. Her fingers groped through drawers in the dark to locate the gun. She drew it against her chest and panted. *What the hell?*

Nick had said no one could get in. She peeked right and then left down the hallway. Nothing.

Shit. She'd clear the rooms one by one. She drew a deep breath, flattened herself against the hallway wall, and checked the guest suite. *No broken glass.* She nudged open the pocket door to the guest bath, but nothing had been disturbed.

Yet, somewhere in the distance, she heard floorboards creaking and footsteps. A rush of adrenaline forced her into high gear as she cleared the master bedroom where everything was serene down to the brass lamp by the bed still on low. Even the safe room door remained fully engaged with the red light blinking every ten seconds or so. She flipped the light switch in Nick's room-size closet. Not a thing was out of place.

Liz moved quiet as a cat down the long hallway, pausing to

glance in the office. The piece of paper she'd seen on the desk earlier was still there. Nothing was broken. She slid against the hallway wall and inched toward the huge living area, gun ready to fire with her heart beating an irregular rhythm. The footsteps started again. Judging by the sound, they were closer.

She tiptoed into the kitchen, silenced the beeping tea reminder on the microwave, and braced her arms on the countertop to shoot if necessary. What were these noises following her through the apartment?

She wheeled around when something rustled behind her. There was nothing there.

Was she going crazy? She shook her head. No—she wasn't imagining these things. She stood watch for several minutes with the gun pointed at the open living area and listened.

Utter quiet.

Maybe Nick had brought in a tenant and they were watching a weird movie? Perhaps the walls lacked insulation in certain areas and the sounds carried through a heat vent or old pipe? Liz set the gun on the counter and retrieved her mug of tea from the microwave. She skipped the shot of booze and stood by the counter, gun in front of her, sipping the hot liquid. She rolled her shoulders, shook out her hands. The silence overwhelmed her frayed senses.

There just had to be a tenant somewhere in the building. The noises had stopped. They must've turned off the TV. That's all there was to it. Maybe in ten years, she'd tell Nick about the night she'd been scared out of her wits in this building. And she'd overdramatize with self-deprecation the fear she'd succumbed to. They'd laugh about it on the way to Ella's recital or soccer game.

She tried to power her phone on again, but it remained

ominously dark. If only she could get some rest so she wasn't this hyper-alert to her surroundings. If she'd gone with Nick, she'd have Ella in her arms, and could've helped them pack up instead of hiding out here dealing with the kinks and groans of this old building.

Liz set her mug in the sink and sighed, then glanced at the ticking clock across the room. He'd been gone almost an hour. He'd be back in thirty minutes or so. Maybe she'd sit in the living room and wait. A floorboard creaked. She froze in place, her erratic breathing the only sound.

The creaks and footsteps grew louder, closer, followed by a distorted voice.

"You thought you'd gotten away with it, didn't you?"

Liz's heart leaped into her throat. There *was* someone in here. She scanned the ceiling. Where were they? She aimed the gun and stepped into the dark dining room, hugging the shadows and following the wall to where a view opened into the long hallway. There was nothing there.

But the footsteps grew faster and floorboards creaked all around her. Someone breathed hard and the soft cries of a baby iced her movements.

"What happened in Iraq followed you home, Lieutenant. I tried to make it easy and quick with the car, but you just weren't close enough."

Liz registered the voice and the words, but the crying baby commanded her full attention. She began to tremble. *No. It's not possible.* But the cries grew more insistent, and her boobs ached. Every fiber of her soul honed into that cry. *It was Ella. That was her hungry cry.*

Panic flooded Liz's mind. Where was the voice coming from? She'd already checked the entire loft and found no one.

Nick and her mother were supposed to have Ella. Or was

Nick trying to call and say he couldn't find her? With the phone not working, he wouldn't be able to get through. An anguished howl escaped Liz's constricted throat.

"Don't you hurt my baby. Where the hell are you?" She looked around the room from floor to ceiling trying to locate the voice.

"Close enough to touch you, Liz. But you'll never find me. Such a pretty little girl you have here. She can't seem to figure out why I'm holding her instead of you."

Liz followed the voice to a vent return in the living room and she climbed onto a chair to take a closer look. Her heart raced when Ella wailed again followed by sniffles and little sobs. "It's okay, Ella girl, Mommy's coming to get you." She pounded the wall with her fist and screamed into the still air. "What do you want from me?"

"You killed my brother in Iraq, you vile bitch."

"I've never killed anyone in my life. I'm an analyst. I sit in an office and juggle numbers and strategies."

"Jazz's diary says otherwise. You were responsible for his safety that day, Lieutenant. His death was a massive dereliction of duty on your part."

"Jazz needed help and counseling." *Lots of freaking counseling.* "He was in the wrong place at the wrong time." Liz swept tears from her face and jumped off the chair. She wouldn't dare tell whomever this was about his suicide and risk angering them. They had Ella.

"That's a lie, and you know it. Little Ella here is in the wrong place at the wrong time, too. I suppose I could leave her somewhere like you did to Jazz. But the evenings are cooling down a little. On second thought, I don't think babies this age know how to swim yet. That would be a quicker end. Listen to how she cries when I pinch her."

Ella's hurt cry pierced the air. Liz's heart stuttered. Fury fueled the adrenaline and terror coursing through her body. She raced to the bathroom and grabbed the extra magazine clip she'd felt in the drawer. When she returned to the living room, she screamed into the vent. "What do you want from me? How can I make this right?"

"I thought you'd see my point of view," the voice asserted. "I want a fair trade. Ella for you."

"Okay. Done." Liz held the gun up to a light, made sure the first bullet chambered. "How do I get Ella back?"

"I'll leave her in the lobby. That lover boy of yours can get her later."

"Whatever it takes," Liz yelled from the kitchen. She rummaged through drawers and quickly lined her thick socks with several of Nick's sheathed kitchen knives. If it were the last thing she did, she *would* eliminate this evil creature one digit at a time. *Screw with my life, blow off my foot, but you will not hurt my child.*

"Meet me in the alley on the east side of the building, Liz. Three minutes."

"You put Ella in the vestibule of the main lobby first. I'll be waiting for you at the door in the alley." Liz wrapped a couple very sharp paring knives in a thick dishcloth and anchored them in the flap of her nursing bra, handles exposed.

"Alright, and Liz?"

"What?" she shrieked.

"Unarmed, please."

Liz tossed a loose knife from her pocket on the dining room table and waited. Could they see her? She hadn't located a camera in the heat vent.

"Atta girl. Unarmed."

Liz tucked the loose knife back into her pocket and lobbed

the drapery remote onto the table. She stood back and listened. No reply probably meant they couldn't see her. She slipped inside the drapes covering the elevator and tapped the down button.

They wanted war? GI Jane was on her way.

37

L iz glanced both ways when the elevator doors opened. To her left was the door to the alley. But before setting one foot outside the building, she had to make sure Ella was in the lobby vestibule. She turned right. The gun at her side, safety off, she ran almost noiselessly through the long, quiet hallway. Pain radiated up her leg, but she ignored it. Harsh automatic lights triggered as she moved. It made sense. The hallway had the markings of a fire exit.

The building was so much larger than she'd expected. She arrived at a door with a glass observation pane, forged ahead, and kept moving to a second fire door, which opened when she threw her body weight into it. Another fifty feet brought her to the third door marked *Lobby Entrance*. She shined the little flashlight she'd confiscated from Nick's kitchen junk drawer on the signs covering the door. *Caution: Building alarm will sound when opened.*

She took a step back. If she activated the building alarm, whoever had Ella might take off with her.

Liz scrutinized the lobby through the glass pane. It was

dark, except for a few shafts of illumination from a streetlight. She couldn't see squat, dammit. The gleaming marble floors reflected the minimal light like a pond in the dark. Ella could be ten feet away, and Liz would never know from this angle. She gave the door handle a tenuous tug. Locked. *Shit.* She swiped the hair off her face and stifled a frustrated sob.

There were only two alternatives. If Ella were in the lobby, she'd be chilly but reasonably safe for a short amount of time. But if she was still with the kidnapper, then she was probably in the car in the alley. It wasn't worth the risk to activate the alarm system if her baby wasn't safe.

She spun around and ran toward the alley. The second door stuck from this direction. She managed to open it just enough to squeeze through, but her prosthetic foot got caught at the bottom. *Dammit.* She heaved at the barrier and slipped into freedom.

Her innocent little girl. Caught up in something even her mother, the hotshot analyst, didn't understand. The flowers, the work personas, the car. Was it all tied together somehow? Damp sweat chilled Liz as she approached the door to the alley. *Had this maniac taken her stroller at the zoo?* Oh dear lord, had this madwoman been close to her Ella that day?

She scanned the alley through the massive glass door in both directions. There wasn't even a streetlight out there. But Ella was nearby. She could hear her crying outside. *Mommy's coming, sweetheart.* Liz cracked the door open, slid into the night, and placed the flashlight at the bottom to keep it from latching shut. Once she got Ella, she'd get back in the building, take the elevator to the loft, and hunker down.

Flattening herself against the wall, Liz inched along the building to a large, dark sedan about twenty feet to her left. Ella's cries tore at her heart. Panic clawed at her brain. *Get the baby. Just get the baby.* The sedan's back door was open. Ella had to be in the backseat. *That bastard never put her in the vestibule.*

Liz climbed halfway into the car, groping the seats, the floor, the ceiling. The crying sounded softer now, gentle baby sobs like when Ella felt alone or scared. Liz couldn't find her in the back and reached over into the front, swishing her arms against the leather.

Liz's feet dangled outside the car when someone tried to close the door against them. *Shit, that hurt.* She flopped onto the backseat and pushed with all her arm and leg strength against the force trying to shut the door. As long as her knee didn't give out, the titanium prosthetic wouldn't buckle under the pressure. She dug deep and with a final, mighty shove, the door flung open. Liz aimed the gun and fired at the dark shadow that had tried to trap her.

Whoever it was sprawled backward against the building.

Liz scrambled out of the car and grabbed a woman's head, slamming it against the flagstone building. "Where's my daughter, you piece of shit?"

But the woman rebounded with force and wrapped both hands around Liz's neck, squeezing with a vice grip, choking the air from her lungs. Shooting stars crossed her vision as Liz tore the glasses from her attacker's face, forcing her thumbs into their eyes.

A knee to the gut took Liz by surprise. She flew back against the car, gasping for a breath. Something hit her head with full impact, and she crumpled into the backseat.

The darkness enveloped her like a bad dream.

38

A gunshot pierced the night. Lana careened headfirst into the driveway, high beams blazing to locate the source. She leaped from the car; gun drawn.

"Security. Freeze," she shouted at the figure climbing into the driver's seat. A bullet rang out and punctured the hood of her Jaguar. The sedan revved its engine and charged directly at her. She rolled out of the way before impact.

The big sedan handily damaged Lana's front passenger side and headlight, sending the other car sliding before jumping a curb and squealing down the street.

That was a mistake, you idiot.

Lana vaulted into her car, spun out, and took off in pursuit as she ordered her Bluetooth to call Nick. He answered on the first ring.

"Lana, what the hell is going on? The alarm notified me a minute ago of a breach to the side door of the building, and Liz's phone isn't working."

"No shit. I'm pretty sure your girl broke house rules and went outside. The next thing I know, there's a gunshot in the alley. I think the perp's got her in their car. I didn't have eyes on. Just a gut feeling. Perp shot at me, tried to run me down." Her heart jackhammered a wild rhythm in her chest.

"Where are you?"

"I'm hauling ass down the boulevard, with the car in my sight. I think it's headed for the beltway."

"Stay with them. I'll catch up with you on the highway."

"I was hoping you'd say that. Locate me. How much distance between us?" *Dang,* there were a lot of dark sedans on the road tonight.

"Fifteen miles. I can make it in ten minutes or less. Don't lose that car, Lana. I haven't got a feed on Liz's location. If she's in that car, you're all she's got."

"No pressure, huh, Boss?" Lana leaned over to grab glare-reducing glasses, shoved them on her face, and glued her eyes to the back of the sedan. It was flying as it took a sharp curve onto the DC beltway.

"They just turned onto 495 North. Driver's got to be going ninety and took the ramp on two wheels."

Lana threw the Jaguar into a higher gear, accelerated, and let it stretch its legs. The bullet hadn't hurt the engine, and it responded right away. *Thank goodness.* She glanced in her rear-view mirror after zooming around a delivery truck and shook her head.

"I've got lights and sirens on my tail. What do you want me to do, Nick?"

"Ignore them. I'll call 911 and get their help."

"Okay. Perp's going over a hundred now. I can still see them."

The cop car gained on her and she hit the gas while Nick had her on hold. "Better make that call fast. I don't want to bust through a police roadblock trying to hold onto that sedan."

It was the longest thirty seconds of Lana's life waiting for Nick to come back on the line.

"It's done. The police know it's a kidnapping in progress and will help maintain eyes on the sedan."

Lana's stomach dipped as she took one of the curves a little too wide on the approach to the Mormon Temple. "How'd you do that? Cops don't like to share."

"Feds don't like to share. Metro police love a good party. They're sending more cars and getting a chopper up."

A patrol cruiser pulled alongside her. She glanced over—the officer nodded.

Nick barked into her ear. "The officer wants to know if you got the license plate, Lana?"

She shook her head. "I was never close enough, and the driver's weaving on these curves."

"Keep your eyes on that car, girl. Let me pass when I catch you in a few minutes."

"Got it." *What the hell was that white thing hanging out of the car?*

"Any identifying marks on the sedan?"

"It's the car with a white object billowing out the window. Maybe a sheet or something."

39

Liz tumbled off the backseat and landed with a thud on the floor. A vicious headache throbbed like a bass drum, and her throat refused to swallow. *What the hell happened?*

She lay there a minute. The rolling tremble of movement under her body gave way to a punch of renewed terror. *Ella—where's Ella?*

She touched her wet forehead. *Blood.* There was a blanket on top of her, and she swiped at the moisture. So much blood. *Why?* Her memory clicked into gear. She moaned, struggled to her knees, grabbed the seat, and pulled up.

An icy voice pierced the dark. "You shot me, bitch. I wish I could've hit you harder." The woman showed her teeth in the rear-view mirror. "You're messy looking now, but just wait until I'm done with you."

Liz laid her head on top of the blanket on the backseat and panted, fighting the panic swarming her body like agitated bees.

"I'm going to enjoy the hell out of killing you. Jazz was

supposed to do it, but as usual, I get to clean up his half-assed messes," the woman mused aloud.

Liz forced herself to swallow in spite of the pain. "Who are you?"

"Jazz's twin sister. Hacker extraordinaire." She gave Liz the one-finger-salute.

The compromised work files. The flowers, the car? "Where's my daughter?"

A peal of ugly laughter erupted from the front seat. "She's fine. I put her in the trunk. If you listen real hard, she's crying."

A fresh assault of anger surged Liz's body. "Stop the car. Get her out of there. Let me hold her. The trunk's not safe."

"You think I give a shit about your baby being safe? She's going to the same place you are."

Horror gripped Liz's heart. She groped frantically under the seats for Nick's gun. But the weapon was AWOL. She must've dropped it in the alley. She crammed her ear against the backseat. Ella's frightened cries grew fainter.

Liz yanked two knives from her pocket, set them on the seat, and hoisted herself into a sitting position next to them. She gripped one, ready to attack, but halted.

This crazy bitch was nuts enough to crash the car on purpose and make sure Liz couldn't get to the steering wheel. *Ella. An accident could kill her.* Liz tucked the knives in the seat crease and balled her fists. She mentally scrambled. There had to be another option.

"Why do you hate me so much?" Maybe, just maybe, the woman would respond to a reasonable conversation and slow down. The vehicle hit a pothole and swerved. Liz bounced violently and hit the ceiling.

"My brother wrote all about you in his journal. He sent me

updates every few days. You turned him in for suspected cyber espionage."

What? "That's a lie. There were a lot of people keeping an eye on him." *Yeah, she had suspicions and had requested they get him out of her unit. Several times.*

The woman swerved into the left lane and accelerated, throwing Liz back against the seat. "Fucking middle lane, always full of slow assholes," the woman shouted. "Jazz intercepted a memo you'd sent up the food chain requesting his transfer back to the states. Don't lie to me."

"I'm not lying. I did request his transfer. Whatever happened after that had nothing to do with me."

"Going home meant returning to prison, and he had no intention of doing that." She sneered into the rear-view mirror. "I'll tell you a little secret. Jazz traded a classified software program for a tidy sum the night before he died. The money's sitting in a Bahamian bank account just waiting for me to show up. You're the last loose end I need to handle before I catch a ride to paradise."

Liz tugged at the blanket on the floor and found the vertical end. The car banked hard on a sharp curve. She slid and slammed against the door. Desperation flooded her thoughts. Ella's car seat was sturdy but tossing like this in a trunk? *Oh my God, what if she's not in her car seat?*

The driver's manic eyes pierced Liz in the mirror. "Get your fucking seat belt on, you idiot. It's the law."

That's enough, you animal. Liz yanked the largest knife from her sock, grabbed the woman by the hair, and stuck the knife to her throat. "Slow down, pull onto the shoulder, and let me get Ella out of the trunk. Now."

The woman wheeled around and pointed a gun at her while keeping one hand on the wheel.

"I'm going to shoot you, Lieutenant. You're a pain in my ass."

Liz threw herself to the floor as the gun went off, shattering the back window. One more wild shot like that and Ella —oh God, she couldn't think about it. Bile rose in her throat as she flattened herself tight against the back of the driver's seat. The next shot hit the upholstery as a puff of padding burst into view.

Liz snatched the blanket, shimmied across the floor to the other door, and let the window down a few inches. It was open just enough to feed the blanket outside to attract attention. The wind tore at the billowing fabric. Liz threw her body weight on the end she'd wrapped around her hand.

"Damn. There's that security idiot again." The woman opened the passenger window and fired several shots at a Jaguar that had pulled up on their right side. "And's there's a cop barreling toward us with lights and sirens." She hooted a frenzied cheer. "Bring it on, assholes. I'm ready for you."

Liz crawled into a ball and held on to the blanket. *What if she didn't pull through the night?* She closed her eyes and prayed for her precious Ella to survive.

Nick would figure it out. He'd be a good father.

40

Nick jolted in horror as the bullets riddled Lana's car
and her Jaguar zig-zagged between two lanes. He
shouted into his Bluetooth, "Lana, are you hurt?" She didn't
answer right away as he held his breath. Seconds later, she
responded.

"Hell, no. But my car's gonna need a shit-ton of body
work. What's the plan, boss?"

He inhaled a gulp of air and relaxed a fraction. "There's
road construction and a traffic jam in three miles. The police
alerted DDOT crew to get off the road and into their trucks.
This perp's going to have to slow down or crash. Stay close
behind me."

Nick turned his attention to his precious cargo in the
backseat. "Arlene, we're going to slow down and stop soon.
My Kevlar vest is on the truck floor back there. Put it on.
Now."

Arlene, wide-eyed and shaking, undid her seat belt,
hoisted the heavy bulletproof armor, and slipped her arms in

the holes. "I'm in." Ella was in the car seat beside her, wide-eyed, gazing at the flashing lights speeding by.

"Good. When I stop the car, I want you to get Ella out of her car seat, set her on the floor, and cover her with your body. Do it quickly. The driver who kidnapped Liz already shot at a car. I want you and Ella protected. Got it?"

"Oh, dear Lord." Arlene swiped tears from her cheeks and nodded. "You be safe out there, Nick. Get my girl back for me in one piece."

"That's the plan, Momma." His brain rapid-fired scenarios, probabilities. But one thought arrested his attention for a millisecond. *Was this pursuit the reason he'd passed two police cars and a fed SUV on Arlene's street as he'd hurried out of the neighborhood? Had the feds realized Liz was in danger?*

Traffic slowed to twenty miles an hour, then to ten. As far as Nick could see, the four lanes condensed into two like an army of ants on a detour. The police car veered left onto the shoulder and continued with lights and sirens. Nick veered toward the right a couple cars behind the sedan as the white blanket drifted like a kite across the trunk.

With no warning, the perp's sedan jerked onto the shoulder and sped off. Nick floored it and pulled right behind them. In the distance, a guy took a leak at the guardrail. He glanced at the vehicles rushing toward him, dropped his pants, and dove over the barrier onto the grass.

A delivery truck made a quick swerve onto the shoulder in front of the sedan, causing it to screech to a halt. The perp reached out the window and fired a shot at the truck. Cars scrambled left to get away from the sedan; the cacophony of horns near deafening.

The truck driver ambled out of his cab. Nick threw his

vehicle into park and leaped out, waving at the driver. "Get back in the truck! Get back in the truck!"

The perp leaned out the window and shot the truck driver in the leg as he scrambled onto the running board. He buckled, screaming, and fell flat onto the blacktop.

The sedan darted left, but another swarm of cars blocked it thirty feet later.

A woman jumped out waving a gun, pointing it in a wide arc at different cars. Passengers screamed and ducked out of view.

Nick dragged the truck driver from the line of fire and advanced toward the woman threatening the traffic. He aimed his gun for a kill shot if necessary.

He spoke into his Bluetooth. "You with me, Lana?"

"On foot, left shoulder, twenty feet behind you. Cop got T-boned by a driver who didn't yield."

Nick grunted. The perp looked familiar. Different but similar. His stomach pitched when he locked eyes with her. *The bar honey.*

She pointed her gun at him. "Fancy meeting you here, Nick Flannery. It's been a while." She snorted loudly and smirked.

It was definitely *not* the flirty giggle that had distracted him weeks ago. "Not long enough, Bonnie."

"Oh, come on now. Didn't you enjoy the lip stain and nail polish? I so tried to be memorable." She swaggered a few feet closer to him, gun aimed at his head.

"Your right shoulder is bleeding. What happened?" He swung slightly left to force her back toward the guardrail.

"That piece of shit you call a girlfriend shot me."

Pride filled his chest. *Good for her.* "Where's Liz?"

"She's dead. In the backseat. You wanna see?" She smiled and cocked her gun.

Nick's heart lurched, and his pulse raced. *No. No.*

Lana spoke into his Bluetooth. "There's movement in the backseat, Nick. She's alive."

Thank God. "Where you at, Lana?" he whispered.

"Fifteen feet from the perp. Hiding in the traffic. Behind her now."

The sedan trunk latch popped, and the back door opened. Liz stumbled out near the guardrail and crawled to the trunk, flung it open, and wailed a heartrending cry. She wheeled around. "Don't shoot her, Nick. She's got Ella."

He steeled his eye on Bonnie's hand and shouted, "No, she doesn't. I've got our daughter, Liz. And your mom."

"Did you ever tell her about us, Nick?" Bonnie sidestepped closer to Liz and yelled over the sound of approaching police sirens. "This man has a mighty fine chassis, Lieutenant. Took me for a ride a few weeks ago."

Liz stood trembling and grabbed a tire iron from the trunk. "I know all about it. He pretended you were me the whole time. Guess you weren't that exciting." Liz twirled the tire iron like a baton and took a step toward her captor. "You tricked me into thinking you had Ella, you vile witch. How'd you do that?"

Bonnie sneered and started boasting. "The day you went to the zoo? I was on you like white on rice and collected information to use later. It came in handy. I recorded her cries when that bird pecked her finger. Then, I pinched her thigh in a tight crowd to get her really wound up. A mother always recognizes her own baby's cries, right?"

She continued, shaking her head. "I should've just killed

you then, but I'm more deliberate than Jazz. I *enjoy* the torment. Fucking up your work files was pure fun. I kept waiting for you to lose your job, or at least your security clearance."

Liz took another step closer. "And my car?"

Bonnie curled her lip and backed up a few feet. "It was supposed to be quick and clean. Merciful—which you don't deserve. You're just too stupid to die."

"That's enough, babe. Move back." Nick stepped into the line of fire between the two women.

Lana's voice pierced his earpiece. "While you guys are up there playing true confessions and who-did-who, I've got a bead on this bitch. You want her dead or alive?"

"Alive. For the feds. No collateral damage if possible." Even so, he refocused his aim for a kill shot. "You still do that kick?" he whispered under his breath, but loud enough for the Bluetooth to catch.

"Hell, yeah. We've practiced it enough."

"Go for it." He took a step closer to Bonnie. "You planning on putting that weapon down anytime soon?"

"Fuck you." She danced a few strides sideways, fired a shot at Liz and missed.

Shock and fury crossed Liz's face. She catapulted the tire iron in Bonnie's direction. It slammed into the woman's chest causing her to stumble backward.

Lana's high-flying kick came at Bonnie from the side and knocked the gun from her hands. Bonnie lunged to grab it, but Lana's reverse kick plowed a combat boot into her face. Nick caught the stunned woman and shoved her face-down onto the roadway, zip-tying her hands behind her back, then her feet.

Bonnie lifted her bloody face and sneered, "You trying to ride me again, soldier?"

"Don't flatter yourself, lady." Nick stood and nodded at the officer who'd abandoned his cruiser and run toward them. The police could take her into custody. A chopper whirred overhead, and the sound of car horns sounded intermittently.

A few steps later, he tugged Liz into his arms. She was a limping, bruised, bloody mess. He kissed her forehead. "I love you, honey. I'll get you to medical as soon as they arrive."

She buried her face in his shoulder and cried. "Please tell me you really *do* have Ella."

He picked her up and strode toward his truck. "I can do you one better, babe. Ella and your mom are right here. See for yourself." He opened the back door and helped Arlene remove the vest. Then, he lifted the crying Ella and offered her to Liz.

Liz choked a sob and wiped tears off her cheeks before reaching for her daughter. "Oh Nick, thank you…thank you." She dotted the baby's entire face with grateful kisses.

Arlene burst into tears. She framed her daughter's face in her hands and looked Liz in the eyes. "I was scared to death listening to the gunshots and car horns. You're alright. I love you, sweetie."

Liz cocked her head and broke a small smile through her tears. "It pays to have a great security team." She lifted a trembling hand and caressed Nick's face. "I only went outside because I thought that woman had Ella. I never would've left the building otherwise. I really believed she had Ella."

"Shhh…babe, it's alright." Nick wrapped his arms around all three of his girls and pulled them close, kissing the top of Liz's head over and over again. He leaned down and kissed Ella's rosy cheek, then Arlene's.

They stood there for several minutes while his heart swelled with gratitude. In all his life, he'd never experienced this emotion of being safe and complete. He nuzzled Ella's chubby cheek again. She belonged to him. They *all* belonged to him.

His family.

EPILOGUE

Three days later

Nick rose from the couch and patted Ella's little butt as he let Derek in through the dining room elevator. He placed a finger across his lips as his friend stepped out of the lift.

Derek set two big bags of carryout food on the table. He peeked at the sleeping baby on Nick's chest and whispered, "She's a pretty little thing, bro. Looks right at home on you, too."

"Yeah. My very own tiny princess, she even reaches for me now." He kissed the top of Ella's head.

Derek smiled. "You know the Sanctuary guys are setting up in the lobby? I kept them from mauling the French chef trying to deliver the food."

Nick barked a laugh. "Mac and Ethan wouldn't take no for an answer. They're covering security the next three days round-the-clock, just in case the hacker had a plan B. I don't think she did, but I'm grateful for their help. And per Major

Chan, Liz's boss, the feds are watching Arlene's house for the remainder of the week, too. That's a big relief."

Derek stuffed his hands in his pockets and looked around. "Speaking of Arlene, where is she? I'm her ride home. Feds are waiting for us downstairs."

"In the guestroom, packing up. I'll walk you back. It's time I put Ella in her crib, anyway."

Arlene zipped her suitcase and turned to them with a broad smile. "Nick, are you sure you don't want me to take the baby home with me?"

Nick hesitated. It had been insane around here the past few days with the doctor, the police, and the FBI. And he knew Arlene really wouldn't mind. But Ella was his responsibility now.

"No, but thank you for offering. I'm not letting either of my girls out of my sight for a long time."

Arlene nodded. "Alright, feel free to call if you change your mind." She stood on her tiptoes and gave him a kiss on the cheek. "Liz is still in the bathroom. I already hugged her goodbye."

Derek grabbed her suitcase, and Arlene followed him down the hall.

Nick laid Ella in her crib and knocked softly on the bathroom door. Liz opened it a few inches. "We're finally alone, babe." He leaned against the doorjamb. How many times had he stood in this same doorway and dreamed of her using this accessible bathroom with the special tub? The pained loneliness he'd felt back then was gone. She belonged here. And, if the evening went according to plan, he'd convince her to stay.

A wide grin spread across her beautiful face. "Omigosh, just us—" She let the door drift completely open.

"Just us. Ella's asleep in her crib."

"Thank goodness. I hope I'm not interviewed, poked, or prodded for a *really* long time." She smiled and leaned toward the mirror to apply a salve to her cuts and bruises.

Nick's eyes enjoyed a leisurely stroll down her body. She was a rock star in her satin panties and bra. "Food's here. How long before you're ready to eat?"

Liz gave him a wink in the mirror. "Just give me five."

"Alright. I'll set it out." He strode toward the kitchen rubbing his hands together.

He'd set up the marble table by the living room window earlier this afternoon and had moved two plush chairs in for seating. He lit the candles and opened the wine. Everything was ready, just the way he'd planned.

He checked the cake. It was perfect, right down to the tiny candy box on top in the midst of the bed of chocolate roses. Butterflies danced in his stomach.

One by one, he unpacked the containers of food. As usual, everything on the menu at *Le Petit Bijou* looked excellent, and he'd ordered quite a bit. Goat cheese salad, Lobster Bisque, Boeuf Bourguignon, Duck Confit, a side of buttered noodles and crusty French bread. She'd love it. So would he. His stomach rumbled in agreement.

Liz sauntered down the hallway in his cozy, blue-striped flannel shirt a few minutes later and stopped in her tracks when she reached the open area. "Nick, it's wow—beautiful. This room really warms up with candles everywhere. And the flower bouquets are stunning." She bent and inhaled a whiff of fragrant yellow roses and traced her fingers across a white hydrangea. "Thank you. You're so thoughtful."

"I'm glad you like it." He walked over and slipped a hand around the curve of her waist. "Wine first? Or with dinner?"

"With dinner. I don't want the food to get cold." She

inhaled a deep breath. "It smells phenomenal in here, like French food and fresh flowers."

He strolled to the counter and handed her a plate. "You first.

Liz set a hand on his chest and peered up at him. "Thank you again. You've been so sweet and have made me feel so special."

Nick swept his lips across hers and kissed her. She tasted like his toothpaste and promises waiting to be kept.

She peeked in several of the boxes. "Oh, you got all my favorites. My mouth is watering." She filled her plate and followed him to the table where he seated her.

He lifted his glass. "A toast, babe."

She raised her goblet and waited.

"To our future. May we take the time to love each other like we promised we would."

A smile lit her face. "Nothing would please me more, Sergeant." She reached over and laced her fingers with his.

A few minutes passed as they ate and admired the sunset. "I asked Ella a question today. She said yes."

Liz chuckled and raised an eyebrow. "What did you ask her?"

"If it was okay for me to be her daddy, in the everyday sense."

Her eyes misted, and a smile crossed her lips as she reached for her wine glass. "And how do you know she said yes?"

"She gave me one of those big, slobbery kisses on my chin. A definite yes."

Liz burst out laughing. "You're really enjoying her, aren't you?"

Nick squeezed Liz's hand. "Yeah, and blowing raspberries on her belly. I could listen to her giggle all day."

"Well, as Ella's proxy, I'm thrilled she said yes." Satisfied, she laid her napkin on the table and sat back. "My goodness, that was delicious."

"Good." His heart clenched. He *was* Ella's father but *becoming* her father was different. Better. Fulfilling. It surprised him how much he looked forward to seeing her now. Even the diaper changes were a chance to interact with the daughter he'd quickly come to adore.

Liz stood and removed their plates. "Since you took care of the dinner, I'll do dishes."

"I'll put the food away." Nick gave a conspiratorial grin. "I have a surprise for dessert."

"Dessert? Okay, give. What is it?" She turned the hot water on and opened the dishwasher.

He hurried to reseal the boxes of food and store them in the fridge. "It's a surprise. I think you'll like it." He leaned against the counter enjoying every sway of her hips as she worked.

"Well, I've had an awful lot of them this week, but if you say I'll like it, I'm game for one more."

Nick stood behind her and pressed her luscious body against the sink, tracing his fingertips across her shoulders.

She leaned against his chest and smiled. "What is it about me doing the dishes that turns you on? You reach for me almost every time I'm in the kitchen."

"Hmmm. I like that your hands are occupied, and I get to touch the places I love without interference." He leaned down and kissed the side of her neck, his hands roaming the round of her derriere. "Like this."

She spun around and caught his mouth in a deep kiss. "Are you my dessert, Nick Flannery?"

"Maybe," he winked. He took her hand and led her back to the table. "Sit. Close your eyes. No peeking."

She cocked her head and gave him a look. "Okay. You're not going to flambé anything, are you?"

"Now there's an idea," he laughed. After making sure Liz closed her eyes, he turned on the huge monitor over the fireplace with the recording of the fireworks behind the Eiffel Tower, adjusted the fiber optic lights in the ceiling, and set the dessert on the table. It was his best imitation of a starry night in Paris. "Are you ready?"

"Yes," she giggled.

"You can open them now."

Her eyelids fluttered. She stood on a gasp and twirled around. "Oh, my. It's stunning, Nick. You're amazing. This is breathtaking. It looks just like Paris at the holidays."

Yes! He pulled her into his arms and kissed her soundly. "I'd love to whisk you away from here and everything that's happened, but we both know it's not possible right now."

Liz caressed the side of his face. "I don't need Paris when I've got you and Ella. The past few days have been the best of my life with the three of us under one roof." She beamed at him.

He kissed her shoulder and whispered in her ear, "Ready for some chocolate cake?"

"Always."

He chuckled. "Got it. Sit down." He cut the big slice just like he'd planned, set it in front of her, and then cut himself a piece.

"Nick," she laughed, "I'll never eat this huge piece by myself. We've got to share it, save yours for breakfast."

He knew she'd say that. "You get the slice with the candy box and the big chocolate rose, Lieutenant. I insist and suggest you dig in."

She giggled. "That little box is edible?"

"Sure is. But you might want to remove the contents before taking a bite." His stomach started doing jumping jacks and cartwheels.

Liz pulled the dainty box from the cake and licked the icing off the bottom. She grinned. "That is amazing buttercream."

Heaven help him. He couldn't wait to haul her into his arms and eat her alive, starting with the little dollop of chocolate in the corner of her mouth.

"Oh look, it has a removable lid." She held it up.

"There's a present in the box, babe." *Shut up, shut up. Let her discover it.* He bounced his knee impatiently.

As Liz looked inside, Nick slid to one knee.

Tears flowed down her face as she pulled out the gorgeous emerald and diamond ring.

He cleared his throat and took one of her hands in his. "Liz, I have loved you since the third day of junior year statistics class. You're everything that's good in my life, the ember in my fire, my continuous heartthrob, my best friend, and the woman I want to spend the rest of my life with. I have never wanted anyone but you. Will you please do me the honor of—"

She slipped to her good knee in front of him, tears trickling down her cheeks. "Oh, Nick. You're the man I've admired most, the one I've dreamt of holding me at night, and my giant among men." Her hands traced his face with tender strokes. "Yes. Yes. I should've said yes the first time."

He nodded as his eyes misted. "You'll do me the honor of being my wife?"

She nodded excitedly, a huge smile lighting her face from within. "Without hesitation."

He pulled her into his arms, kissing every inch of her face over and over again. "Looking back, saying no in Paris was the best thing you could've done. We have Ella because of it. It all worked out the way it was meant to. I love you, Elizabeth Nelson."

Liz swiped the tears from her cheeks. "I love you, too. So much."

Nick slipped the ring onto her finger. It fit perfectly and would endure the decades.

Just like them.

ACKNOWLEDGMENTS

Thank you to the friends who believed in and encouraged me. Thank you to my Greek Adonis who ate way too many crockpot dinners, giving me the time to write and finish this book. I am so grateful.

Special thanks to authors Rebecca Rivard and Cate Wells. Your mentoring made all the difference.

ABOUT THE AUTHOR

Nonna Henry hid under the covers as a kid and devoured every Nancy Drew mystery she could get her hands on. Her dad bought her a flashlight, so he could have his back. A lifetime reader of everything, she especially enjoys the Bible (what an adventure), all romance stories and happy endings. She writes romantic suspense and contemporary romance.

She has a degree in theology, lives the life of an entrepreneur and her favorite place is on a beach with her hero and their family. A Jersey girl at heart, she currently lives in Maryland.

You can find her on FB and by visiting her website

www.nonnahenry.com

ALSO BY NONNA HENRY

SANCTUARY, INC. SERIES